breaking yawn

THE SECOND BOOK IN
THE TWISHITE SAGA
A PARODY

STEPHFORDY MAYO

Michael O'Mara Books Limited

First published in Great Britain in 2011 by
Michael O'Mara Books Limited
9 Lion Yard
Tremadoc Road
London SW4 7NQ

This book is not endorsed by nor officially associated with
Stephenie Meyer and the *Twilight* series.

Papers used by Michael O'Mara Books Limited are natural,
recyclable products made from wood grown in sustainable forests.
The manufacturing processes conform to the environmental
regulations of the country of origin.

ISBN: 978-1-84317-549-0 in hardback print format
ISBN: 978-1-84317-792-0 in EPub format
ISBN: 978-1-84317-793-7 in Mobipocket format

1 2 3 4 5 6 7 8 9 10

Cover design: www.lucystephens.co.uk
Cover image: Getty Images
Designed and typeset by K DESIGN, Winscombe, Somerset

Printed and bound in Great Britain by Clays Ltd, St Ives plc

www.mombooks.com

preface

My short life has seen too much horror. A decapitated corpse reaching out toward me. An innocent young man burnt beyond recognition by hot oil. Crowds running in fear of their lives. And entrails, so many entrails.

But worst of all is the chilling vision that haunts me every time I close my eyes. A dark room. A crowd of sinister ghouls staring at me from the shadows. I can feel their eyes upon me, feel their envy and hatred, as I shuffle unwillingly through their midst. Eerie organ music deafens me; its relentless pounding seems to control my feet, driving me onwards, onwards toward a terrifying fate I can barely imagine. . .

'Oh, come on now, Heffa. Be fair. Our wedding was lovely, not like that at all.'

'Shut up, Teddy, darling. I'm creating an ominous mood of supernatural dread to draw the readers in.'

'Oh, right, sorry, love.'

My name is Heffa Lump. And this is my story.

'And mine too, darling.'

'Yes, all right. It's *my* story, the story of my love for Teddy Kelledy, the world's most eligible teenage vampire.'

'Yo, what am I, chopped liver?'

'Oh, God, honestly! Fine. It's also the story of how our love was tested by Joe Cahontas, über-hot werewolf best friend. Everybody happy and feeling included now? Then let's get on with it, shall we, before those who still can die of old age. . .'

chapter 1

hard times

I pulled the duvet tighter round me and listened to the rain hammer on my window. It had been pouring down for a whole week now. And the week before that too. It had stopped for about eleven minutes last Tuesday, but otherwise Spatula was living up to the boast on the town sign: 'America's Rainin'-est City'. I'd gotten used to the damp in the year I'd been living here, and ordinarily I wouldn't have let a couple of feet of rain stop me from going about my important business. But since graduation at the start of the summer, life in Spatula had gotten quite sleepy, and I had dozed off with it.

Don't get me wrong – a bit of peace and quiet was a welcome change after all that had happened since I moved here. When I'd arrived, I'd been just another ordinary teenager. Sure, I might have been far more intelligent than my peers, although I wouldn't dream of bragging about it. And maybe I was rather more jaw-droppingly beautiful than the other girls, with my long dark hair, my unblemished complexion, and eyes as deep and rich as wells of emeralds. But I was modest enough to take that in my stride, just plain old Heffa Lump (not plain in that sense, though. I was gorgeous).

But then I'd met my one true love Teddy Kelledy. At first I'd thought that the pale, sinister, fanged fellow student was just another average kid like me, but after only a few short days, a lot of hints being dropped, and some blindingly obvious demonstrations of his spectacular non-ordinariness, I finally realized the truth. Teddy Kelledy was a vampire. Yes, a vampire. You've probably never read about anything like this before, a girl falling for a supernatural creature, but it's surprisingly common; there are support groups on the Internet and everything.

Anyway, Teddy and I soon realized that we were meant for each other, and nothing could ever keep us apart. Things that attempted to keep us apart included my father, my human friends, my werewolf best friend Joe Cahontas, a gang of murderous goths, an army of zombies and, most recently, our ongoing disagreement about whether or not Teddy was allowed to make me a vampire.

I won't recap all the details, as that would be a cheap way of padding out the chapter; just believe me when I say that you could have filled a book with all the wild things that had happened to me in the last twelve months! (Author's note: *New Moan: The First Book in the Twishite Saga* is available in all good bookstores now.)

So I was enjoying a bit of downtime at last, and life was sweet. My father Chump Lump had given up being a private detective. The mayor had been so grateful to Chump for his efforts in fighting off the massed ranks of the undead that he'd been reappointed to the town police force, and Dad was over the moon to have his old job back. In my experience, Chump couldn't crack an egg without help, let alone a case, but Spatula wasn't a crime hotspot like Port D'Angerous. Apart from the occasional blood-drained corpse turning up a couple of times a week, it was mostly routine community stuff. It was great to see him so happy – his good mood made him much easier to borrow money from.

Not that I wanted for much. Teddy's family was rolling in dough, and he just couldn't resist spoiling me. CDs by that hot new band that we both liked, romantic meals, and enough new outfits to make Kate Middleton turn attractive with jealousy... my boyfriend was everything a girl could wish for. If only he wasn't so insistent on turning me into a vampire right away. He said 'it would bring us closer together' and that 'it might hurt at first but I'd soon enjoy it', but something was still holding me back. Maybe it was because I felt I was too young to make such a big commitment to a guy. I was still only eighteen, although I was very mature for my age. Or maybe it was because of how my werewolf best friend Joe felt about Teddy.

Their feud had started before I arrived: Joe resented the prices that Teddy's father charged in his butcher's shop, and Teddy was infuriated by the amount of hair that the werewolves shed. But I had given them something meaningful to fight over. Me. Could I ever be happy with Teddy if it meant losing Joe? Not that Joe and I were talking anyway; he was still angry that I'd chosen Teddy over him.

My serenity shattered by thoughts of my ongoing man trouble, I turned over in bed and saw the alarm clock on my nightstand. It was already 4:30 in the afternoon, nearly time to get up. I put the bag of tortilla chips that I'd been cradling on the nightstand and yawned wearily as I threw the covers off. School might be a thing of the past but I still had to keep house for my father, and he would be home from work soon. I brushed the crumbs off my pajamas and went downstairs to the kitchen to get started on a casserole for dinner.

Sometimes I resented having to do all the cooking, but the simple fact was that I was a culinary genius, so it was a burden I would have to bear. Besides, on the rare occasions when Chump had tried to cook something for me, it always led to painful and patronizing descriptions of 'burned noodles' or something similar, plus awkward attempts to make my father seem like a humorous character rather than just a dull cipher, and I couldn't face it anymore. Better that I quietly got on with it in my modest and understated manner.

The casserole was bubbling away very happily when Chump came through the door an hour or so later. 'Hey, Heff, how was your day?' he greeted me in his usual style. I sighed deeply and stopped stirring the pot.

'Oh, okay, I guess, Dad. I spent most of it pining for Teddy, and the rest of it worrying about Joe. Not that you would understand, because no one has ever loved like me before.'

He sat at the table and opened the paper. 'That's great, darling. What's for dinner?'

I turned back to the stove and continued stirring the pot. He knew the answer; it was casserole. It was always casserole. I didn't fully understand my fascination with the simple hearty magic of a well-prepared casserole, but I had cooked it for the last 278 days in a row, and I wasn't bored yet. It also made Stephfordy's life a lot easier as she didn't have to think of a new menu every day. She's a writer after all, not Gordon frickin' Ramsay.

'Oh hey, there was this note for you in the mailbox.' Dad waved a clumsily folded sheet of notepaper in my direction.

I snatched it from him gratefully. 'Why didn't you say so before? It could be urgent, Dad, honestly!' I unfolded it and gasped as I read the first line:

I'M GOING TO MURDER YOU AND DEFILE YOUR CORPSE!!!

Then I noticed that the words had been hastily crossed out by whoever wrote the note. Beneath that there was another line that read:

I hate you, Heffa Lump, I hope you and your stinking vampire drop dead.

Well, that was better than threatening murder... though it had also been crossed out. Someone was clearly struggling to organize their thoughts. The childish looping handwriting was somewhat familiar to me. The third line, which wasn't crossed out, read:

Actually, I still like you lots, Heffa, but we can't be friends anymore because of Teddy. Vampires and werewolves are mortal enemies. In case you'd forgotten.

I realized the note was from Joe. He was obviously still hurting, just like I was. There was one final line:

P.S. My dad says I should have rewritten this note in neat, without all the death threats at the top, but I only had one sheet of paper so I just crossed 'em out. Please ignore the death threats and just read the third line, okay? Love, Joe Cahontas.

I was torn between being relieved that Joe wasn't going to murder me and sad that he had made me choose between him and Teddy. Why couldn't we just hang out and fix motorcycles like we had in the old days? I used to love sitting there in the darkness of his garage, watching him grappling with his huge wrench, tweaking his nuts and screwing my parts. My motorbike's parts, I mean. I dropped the note on the table and returned to stirring the casserole wistfully. After about ten minutes, during which I sighed with increasing frequency and volume, Dad looked up from the paper.

'Everything okay, kid?'

'That note was from Joe Cahontas. He just wanted to let me know that he still hates Teddy and still can't be my friend anymore.'

'That's a bit weird, isn't it? Does he think you've got amnesia?'

'It is chapter one, Dad, there's no harm in a thorough recap is there?'

'I guess not, darling. Come and sit down for a second, I want to talk to you.'

He folded the paper and set it down on the table. I drew up a chair and sat expectantly, licking the casserole spoon clean while he frowned quietly. I recognized that expression – Chump was about to stretch his limited conversational abilities with an extended passage of dialogue.

'You know I like Teddy, don't you, Heffa?'

I nodded.

'But, let's face it, Joe is *much* better. He's way taller and more athletic looking. Healthier looking all round, actually. And he likes sports. Teddy doesn't even know the difference between baseball and golf; it's embarrassing. If you want my advice, you should dump Teddy and go out with Joe.'

I was shocked, not only that Chump had managed to string so many words together coherently, but also by the very idea that I would ever give up Teddy. Since the first moment we had met, we had been destined to be together, and nothing could change that. He was my soulmate. Goths and zombies and whatnot had tried their best to separate us and failed. We certainly weren't going to be torn apart by the narrow-minded prejudices of some podunk sheriff. Before I could compose a suitably scathing answer, I heard the unmistakable roar of a sports car engine in the distance. Teddy was here!

I ran to the door and threw it open just as his car squealed to a stop outside. He didn't usually drive with such urgency – was something bothering him? The gull-wing door opened, and he swung out with balletic grace. I never failed to be amazed by the sight of him, and I never failed to use the fact of seeing him as an excuse to describe him all over again.

His perfect skin was always the first thing I noticed, so pale and flawless, and smooth like polished marble. His face was perfectly proportioned, and the sight of it was still over-whelming to me. Imagine that every artist there's ever been had taken all the works of art they'd made and smashed them all up and melted them down and combined them into one perfect object called Teddy Kelledy. You wouldn't even miss all that other junk if you could only look at him once. His forehead was as wide as the Mississippi and his cheeks were as angular as cut diamonds. The rain trickled between his neat blond eyebrows and ran down his elegant nose. His eyes were purple beneath his noble jutting brow, and as his gaze met mine he smiled, revealing a row of perfect white teeth, with just a hint of long sensuous fang at the corner of his mouth. My stomach flipped over, and I steadied myself against the doorframe. He jiggled his long, probing fingers in a cheery wave, then took a plastic bag from the car and held it above his head as a makeshift umbrella. Turning up the collar of his perfectly tailored raincoat, he ran to join me in the shelter of the veranda. When he wanted to, Teddy could use his vampire super-speed to run incredibly quickly, but for everyday activities like this he ran like the rest of us, only a thousand times more gracefully. He put his arm around me and led me back inside.

'My darling, I thought I would never see you again!' he exclaimed melodramatically. 'I felt sure that some awful fate must have befallen you since I left this morning. Perhaps a rogue vampire had murdered you, or your house might have been incinerated, or you might have slipped in the shower and fatally banged your head.'

Teddy was often like this; it was really moving that he was so worried about my safety. I reassured him: 'Don't worry, I haven't had a shower for days.'

He let go of me, and moved away slightly. My dad was looking at us with the frustrated expression he put on every evening at this time. I knew he liked Teddy, because he repeatedly told me so; he must have just been tired after a long day at work. Teddy greeted Dad warmly and joined him at the table. I busied myself in the kitchen while they chatted.

'Whatever you're cooking sure smells, Heffa, why don't you serve it up so we can eat? The game starts soon. Join us for some dinner, Teddy?'

'No thank you, sir. I already partook of my evening repast with my family.' Of course Teddy didn't want to eat with us, even the most brilliantly prepared casserole in the world, which I started to dish up, couldn't nourish him. He craved blood and blood alone. Sweet human blood, preferably.

Of course, the Kelledys didn't prey on humans. Teddy's father Joseph had brought them up to drink only blood that was willingly donated, so breaking into the local hospital once a month to steal the blood-drive donations kept the whole Kelledy clan from having to do anything evil.

Dad grunted. I knew that he thought Teddy was rude to refuse our hospitality every evening — and to be frank it (probably) wouldn't have killed him to taste the darn casserole after all the effort I had gone to.

I brought the plates of casserole to the table and Teddy cleared space for me to put them down, gathering the day's post and the paper into a neat pile. Suddenly he grabbed the newspaper with both hands and stood up. His mouth was open and his indigo eyes were wide with what, on anyone else's face, I would have taken to be fear. But Teddy wasn't afraid of anything, was he? I dropped the plates on the table and grabbed the paper from him. The front page read: 'Worrying Headline Points To Imminent Plot Development!' What on earth did that mean? Puzzled, I looked up, and saw Teddy and my father exchange concerned glances. With a feigned lack of interest, Teddy took the paper back from me, folded it several times, and put it in his coat pocket. He laughed half-heartedly, looking to Chump for support. 'The things they print these days, such nonsense.'

'Yeah, I know, I don't know why I bother to read it. Anyway, let's chow down before it gets cold.' Chump started to eat with his usual single-minded enthusiasm, and Teddy sat down again, idly tapping his fingers on the table and whistling a tune I recognized as one of his own classical piano compositions, 'Waltz for a Decapitated Girlfriend'. I couldn't help thinking there was more to that newspaper headline than they were telling me.

After shoveling the last of the casserole into his chasm-like mouth, Dad sat back in his chair and said, with studied nonchalance, 'By the way, Heffa, it might be best if you don't go to Port D'Angerous ever again.'

Before I could react, Teddy chipped in with, 'In fact, you should think deeply before going into Spatula as well.' Chump nodded enthusiastically and Teddy continued, 'Actually, on further consideration, it might be wise not to depart the safety of this abode at all.'

'Suits me,' I shrugged, wiping my mouth with my pajama sleeve. My father breathed a sigh of relief, and Teddy – who hadn't really needed to breathe since becoming undead – pretended to.

'Anyway, I'm going to watch the game,' Dad announced, grabbing a six-pack from the fridge and heading for the living room.

After we had washed up, Teddy and I sat at the kitchen table talking about nothing much. He seemed to have something on his mind, but I knew he'd tell me when he was ready; we had a very frank and honest relationship. In the meantime I was still thinking about the note I'd got from Joe. We had been so close before, and I hadn't realized until today just how much I missed having him around. Teddy put his hand on mine. It was ice-cold – as you'd expect from a walking corpse – and although I usually adored his frosty touch, I shivered, thinking about how warm Joe Cahontas was in comparison.

'You seem distracted, my darling. Is anything wrong?'

'Huh? Oh no, I was just thinking about. . . a nature program I saw, about wolves and their, um, mating habits.'

Teddy frowned. 'You know I don't like you watching those programs. The content is so unseemly and graphic. You haven't heard a word I said about the new CD by that band we both like!'

'I'm sorry; it's just been a really long day. Let's go to bed, I'll be fine after a good night's sleep, and I'll sleep better knowing you're sitting there in the dark, watching me. There's nothing a girl finds more reassuring.'

'I eagerly anticipate my nights looming over your bedside, but before we can enjoy the intimacy of your boudoir, there are some serious matters we must discuss.'

I stood up angrily. I had heard this speech before, and I knew where it was heading. Teddy was going to ask permission to turn me into a vampire, again. We'd been over it a million times, and he wouldn't shut up about it. I gently explained that I wasn't in the mood to discuss it right now.

'For Chrissakes, are you going to start giving me grief about becoming a vampire? Giving my soul over to eternal damnation in return for a warped half-life living in the shadows, shunned by all that is decent and holy. . . it's a big commitment. Stop pressuring me! I've told you, maybe one day I will, but right now I'm young and I've got my whole life ahead of me.'

Teddy looked sheepish but protested, 'Eighteen isn't young. It's a perfectly decent age to become undead.'

'Well, maybe I'm not convinced that you're the right vampire for the job, did you think of that? You can't expect me just to roll over and bare my neck, you need to woo me, pursue me.'

'Pursue you? Through the forest? With you dressed only in a nightgown? While tree branches scratch your lily-white skin and thorn bushes rend your flimsy garment?'

Teddy was getting carried away. I saw his eyes start to turn red, which was usually bad news for someone. I wasn't entirely against the idea of finding myself at his mercy alone in the woods, but it was still raining.

'Calm down, will you? I'm trying to explain that you can't take me for granted. You need to show that you care, buy me presents, romance me, buy me presents. Or buy me presents.'

He nodded and his eyes returned to a dark green color. He somberly picked up the plastic bag he'd brought in with him and put it on the table in front of him.

'Ooh, is that a present?'

'Not exactly, although you will thank me for it, I'm sure. I said we had some serious matters to discuss. You know that I love you, and I want to provide you with the best of everything. Whether it's a first-class education, or a fine place to live, or...'

'Diamond necklaces? A solid-gold toilet? A butler?'

'Yes, I would give you all of those things, if only I could.'

I didn't like the way this conversation was going. Had Teddy's father cut his allowance? '"If only you could"? What does that mean?'

'It is somewhat awkward to discuss. You may be aware that the economy has been going through a slight period of uncertainty for the last couple of years.'

'It has?'

'Yes, the global recession, mortgage crisis, total financial meltdown? Do you recall?'

I didn't have much to do with the world of finance. I just held my hand out until Chump filled it with dollars. Could this explain why he had used one of his kidneys to pay the last set of utility bills? But what did that have to do with Teddy and his family? They were the richest people in town. Thanks to their habit of not dying, they had had several lifetimes to accumulate a fortune.

'Anyway, whether you noticed or not, times are rather trying. Some of Father's investments have performed less well than anticipated. It's very puzzling; they sounded so promising on paper. Low-cost mortgages for unemployed meth addicts, deep-water oil exploration in Florida, Adam Sandler's kabuki theatre company... they have all come to naught!'

'Naught? How much naught are we talking about?'

15

'A large corpulent naught, I'm afraid. Apart from the castle, which we own outright, and a few other trinkets, the Kelledys are completely bankrupt.' He held his head in his hands. I wanted to rush to him, hold him and offer him comfort, but there was something I still needed to know.

'So just to be clear — that bag? Not a present?'

Teddy forced a smile and removed a sheaf of papers from the bag. 'No, not a present, but something that will reward you in time.'

'A load of forms? Do I have to mail off to get my present?' I hoped not, I hated waiting.

'You are delightfully droll. I simply can't be depressed when I'm around you. If we can't rely on Father's investments to provide an income for our future, we must secure an income for ourselves. These are application forms: it's time for you to get a job!'

Get a job? This was all too much to take in — didn't I already have enough on my plate with looking after Dad and keeping on top of the daytime soaps? It had been a hell of a day, and my head was spinning. I reached for the edge of the table, but my grip was too weak to steady myself. As I fell, I felt a tidal wave of darkness hit me, and heard Teddy's voice, many leagues distant. 'I'll start filling in the basic details for you and when you wake up you can work on your personal statement...' And then all was silence.

chapter 2

working girl

I woke up in bed, and it was morning. My darling Teddy must have carried me to my room and tucked me in, in his perfect sensitive caring way that I loved so dearly. I was snug beneath my blankets, but the chilly summer wind whistled through the open window and rattled it in its frame. Teddy had been asking me for some time to get a handle put on the outside so that he could close the window behind him when he left, like the well-brought-up fiend he was. I couldn't ask Dad to break out the toolbox without giving him a good reason, though, and I knew that his simple mind would never be able to understand the truth nor the romance of my need: 'so that my undead vampire boyfriend can illicitly enter our house each night to watch me sleep in my adorably sleepy way'. He'd never believe that all Teddy did was watch me sleep; no one would.

Teddy kept me safe through the long dark hours of the night, but he always left before I woke. 'I simply must be home before *Daybreak*,' he had explained. He was such a big Adrian Chiles fan. So each morning I awoke alone to the sounds of the ancient forest that surrounded my modest home. Amidst the creaking of the mighty branches and the rustling of the leaves, I felt totally in tune with nature, like my bottomless well of empathy for all living things was kept topped up by this daily communion. In the distance, I heard the comforting hum of the woodcutters' chainsaws. Externally, at least, all was well with the world.

Usually I slept well, my conscience being utterly untroubled by any of the selfish acts or unkind thoughts that keep less highly evolved souls awake at night, but today something was wrong. I felt as if an enormous weight was pressing down on me. Looking down, I saw the pile of job application forms stacked neatly on my chest. Teddy had left me one of his subtle hints. The note on top was written in his familiar perfect copperplate hand.

> My darling Heffa, I have failed you. I strove long into the night to fill in these application forms, but was utterly unable to encapsulate your unique abilities in such a way as to make you sound even vaguely employable. I am afraid this task must fall to you. Must dash, Adrian is interviewing J-Lo this morning. All my love, Teddy.

I tossed the note aside in disgust. It looked like I would have to do everything for myself, as per usual. I scowled for a few minutes to focus my resolve and was about to get out of bed when I realized with horror that Teddy had forgotten to pull back my blankets; there was no way I would have the strength to yank them aside myself. I was trapped, pinned down beneath the heavy bedclothes. I would have to spend all day in bed, unable to apply for gainful employment, as I really, really wanted to. Fate, you have coughed up a hairball in Heffa Lump's casserole once more!

Resigned, I decided to go back to sleep until Teddy arrived that evening to free me. He could fill the forms in under my supervision.

Then I heard my father's clomping footsteps approaching. He popped his head around my bedroom door and I gave him a nonchalant smile that said, 'Keep moving, officer, nothing to see here.' Yet he snorted with alarm, and with his two strong hands – which had 'solved' so many crimes without troubling the overworked court system – he dragged my helpless body out from beneath the heavy blankets and the teetering pile of paperwork.

'Darlin', you know females aren't strong enough to handle two blankets. Lucky I stopped by, you'd have been trapped there all day,' he said.

'Yeah, thanks a lot, Dad, now I can get up and spend my day filling in dozens of forms. I can never repay you.' Except by slipping some laxatives into tonight's casserole.

He smiled and tousled my hair in the fatherly way I had always hated. 'Looking for a job, huh? Good for you.' He picked up one of the forms. 'High School Guidance Counselor? Are you sure you're qualified for this? It says, "Slayer powers a definite advantage."'

I waved away his trifling objection; I knew that I could achieve anything I set my mind to. Right now I was concentrating on making Dad leave me alone. He picked up another job application. 'Waitress – Morlocke's Bar and Grill. "Must be willing to go with bar owner, no shapeshifters." Jeez, that's just perverted.' He tossed the form aside and stood up, his hand resting on his gun. Seeing him there, smug with the unearned authority of the uniformed crypto-fascist, gave me an amazing idea. Filling in job application forms is only for people without contacts. My dad was sheriff; he could get me a job through the power of necrotism.

'I'll come and work for you as a policegirl!' I clapped my hands excitedly. 'I'd be brilliant at it, I love telling people what to do and I'm always right. Lend me your nightstick, Daddy, I want to practice cracking hippy skulls before my interview!'

Chump was unimpressed by my sudden eagerness to go into the family business with him. 'It's not all about fixin' social deviants, darling, you've got to learn about solving crimes too.'

'Oh, I know all that,' I assured him. 'I've watched all the cop shows. You just find the clues, look at them through the micropoke and then shout at that week's guest star until they confess.'

He shook his head violently with admiration before trying to put me off again. 'Sorry, honey, it's just too dangerous.'

'But Daaad! I've faced deadly danger a thousand times. Why just last week this rogue vamp...' I clapped my hands over my mouth; I had nearly said too much. Chump could never know about my secret supernatural life, his fragile mind would never be able to take it, and he'd be even more insistent about that dusk curfew. I backtracked, disguising my sudden change of heart with some well-placed flattery. 'I guess you're right, Dad, I'm just not big or dumb enough to be an emotionless goose-stepping pig.'

He breathed a sigh of relief. 'Finally you're talking some sense, kid. Tell you what, I'll ask around town on my rounds today, see if there are any vacancies for you. I'll see you this evening.'

I shrugged with gratitude. I didn't imagine that Chump would turn out to be much help in this matter, but if it gave him something to do and kept him out of my hair, then I was all for it. He left the house whistling in his gratingly atonal way, and I sat on the bed planning my next move. I gathered the scattered forms back into a pile and flicked through them. They were long and complex, and the boxes were far too small for my endearingly childlike handwriting. And the questions were deeply intrusive: what business was it of theirs what my SAT score was? Heffa Lump is a sensitive and private person, not some lab specimen to be pinned out and poked with the pointy knives. I knew then that the traditional job search route would not work for me. Not because I had no skills or experience, and not because I lacked motivation to achieve anything beyond satisfying my basic physical needs. No, it was rather that I was beyond the petty concerns of these bureaucratic 'employers' with their so-called 'opportunities'. I was on a higher plane entirely. I had a boyfriend who was a vampire. And that made me simply too darn special to look for work, whatever he might think to the contrary.

On the other hand, maybe it would be nice to have something to do on the days when Teddy was busy. Despite my young age, I had already read all the worthwhile works of world literature, and there were only so many episodes of *LA Ink* a girl could watch in a day. I resolved half-heartedly to continue my search for employment.

But where was I to look, given that the normal options were closed to me due to excessive specialness? I considered this dilemma as I dressed (I'd decided not to shower until I had found a job). I marveled once more at the incredible range of clothes in my wardrobe; each outfit suited me better than the last. I knew that I would look ravishing in just a potato sack. Many young girls with this talent would feel some sort of vast egotism about it, but I prided myself on my total modesty in the face of this irresistible hotness, and I rarely dressed up. Why bother when I turned heads wearing merely . . . this old T-shirt with BBQ sauce down the front and . . . my favorite sweatpants; (sniff) they had a couple more weeks' wear in them yet, for sure. I admired myself in the mirror, and the sight of me looking so amazing made my thoughts click into place. I would go and visit Teddy's sister Bobbi out at the remote Kelledy castle deep in Spatula's darkest woods! She was almost as stylish as me in some ways, and with her relentless perkiness she was sure to be eager to help me out with my problems. Teddy was off hunting with his brother Jack, so it would just be us girls.

With a renewed sense of purpose, I skipped down the stairs and out the front door. The hulking black armored car that Teddy had given me as a graduation present sat on the driveway, daring people to come within its deadly range of fire. I called it 'Mabel'. I smiled at its quirky cuteness, so reminiscent of my own personality, and climbed aboard.

I made good time on my drive out to the Kelledy castle. The roads were wet with rain, but this was no problem for Mabel's all-terrain tires. There was some nasty mid-morning traffic clogging Main Street – Only Street would have been a more appropriate name – but a few warning shots from Mabel's turret-mounted 50mm cannons convinced the good folk of Spatula that I had the right of way.

Soon I was alone on the country road that led into the forested hills above town. The trees closed in around me, the wind and the rain lashing their branches. It was almost as if they were shivering with fear at some as yet unrevealed horror passing close by them. Then, round a bend in the road, I saw Castle Kelledy at last. It loomed above the trees, as threatening as ever in its stolid grayness. Two mismatched towers rose above the main keep, and I could swear the taller one was leaning to the left even more than usual. It felt very homely. From a distance you would swear it was one of those European castles that had been shipped over brick by brick. It was only close up that a rapped fist on the moss-covered wall revealed that the whole thing was made of fiberglass.

Bobbi Kelledy was Teddy's younger sister, although they weren't really blood relations – except in their shared lust for it – they just referred to each other as brother and sister so that everyone would know there was no funny business going on. Except there was, because Bobbi was involved with her other 'brother' Jack. All a bit seedy, now I came to think about it. Anyway, Bobbi had become a close friend; her constant good mood was exhilarating, even though it was only a mask hiding the darker, more homicidal side of her character. Her style advice was always invaluable and she was always ready to get involved in the latest Kelledy wheeze. Whether it was organizing a party, organizing a massacre, or just helping me to avoid grown-up responsibility, her 'can-kill' attitude was a real tonic to be around.

I found her in the TV room, lounging on the sofa with a blood smoothie. 'Oh, it's you again,' she greeted me rapturously. 'You know Teddy's not here, right?'

'I thought we could hang out, just us girls,' I said. 'Oh, Bobbi, life is so hard at the moment, no employer is likely to recognize my unique abilities, I just don't know what to do!'

'Sssshhh,' Bobbi hissed through her fangs. 'I'm missing the good bit!' She nodded at the enormous widescreen television. On the screen a vampire was standing in the middle of a fearful dungeon lit with disco lights. She was frowning in concentration, but I wasn't sure why. Then the viewpoint switched to three ghastly ghouls sitting in a row behind a huge sarcophagus. One of them looked very familiar. He had an oily quiff, a ruffled shirt with pink buttons and long painted fingernails. It wasn't till he spoke that I remembered though – I'd never forget that high-pitched drawl. It was D'Arcy D'Acula, ancient vampire and adult film mogul, last seen in Romania trying to get my Teddy to expose himself to the world! I gasped in horror; what was he doing on TV?

'Well, darling, I just don't quite get what you're doing,' the foul fiend said. 'What's your talent again?'

'I'm protecting the entire audience with an invisible forcefield,' the vampire on screen said proudly. 'Try to read my mind; it won't work!'

'Read *my* mind,' the second horrific beast on the panel growled, with a sneer so fearsome I felt quite frightened myself, though on looking again his hair was probably scarier. 'That is a bloody awful talent.'

'I agree,' said the third judge, a young-looking woman with a wide blank face. She wore a bizarre hat made from a fax machine and was wearing enough make-up to paint a battleship; I could not even begin to imagine how hideous she would look without it. 'It's thumbs down from Lady CooCoo too. I'm sorry, but you're... *fired.*'

By now all three of them were holding their thumbs down. The auditioning vampire barely had time to scream before a jet of fire burst from the floor and set her ablaze. Bobbi sighed with satisfaction.

'What on earth are you watching?' I asked.

'Duh, Heffa, it's only *Undead's Got Talent*, TV's premier supernatural talent show. Where have you been? This program's huge, the underworld tabloids never talk about anything else: *Flay, Scream!, Gore*, they're always full of the latest gossip.'

'I thought D'Arcy D'Acula was our arch-enemy,' I pouted. 'Why are you helping his viewing figures?'

'Oh, he's the nice one,' Bobbi explained. 'The ones you really have to watch out for are Lady CooCoo and Cowl. They say CooCoo's some type of shapeshifting banshee, and Cowl... well, no one really knows quite what he is, but it's definitely not human. They judge the contestants, and they're harsh; people call them the Vindicti. Ooh, this is the bit where they throw the losing contestants to the lions!'

'Do you mean the relentless media exposure and snarky belittling that makes them regret the day they ever tried to get famous?' I asked, remembering previous reality TV shows I'd watched, like *America's Next Top Vampire* and *Pop Igor*.

'No, I mean the actual lions, dummy,' Bobbi shouted enthusiastically over the sounds of roaring and feasting emanating from the television. 'Hey, Heffa, why don't you enter? If you gave up your silly reluctance to let my brother turn you into a soulless murdering beast, you could go on the show and make your fortune that way; no more of this work business. Also, if you lost and the Vindicti had you fired, that would be okay too,' she added.

'Aw, thanks Bobbi, it's nice to know that win or lose I'll get just as much support from you,' I responded. She could be so thoughtful. 'But I don't think that kind of showing off is for me, and I'm still not quite ready to die. Thanks anyway.'

Bobbi shrugged and turned back to the television, leaving me feeling somewhat under-comforted. I was so tired of vampires thinking that me becoming one of them could solve all my problems. I wanted to make something of my life *my* way. Perhaps I'd made a mistake in coming to see her. I had a human problem; perhaps the answer was to get some human advice. But since coming to Spatula I'd mostly hung out with otherworldly beings, so a lot of my old friends were dead to me, and quite a few were actually dead. I wondered who was left. . .

There was always Piper Thinne. She'd been in the group of people at school I'd affectionately called 'the evil ones' due to their inability to be happy when I'd landed the hottest boy in our year, but I was running out of options. She'd have to do.

Piper lived on the other side of Spatula, in one of the less well-imagined parts of town. Stephfordy had thought about some areas in a lot of detail. My house, Main Street, the Kelledys' castle: these were all richly imagined and lovingly described, but not everywhere was lucky enough to get the full writerly treatment. As well as playing host to the rain that was a reassuringly soggy presence in all our lives, the more vague areas of Spatula were shrouded in a blanket of fog that lent them an aura of unreality. I usually stuck to the more solid areas if I could; it was a bit too much like Silent Hill round the misty parts. Only with more misshapen freaks.

Piper looked somewhat surprised to see me when I rang her doorbell. 'Uh, Heffa, I'm kind of busy. . .' she began, but I brushed her objections to one side, as well as her body, and went in.

'I'll help with whatever you're doing if you like,' I said. 'Oh, you're writing college applications; I can do that for you! All you need to do is add the bit where you explain how your boyfriend's family can build a new library and they'll let you in, no questions asked.' I sighed, remembering how easy it was all going to be until Teddy dropped his insolvency bombshell.

'Er. . . thanks,' Piper said, moving her bits of paper out of the way so I could sit down. 'So, what brings you here?'

'What, I can't visit one of my oldest friends? Oh, Piper, my life sucks, and I knew you'd understand since yours obviously does too. I can't get a job, I can't afford to go to college, and I just don't see why I have to make all this effort! I was so sure that once I'd graduated the Hollywood talent scouts would be all over me, but apparently their moody-teen quota is full this year. It's so unfair!' I burst into a very wild and convincing wail of grief; those Hollywood film-makers didn't know what they were missing.

'Er, hey, oh, I have an idea!' Piper said. She ran around the room in a frenzy of excitement, rummaging through drawers and pulling books off shelves with wild abandon. She seemed keen to help me, but after a while I started to think that maybe she didn't have an idea after all. I was about to adopt the mortifying frown I reserved for close friends who disappointed me, when she grabbed the previous day's *Spatula Gazette* from the floor. She scanned through the pages with feverish eagerness. 'Um, um, um, no, no, maybe, yes! Look, this would be perfect for you and if you leave right now, you can make the audition.' She thrust the paper under my nose, and I sniffed and heroically suppressed my sobs.

'TODAY. The Spatula Humdrum Amdram Collective auditions for *Worrying Heights*, a new musical based on the classic novel by Emily Borëonallday. Rec center, 3 p.m.,' I read aloud. 'Piper, you're right, I'd be perfect for the main part! I must leave immediately.'

'Oh, thank God,' Piper said. 'I mean, brilliant, Heffa, go you! Go, go, go. Please.' She helpfully pushed me out of the door and waved frantically. She was such a kind friend.

I raced to the rec center as fast as my armored car would take me. I had read and loved *Worrying Heights*, along with every other book in the world, and quickly reminded myself of the plot. Clingy, the beautiful, wild heroine, was forced to choose between two men: the boring reliable one and the intense crazed one who loved her even when she was dead. Something about that seemed rather familiar but I had no time to draw out the painfully obvious parallels – the audition would start any minute.

I thrust open the church hall doors with a bang, startling several old ladies into falling over. Brilliant, that was the dramatic entrance sorted. 'Look no further,' I announced. 'It's me, it's Clingy, I've come in now, oh oooh, oh.'

I paused to gauge the effect. Silence reigned as the entire hall struggled to cope with my amazing personification of Clingy's tortured soul.

Up on the hall stage, the director cleared his throat. 'That was very... enthusiastic,' he said, 'thank you. Why don't you join us on stage? What's your name, dear?'

'Heffa,' I announced, with a winning smile. 'Heffa Lump. You've probably heard of me.'

'Um, I'm not sure...'

'Oh, you card,' I giggled, elbowing him playfully in the ribs. 'Now I know you'll want to give me the part straight away, but I guess we've got to preserve the niceties and audition the no-hopers. Who've we got?'

The director was wearing the awed expression that people often seemed to adopt around me; it was rather sweet. 'Er, you and, um,' he consulted his clipboard, 'Wanda Mensional.'

'What, WANDA?' I gasped. 'What are *you* doing here?'

Wanda Mensional had been a school friend of mine, one who'd secretly maintained a double life as teen pop sensation Winona Arizona, the two-faced cow. The last time I'd seen her she'd been eating her way through the prom-goers, having been unfortunately and I'm sure accidentally turned into a vampire by Teddy's father Joseph in a moment of weakness.

'I might be world-famous, but I like to slum it and give something back to the little people, especially when they look so tasty,' the black-clad, white-faced, brown-wigged traitor said, sneering at me from the side of the stage. 'Good luck with the audition. I know they want someone who can sing *and* dance *and* act, but none out of three ain't bad, I'm sure you could get the part of the boring old housekeeper Mrs. Smelly if you try really hard.'

'You just watch,' I announced. 'Right, Mr. Director, I'm going first.' I took the card with the audition speech on it and drifted in a tormented, lovelorn way to the center of the stage.

'Has there ever been such a poor girl as wot I am?' I declaimed in my best English accent. 'Oh, lawks, how sad is I? Here am I trapped upon the lonely moors of backwards nineteenth-century England before they had dentists or dry cleaning, torn between dashing, homicidal Cliffledge and dull-but-loaded Edgar. Cliffledge is reckless and sexy and I would love to throw myself upon him but he is also rude and smelly, while Edgar is boringsville but he does have a house and a nice carriage. Why, gadzooks, 'tis just like me and Teddy and Joe Cahontas. For while Teddy is prim and proper and wants to marry me and give me wealth and so forth, Joe is violent and all muscly and jumps off cliffs and wants to ravage me on the back of his motorcycle... *what?*'

'If you could just read the bit on the card?' the director said, as he stopped waving his arms wildly in desperation. 'Also, Stephfordy would like me to add that you're missing the point: Teddy is totally Cliffledge, what with the obsessive love, and Joe is the conventional option; please can you stop messing up her carefully inserted references to classic works of literature?'

I thought about this for a while. 'Nah, I don't think so. Joe's the rugged, poor and hairy one; Teddy's all respectable, except for the occasional blood-drinking. Are you sure she's thought this through?'

The director shrugged. 'Don't ask me. Just read the frickin' card, would you?'

'Fine.' I squinted down at the bit of paper, and screamed, 'Oh, *CLIFFLEDGE!!*'

Once the tinkle of breaking glass had faded away, a hush descended over the room. I waited for the rapturous applause, but the director only winced, removed his fingers from his ears, and said, 'Thank goodness that's over. Ms. Mensional, your turn.'

Wanda Mensional raised her arms to the heavens, bared her fangs and moaned, 'Ohhh, *Cliffledge*...'

I was swept away with emotion. Her acting prompted such a dark, deep response, such a tidal wave of raw untamed feeling. It was a revelation. I felt it from the bottom of my soul: *I hated Wanda Mensional.*

'Well, that's easy!' the director announced, smiling. 'Wanda, you *are* Clingy. There's no doubt in my mind.'

'Why, thank you,' Wanda simpered. 'Now, when do the group rehearsals start? I'm ravenous... with the urge to start acting, obviously.'

I had never been so insulted in my life. There was nothing for it but to leave with dignity. I extended a trembling hand and said solemnly, 'You'll regret this one day when I'm the most famous person in the world and you're still stuck in this provincial hellhole, you blinkered idiots.' And with that I left the stage and flounced off in pure Clingy style. They'd soon find out what they'd lost by rejecting me.

As I sat in the car mourning the death of my barely-even-begun amateur dramatics career, I realized that perhaps this latest setback had shown me the way forward after all. Wanda thought she was so amazing, with her talent and her platinum album and her pointy teeth, but I knew she had less than a tenth of my awe-inspiring abilities. There was nothing for it: I'd have to get famous too. When crowds were begging *me* to sign autographs and adopt their children she'd understand how foolish she'd been to think she could compete. Plus, if I was a superstar, that would take care of all my financial woes too. It was win-win!

For a brief moment, I felt doubt. Was I strong enough to cope with the pressures of fame? What if it went to my head and I got snooty or addicted to diets or something? Also, I hadn't quite figured out how exactly I was going to become the most popular girl in the world. There was only one thing that could reassure me, one person who believed in me absolutely. My beloved, my only, the beautifullest man in the world, Teddy would wrap me in his icy arms and take all my troubles away. I set off at once to find him.

chapter 3

gruesome threesome

Darling, what's wrong?

I read the note and glanced over at the vision of pure hotness
that was Teddy Kelledy frowning in concentration at the table,
looking for all the world as if he had not been writing
illicit letters to me. I took my pencil out and scribbled a
response:

**That director was so mean to me. I could have died of
embarrassment.**

Teddy read the scrap of paper, stuck his tongue out the side of
his mouth endearingly and wrote in reply:

*I would never let you die of embarrassment. I would be
right there beside you, doing something so outrageously
gauche that all attention would have been focused on me
instead. Darling Heffa, I will never let you die, period.*

I thought about this.

What if I had terminal cancer?

*I would search the world for compatible blood, organs and
bone marrow and ensure your survival. And if all else
failed, turn you into a vampire.*

How about if we were trapped in a sinking ship?

*I would use my inhuman strength to rend a hole in the
side of the vessel and swim to land. And if necessary
turn you into a vampire.*

Freak chainsaw accident?

I would sew your mutilated body back together with loving care and running stitch. And then turn you into a vampire.

I gazed at him. Surely I was the luckiest girl in the world. Who else had a boyfriend so devoted he was prepared to murder people for organs, swim halfway across the globe, and live with a horrific re-animated corpse? Who else had a boyfriend so careful and considerate he would plan for all these eventualities? Why, I wouldn't have been surprised to learn he had a perfect match for my blood type already locked up in his house in case I should ever need it. That was the kind of love every girl longed for, but only I had it. Every other girl could just dream. And weep into their pillows at night in the knowledge that they would never experience the pure passion I could inspire without even thinking about it.

I just have one more question.

Ask it, my love.

Why are we writing notes to each other? You're sitting right there.

Teddy looked up from his careful perusal of the steakhouse menu and frowned at me. When he'd seen me so distraught earlier, he'd immediately rushed me off for a romantic meal; I hadn't anticipated that we would spend the first ten minutes of it passing notes across the table to each other.

'I'm not sure,' he confessed. 'It is true that a conversation like this would have been better expressed verbally. I can only assume that Stephfordy Mayo wants everyone to appreciate the contrast between my perfect copperplate handwriting and that werewolf's uncouth scrawl back in chapter one.'

It was a bit mean of Stephfordy to keep making it so obvious that Teddy was utterly superior to Joe in every conceivable way, but I appreciated it – if it wasn't continually pointed out to me, it was entirely possible I could get bored with Teddy and run off with Joe, who was after all tall, built, handsome and a dab hand with his tools. Still, only Teddy could really match my perfection. He was such a gentleman!

The waitress came by to take our orders: an excessively rare steak for Teddy, as usual; pasta alla puttanesca for me. 'Thanks, guys,' she said. 'And if there's anything else you need – and I do mean anything,' she purred, winking at Teddy, 'just ask!'

'What a pleasant waitperson,' Teddy commented as she stalked off with an unnecessary sway. I could see what she was trying to do, but it was hopeless. Teddy only had eyes for me, and had done ever since he'd first smelled the sweet scent of my blood. Even my completely ordinary O-positive was somehow better than anyone else's. The waitress had no chance against destiny.

'Oh, Teddy,' I said. 'Everything else about my life is difficult, but at least I know I have you. For ever and ever and ever.'

'Yes, my love,' he whispered gently. 'Our love is indeed eternal. I knew it would be since I first met you and my fangs extended involuntarily. It was most perplexing.'

'There are so many memories,' I sighed. 'It's hard even to put them in any kind of ranking order.'

Teddy reached out to stroke my neck, his ice-cold digit running softly up and down my jugular vein, as was his adorable habit. 'But, Heffa, how can you put them in order of excellence? Surely all our moments together are so spectacular they can barely be distinguished?'

'You've got to have a top ten,' I argued. 'For one thing, that's how Stephfordy thinks teenagers are, all angsty lists in diaries and so forth. And for another, if I don't rank your amazingness, how will I be able to let you know when you're falling below expectations?'

'That is a valid concern,' Teddy agreed. 'Very well, I shall tell you mine, if you will tell me yours.'

'Great!' I reached into my purse for the list I'd compiled for this very occasion, with Teddy's behavior, hair, outfit and protectiveness level carefully graded for each incident so I could be sure it was as comprehensive as I could make it. 'Let's see – there was that time you told me you loved me. And that other time you told me you loved me. And that time

31

you ripped apart a lot of annoying goths and then told me you loved me. And the time we were flying back from Europe and I told you I'd never let you out of my sight ever again, and you told me you loved me. That's the top four, anyway, the rest are all the times you gave me CDs and jewelry and outfits and cinema tickets, but I might have to discount those since you're poor now and won't be able to give me things anymore.'

'I give you my heart, Heffa,' Teddy said earnestly. 'If you wish, I will rip it from my chest this very instant!'

'But enough about you,' I said winsomely. 'What are your top ten memories of me?'

Teddy stared mistily into the distance. 'The incident I cherish the most was tearing apart that evil vampire coven while you lay unconscious and helpless. That said, the occasion where I rescued you from certain death beneath that over-inflated prop *thingy* was also most satisfactory; I relished the opportunity to utilize my super-speed, and you were so terribly adorable, lying there unconscious...' He paused for thought.

'Then there were the many nights I watched as you slept, as you writhed under the covers and shouted my name... and I will never forget your look of utter desolation when you fainted after I told you I was leaving. As you slumped to the floor, I knew once and for all that anyone who could respond to my words in such a pitiful way was the woman for me! Submissive, mostly silent, frequently unconscious...'

I reached over to squeeze his arm. 'And just think, when I finally begin to get wrinkles and let you make me into a vampire, I will never need to sleep again, and we will make even more beautiful memories in which I'm conscious!'

A look of confused adoration crossed Teddy's perfect marble features. 'Yes... long aeons of constant wakefulness will certainly be something to look forward to...'

Our food arrived, interrupting the latest perfect moment we'd shared, and I took the opportunity to glance around the steakhouse; I did love the chance to hone my descriptive skills and waste pages upon unnecessary details. Yet in this instance I found myself sadly uninspired. The check tablecloths, ketchup-stained tiles, rustic wooden-paneled walls, dull sad faces... there was nothing in Spatula worth immortalizing in the fascinating story of my life. How could a town with one school, two roads, one crossroads, and one diner deserve a starring role in the romance of the century? If I described it in any great detail, the locals might try to develop it into a tourist attraction and I couldn't have that. Just looking at their pasty faces, sagging guts and bad taste in clothing made me feel sick. In comparison to the glowing brilliance of the Kelledy family and my reflected glory as Teddy's girlfriend, they were nothing.

'Wait a darn minute!' I shouted.

'Heffa, what?!' Teddy leapt up, his eyes flashing turquoise in panic. 'What is it? Do I need to rend someone limb from limb for you?'

'Much as I love watching you indulge your sexy over-the-top violent side, now is not the time! Teddy – I've just realized the answer to all our problems.'

'I wasn't aware we were burdened with any problems,' Teddy said, his beautiful brow clenched in confusion.

'Only the lack of financial support for the lifestyle I wish to be kept in,' I reminded him. 'But now I know what to do. Look around you – what do you see?'

Teddy examined the other diners. 'Dessert?' he suggested.

'Right!' I said. 'Well, not exactly, but think about it, we're better than them in every conceivable way, correct?'

'I am at the pinnacle of the food chain, they are as cattle to me,' Teddy agreed, salivating only slightly.

'So don't you see? All we need to do is share the story of our love with the world and we'll become superstars! We'll be the next Bennifer, Brangelina, TomKat! All we need is a cutesy combination of our names and a few interviews with gossip mags and we'll be set.'

'Would we not first need to become famous for some marvelous achievement?'

I smiled at his sweet naiveté. 'Not anymore, darling, where have you been? We live in a world where Snooki is famous. Now, what shall we call ourselves – Hefward might work, I'm not so sure about Tedeffa. Maybe Heddy?'

'Um.' Teddy was playing with his knife, awkwardly, but so far managing to keep it away from anyone's wrist, I was so proud of him. 'I do not know that I concur. Is this shallow vision truly how you envisage our future together?'

'Full of fame and fortune? Of course – how else would we ever be happy? Why, what do you want from our lives?'

Teddy blinked and looked bashful. 'Oh, it is just... I am an old-fashioned vampire; it is the way I was raised. I have this dream of the two of us... me going out to work in my father's butcher's shop, coming home to find you waiting with a bloody Mary on the porch, in a little apron with frills, and then we would hunt dinner, and talk about our days, and not sleep in each other's arms, vampire and wife for all eternity.'

I rolled my eyes. I suppose he couldn't help being an old man of thirty trapped in the body of a gorgeous teenager, but he wasn't even making an effort to overcome it. 'You really expect us to get married and for me to stay at home fixing you Bloody Marys?'

'It wouldn't just have to be Bloody Marys,' he said earnestly. 'Bloody Lucy or Kate or Mark would be fine too; I am not fussy.'

I sighed. 'I'm sorry, Teddy, but we live in the twenty-first century now. We don't have to be married before you vamp me, and I'm completely happy for you to endow me with all your worldly goods right now. I'm a modern woman – I don't want a ring on my finger. I want lots of rings, and some necklaces, and maybe a Ferrari, whatever's going.'

Teddy's eyes darkened to a chocolate brown. 'I disapprove of the idea of you working,' he said. 'It is a man's duty to provide for his woman.'

'Whoa, whoa, whoa,' I said. 'I didn't say anything about working – if I've learned anything from the last few hours, it's that there isn't a profession in the world that can fully allow me to express myself. The only way I'll ever be happy is to be Me, full time. And if we share our story with the world that can happen! Anyway, it goes against forty years of feminism to think you have to be married before spending all your boyfriend's money; I'd be quite happy to do that right now, but you don't have any. This is the fastest way to get some.'

'I just don't know,' Teddy said. 'I'm a vampire, remember? My specialty is lurking in the shadows and keeping myself hidden from the world. I fear going on *Oprah* is not the way to maintain that tradition.'

I could barely keep myself from crying. After all his protestations about loving me until (and beyond) death, I couldn't believe he was being so selfish about keeping me from my dream career. Why, in preventing me from spilling the beans about our amazing romance, he was also denying a whole generation of girls the chance to dream of the day they'd find their own pale imitation of Teddy Kelledy. Couldn't he see he was destroying their lives as well as our bank balance?

Well, fine, but this wouldn't be the end of the matter. I was sure I'd be able to persuade him of the brilliance of my plan, given time and the withholding of his neck-sniffing privileges.

Our awkward silence was interrupted by the feedback crackle of a microphone. I looked up from mournfully gazing at the spot on my wrist where a Rolex ought to have been, and was shocked to see Joe Cahontas and his fellow werewolves standing on the stage at the far side of the restaurant. I'd noticed the sign promising live music, but hadn't realized it was Joe's band The Protection Racket playing. It was the first time I had seen Joe since our falling out, and my heart flipped over with entirely platonic pleasure. He seemed taller than ever, although that might have been because he was standing on a stage. His ample muscles strained to escape the confines of his simple plaid shirt, and I found myself willing them to succeed. He brushed a lock of his long black hair from his eyes and came forward, acknowledging the audience of diners with his easygoing, radiant smile. I hadn't realized until this moment how much I'd missed his homely unpretentious warmth. I glanced at my snooty cold pretentious boyfriend Teddy, in case there was any chance he was about to lose control and attack Joe with a thrilling display of manly rippling. He was grinding his teeth so hard that they began smoking, and repeatedly stabbing a nearby diner in the leg with his fork, but apart from these subtle signs he was keeping his rage in check.

'Awright Spatula!' Joe howled into the microphone. 'We've got a set that will put hair on your chest, hands, and maybe some other places. Ready, guys? A-one-a-two-a-one-two-three—'

With a wild thrashing of drums and guitar they launched into 'Hungry Like the Wolf', followed by 'Werewolves of London', 'Teenage Lycanthropy' and a rousing rendition of 'Who Let the Dogs Out?' As their sweat flew and the guitar shredding grew ever shreddier (they probably ought to have cut their fingernails), the audience's excitement mounted: girls abandoned their dates; wives abandoned their husbands; small children ran from their parents – there was just something undeniably magnetic about the raw animal energy of a bunch of hairy, leather-clad musicians.

'Heffa!'

I broke away from my head-banging reverie to see Teddy looking at me, worry and terror all over his divine face. 'Yes, my love?' I asked dreamily.

'You were nodding along rather enthusiastically. You can't be... enjoying this, can you? They stink! Both in the olfactory sense and the musical one, I should clarify.'

'Oh, my beloved, you know Joe and I are just friends, even though he hates me at the moment. I miss him, that's all.' I hurriedly scrunched the napkin where I'd written my phone number and a time for us to meet into a ball, and hid it in my lap.

'Hmmm,' said Teddy, only slightly convinced. It was hard to believe that such a fine specimen of inhumanity could possibly be jealous of another fine specimen of inhumanity, but then again both he and Joe were fighting over *me* – and I was clearly the biggest prize in Spatulan dating since, well, ever.

On the stage, Joe was fending off attempted stage invasions by any audience member with an XX chromosome. He caught my eye after a particularly ruthless swipe of the mike, and winked.

He was *so* naughty, I thought to myself. He knew I'd never choose him over Teddy and yet he persisted in flirting with me outrageously. Anyone would think he was trying to use his wolfish charm and dozens of screaming fans to prove that he was the hotter option.

Still, having said that… I had no doubt that with his sexy blue-collar image and howling voice Joe could storm the charts if he ever devoted all his attention to his music, rather than splitting it between auto-repair, pining after me, and wandering round the woods in the nud. With me at his side, as his manager-cum-girlfriend, we'd hit the big time as the rock world's alpha couple within weeks at the outside: all the fame and fortune I'd ever need…

But how could I be thinking like that, when Teddy was sitting beside me clenching his teeth and growling in a state of fury? How could I possibly consider betraying him like that, simply because I wanted cash?

Okay, I admit it. It was totally easy.

But overall I still thought Teddy was my first choice. After all, he was a lot less sweaty, and the only boyfriend who could make me immortal. I just needed to persuade him to go along with my brilliant money-making scheme. And if I pretended that I might dump him for Joe, he was bound to do whatever I wanted to guarantee I'd stay with him.

Heffa Lump, you modest, humble, lovely evil genius, I congratulated myself, and moved to put my plan into action.

'JOE! THAT WAS AMAZING! I THINK I MIGHT LOVE YOU AFTER ALL!' I shouted across the restaurant. Subtle, but I thought he'd get the idea. Joe was signing autographs by the stage edge, but on hearing my voice he dropped his pen as if he'd been shot. The fan he'd been signing rolled down her T-shirt with disappointment. Joe shoved her aside and bounded up on to the closest table, sending dishes crashing to the floor. His wolf-brothers looked nervously towards the bar, where the manager was busy deducting the damages from their earnings.

Joe leapt from table to table, reducing the band's profitability as he headed towards me like a hairy cruise missile. He arrived in a final clatter of breaking crockery and looked into my eyes. 'Heffa, are you serious?' he asked, drooling with excitement.

'No, of course not, why ever would you think that?' I asked, shocked. 'I love Teddy! Remember? I just thought, you know, I could totally do you too. Except I wouldn't because I love Teddy. It's really very simple. No room for misinterpretation there.'

I sat back and smiled as his hackles rose. 'You think I'm gonna give in that easily? I ain't giving up, girl. I'm the right husband for you, honest!'

Again with the husband thing, did they think I had no other ambition?

'That's sweet of you, Joe, but I'd hate for you and Teddy to fight over me...' I glanced at Teddy, whose divine talons were shredding the tablecloth into confetti. 'After all, I wouldn't want to have to judge whose love is purer by who can rip the other person into itty bitty pieces, that would be silly.'

Joe and Teddy just looked at each other, confused. I sighed. Boys were so dense. 'Though, you know, if you really *wanted* to...'

'Heffa, do not fret,' Teddy said through clenched fangs. 'Though nothing would give me greater pleasure than turning this mangy cur into a wolf-skin hearth rug, I will bow before your womanly weakness and withhold my wrath. However, I must insist that you never see, speak, or come within two miles of him, and I am prepared to enforce my will by fitting you with an electronic tracking device if I have to.'

'But—'

'Who are you to order Heffa around?' Joe demanded. 'What are you gonna do, lock her in a coffin?'

'If I have to do that in order to protect her from you, then indeed I shall!' Teddy announced.

'No one puts Heffa in a coffin!' I said sternly. 'I've had it up to here with all this posturing. If you're not actually going to fight, then I think I should go home. Come on, Teddy. Joe, I'll try to slip away and come spend some time with you later, okay?'

'You will not!' Teddy said, pouting.

'Will too!' said Joe.

'Will not!' said Teddy.

'Will—'

'Okay, seriously, that's enough,' I interrupted. 'Stephfordy's idea of will-they-won't-they tension may be stuck at third-grade level, but I don't have to go along with it; all this testosterone is giving me a headache. I'll see you – *both* of you – later.'

I walked away, leaving Joe and Teddy to glare at each other. The atmosphere between them was almost unbearably tense, but the other diners in the restaurant seemed energized by it. As I headed for the exit, I heard snatches of excited conversation; they had really been hoping to see a fight. Typical Spatula mob, always eager to gather round their betters for a good gawp.

Back home, I went to my room and flopped morosely onto the sofa. Life was so darn complicated. I felt the need to have an overwrought visual metaphor to explain my feelings so I wandered into the kitchen and looked around. Teddy and Joe were... just like a knife and fork, always clashing, leaving me as the spoon. No, that didn't sound right. I shut the cutlery drawer and turned to the fridge. Magnets? ... No, that was ridiculous. I opened the door. Perhaps Joe could be bread and Teddy the mayonnaise? And I was the lettuce, preventing the sandwich going soggy. Hmmm. No.

In despair, I opened the cupboard. Teddy was like water, smooth and eternal; and Joe was oil, slightly sticky and greasy. And there was no way the two of them would ever mix.

Unless someone threw in a match... and I was a real fiery character, I was sure I could cause an explosion sooner or later. And once the town was aflame with gossip about the Teddy vs. Joe grudge match, then I'd be one step closer to being the name on everyone's lips.

Satisfied with my day's work, particularly the fire analogy, I put the olive oil back in the cupboard and went upstairs to my bedroom. My bed was calling to me. *Come here, Heffa,* it seemed to be saying. *Rest your weary head in my soft embrace.* I sighed. If only everything in my life could be as reliable as a pillow... I wasn't sure I could cope with the sheer effort and out-of-the-house activity involved in getting Joe and Teddy where I wanted them.

I thought briefly about shutting and locking the windows, to send a message to Teddy that while he might be the most committed night-time stalker in the world, a girl had other needs too. But I knew to my cost that Teddy's urge to watch my slumber could not be prevented by latches, and I didn't want my beauty sleep interrupted by him breaking in — shattered glass made the bed uncomfortably crunchy. I opened the window wide, then hung my emergency garlic from the frame. Of course, this would have no impact on Teddy, but I hoped he'd get the message: he could lurk as lovingly as he liked, but until he shaped up and did exactly what I said at all times, the bad odor would remain between us.

chapter 4

playing away

Forty-eight hours later, I was still pretty angry about my argument with Teddy. I knew he was watching over me at night from the stack of poetry books left by the side of my bed, bookmarked at the most soppy passages, but we hadn't spoken for two days as I was so cross. This was drastic stuff – the longest we'd spent apart since the time he inexplicably dumped me for no reason and ran off to Romania – but I had to let him know how I felt. I'm a reasonable person and always willing to listen to rational arguments, but he had no right to ban me from seeing Joe. Imagine, trying to tell me who I could see, and flirt with, and maybe cheat on him with if it seemed like it would help me realize my dream of fame and fortune.

Teddy and I might be soulmates, destined to be together throughout eternity, but he didn't own me, and if I wanted to dabble with selling out everything our relationship was based on, then that was up to me. I hadn't seen Joe either though; I didn't want him to get the idea that I was in the bag yet. It's true what they say about being a modern woman – it's all about multitasking, keeping a lot of balls in the air at once, and I was starting to get the hang of it. Oprah would have been proud of me. I looked out of my window at the sun bravely trying to burst through the thick bank of cloud that hovered permanently over Spatula and I felt close kinship with that seldom-seen heavenly body. Wasn't I trying to shine too, to break through the clouds of indifference and bathe the whole world in my radiant light? I would have to keep an eye on the sun; it could be competition. It wasn't doing too well at this very moment, however; the rain looked set in for another day.

But I wasn't disheartened, unlike that quitter the sun. Today was too important to waste on brooding – something I never thought I'd say. Much to my amazement, my dad had set up a job interview for me, and it was just my sort of work. There were some great advantages: it wasn't too physical, and I'd get to meet all sorts of people, and help them solve their problems, something I think I've already proved I have a gift for. But what had really impressed me was how many people had found fame after working in a place like the one I was headed to. Pink, Sharon Stone, Shania Twain, heck, even the President of the big ol' US of A had put their hours in, and as Chump said, look where they ended up! There was clearly something about this job that guaranteed future success; I mean, think about what Pink had achieved! I threw back the bedclothes and raced to get ready for my interview.

I was so eager to get the job that I arrived fifteen minutes early. I announced myself at the front desk and the girl said something about how I'd have to wait. I knew my prospective boss would realize the moment he saw me that I was just what he'd been looking for, so to save him from wasting any more time (because a good employee is always trying to bring solutions to the table), I shoved her aside and headed for the manager's office.

A spotty kid carrying a huge bag of frozen french fries blocked my path. 'Hey, you can't be back here without a hairnet!' he exclaimed, but I could tell from looking at him that he was already worried about me being promoted ahead of him, and was desperately trying to save his ass with this bureaucratic guff. I gave him a good shove to show him that this lady could smash through any glass ceiling and he staggered backwards towards some sort of tank full of cooking oil. Clumsy dope. I marched on and didn't look back; he could try to distract me with his strangulated cry of agony and his strong smell of scalding flesh, but I wasn't going to fall for it.

The door to the manager's office burst open and a sweaty man with a terrified expression raced towards me. I held my resume out in front of me and, ignoring the trivial medical emergency behind me, announced in my most determined voice, 'I'm Heffa Lump, and I'm here to accept the job of

"Junior Trainee Burger Selection Counselor" that you're about to offer me.'

The manager paused for a second, distracted from the brilliance of my interview technique by the sound of the ambulance screeching to a halt outside the restaurant. He looked at me quizzically, probably because he couldn't quite believe how lucky he was that the answer to all his business problems was standing right in front of him.

'Heffa Lump, you're Chief Lump's daughter, aren't you?' He clutched his face and groaned with relief. 'He told me you'd be coming by. You're hired, but tell your dad that our, um, friends at the environmental health board better remember not to drop by any time soon, that was the deal.'

I was elated. He'd seen my potential straight away; I didn't even have to feed him all that baloney I'd made up about volunteering at the homeless shelter. 'You won't regret this, I promise.'

He shrugged. 'Fine, whatever, just try not to maim any more of my staff, please, otherwise there won't be a business around for your dad to shake down.'

I smiled and headed for the changing room. The job was mine and I was thrilled, even though the restaurant wasn't particularly glamorous. In fact, it was a real mess. That stupid spotty kid had dropped fries everywhere when he blacked out with pain, and I had to kick the paramedics' bags out of the way just to clear my path. This was a business crying out for a touch of Heffa Lump magic.

So there I was, behind the counter at Dirtee Burger, always ready with a smile and a helping hand, making sure that our customers/guests/victims – whatever you wanted to call them – found the foodstuff-like menu item that was right for them. Quite the responsibility, but over the course of the morning I had already proved to myself that I could handle it.

'I'm sorry, sir, but if you order that, you won't be able to get your ass back out through the door when you're done.'

'You with that complexion, and you want large fries?'

'Sweetheart, order whatever you feel like; after all, comfort eating is probably the only comfort left to you.'

I was making new friends, and I was making a difference. Best of all, it was keeping my mind off the Teddy and Joe situation, which was great news because my tangled love life made picking any three items from the Filthee Combo Saver Selection Menu for only 99 cents look like child's play. In fact, I'd just finished helping a child to get a balanced meal by selecting four different flavors of ice cream when I heard a familiar growl, and saw Joe Cahontas grinning at me from the other side of the counter.

'Yo, Heffa, Laddie said you were working here now.'

I was excited to see Joe after our steamy platonic flirtation at the steakhouse, although obviously it wouldn't do to let him know that. 'Huh, how did Laddie know already? I only started a few hours ago,' I said nonchalantly.

'I guess your dad must have mentioned it to his mom, Lassie; they've become quite good friends since Laddie's father Daddie was murdered during that wolf-hating woodcutter's crazed axe rampage.'

This was brand new information to me, and obviously distressing. Dad had a friend? We'd see about that. Joe enjoyed his first ever moment of knowing more than me. He stood there grinning, crossing his tree-like arms in mockery of my indignation. His muscles rippled beneath his tight black T-shirt, and I imagined holding him, burying my face in his soft warm fur. I felt light-headed and queasy, but that might have been the three Dirtee Sausage Muffins I'd eaten. This was Joe Cahontas, my best friend in the whole world, notwithstanding the temporary vendetta issue between us. My feelings towards him were pure and sisterly, weren't they? He might be tall and handsome and as smokin' and steamy as a spring break sauna party, but I could never betray Teddy... could I?

The air was thick with tension, and the smell of rancid cooking oil. He broke the silence.

'So anyway, I'm getting pretty hungry, Heffa. Are you going to service me or what?'

I blushed and grabbed the till to steady myself as I felt my legs give way. 'Yes, Joe, of course, what in here looks good to you?'

'Well, I don't know, me and the pack don't really eat this sort of thing, we tend to go for dry food, enriched with vitamins. It keeps our fur really glossy and our joints supple, and you don't need to eat as much as with the canned chow, y'know? How's the Dirtee Burner Burger?'

I was relieved to be able to talk business again. 'Oh, it's great. It's really big and brown and meaty, and so strong. Tasting. But sweet as well. Some people don't like that it's a bit hairy, but I don't mind that. In fact I love it.'

He nodded. 'Uh huh, and how about the Cold Fish Filet Burger?'

'That's great too; the meat is really white and pale, and although it's ice cold, you still feel really comfortable with it, and it's got a lovely rich taste. You wish you could go on eating it forever.'

'Jeez, Heff, you make them both sound great, but I betcha neither one is really as good as you think. It's probably all made from low-quality ingredients that have been slung together as cheaply as possible. Tell you what, my van's outside, why don't you ditch work and we'll head back to the reservation? I'll cook you up a chili dog that'll put hairs on your chest.'

'Joe, that's crazy. I can't be seen with you. Teddy would go nuts, and I can't have another busload of dead priests on my conscience, not after last time. And besides, I've got my career to think of now. And I'm not even sure I want a hairy chest.'

They were all good reasons, but I knew that I didn't believe them in my heart. I'd already proved that I could get any job I wanted, and who cared about a few priests? The Pope could easily get off his ass and make some more. And as for the hairy chest, it might be a good look for me. Maybe if I saw a bit more of Joe's, I could get used to the idea. Joe stood patiently as I wrestled with my indecision, an annoyingly smug smirk on his full red lips. He knew my decision had already been made. I couldn't resist. A nice long ride with Joe, followed by gulping down his big juicy chili dog. Throwing my career away for a guy, what a putz. I left on his arm.

Joe was quiet on the drive back to the reservation. He glanced over at me and smiled every few seconds, but otherwise he kept his eyes on the road and his hands on the wheel. The silence in the van was oppressive, and my mind was no help either, with its deafening cries of 'what are you doing – you love Teddy, you slutty moron!' alternating with 'but Joe is nice too, what can possibly go wrong?'

The road snaked precariously around the edge of the cliffs and I looked down at the turbulent sea far below. It seemed so deep, and so icy cold, yet despite its tempestuous moods I was drawn to it. On the other side of the road stretched the ever-present forest. The mighty trunks thrust towards the sky, solid and dependable, the darkness between them moist and inviting. The road ran straight and narrow between the two of them, sea and forest. In some ways this was just like my life, trying to walk the right path while torn between two opposing elemental forces. If you hadn't spotted that already, then Stephfordy says you need to read a bit more carefully from now on, her metaphors aren't always going to be so obvious, so pay attention!

Eventually, the road curved away from the cliffs and headed into the forest towards the Utensil Indian reservation. The reservation had been undergoing a lot of development work recently. I hadn't seen the place since the new buildings had gone up, but Chump had talked about it a lot. He was all in favor, said it was great that the Utensil tribe had a steady income again. Things had been tough since the late seventies, when the bottom had fallen out of the hand-carved wooden salad tong market.

'I hear the old place has become quite fancy since the last time I came out here,' I said to break the silence. Joe steered the truck round a long bend and pulled over at the side of the road. The Utensil reservation stretched out before us.

'There it is, Heff, home sweet home.'

It was certainly an impressive sight. The gateway was flanked on either side by enormous wolf statues, at least twenty feet high. They were rearing up on their hind legs, their snarling jaws open mid-howl. Their eyes were spotlights that swiveled back and forth illuminating the sign that stretched between them across the entrance: 'The Happy Humping Ground Casino and Resort.'

The road curved down through the woods to the main casino building, a bunker-like concrete structure, which looked more like a nuclear shelter than a pleasure palace.

'We kind of blew the budget on the wolf statues,' Joe explained apologetically as he drove on towards the hulking grey monolith.

'Aren't we going to your father's house?' I asked.

'No. Do you see how much parking space there is?' I nodded. 'We kind of had to choose between that and the old village, and everyone had to move into town after it was bulldozed. Dad lives above the video store now, it's really good for him; he never has to pay late fees.'

I shook my head disdainfully. I knew Teddy was a relentless modernist with little time for beautiful ancient traditions, but I'd thought that Joe was a deeper soul, what with being a Native American and everything. He'd better have some beautiful legends about mystic events in the tribe's past up his sleeve; otherwise I might be forced to think again about this dalliance. He must have seen my frown.

'Don't worry, Heff, there's still a great place for us to hang. Me and the rest of the pack have been taken on to provide security for the resort; we've got a whole building to ourselves round the back.'

'Wow, security for a casino, that almost sounds like a proper job. I thought you guys were anti-corporate anarchists?'

Joe shrugged. 'Well, we don't actually do a whole lot of work, to be honest. When the boss is around, we spend hours talking about "patrolling" and "perimeters" and coming up with elaborate plans about who's going to run where and sniff what, but it's just for show. Most of the time we're just hanging in The Doghouse, getting high and getting our groove on.'

He pulled the van to a stop outside a windowless tin shack. The bass rumble of the music coming from inside rattled the frame of the building, and the sound of barking laughter confirmed the presence of other members of Joe Cahontas's werewolf pack. Joe rushed to my side of the van and opened the door for me. I climbed out warily. I was here to spend time with Joe, ideally alone. I wasn't sure I was ready for whatever was going down in The Doghouse. Joe opened the door and waves of pungent smoke wafted out. I breathed a last deep breath of clear afternoon air, and followed him inside.

I couldn't make out a whole lot of detail through the haze, but I could see that several pack members were there, and that their taste in interior design hadn't improved since the last time I'd seen them. The room was dimly lit with lamps that had been draped in tie-dyed cloth, making the light that bit more classily atmospheric. Couches that moldered in various stages of decay took up most of the space, and on each one slouched one or more recumbent wolf-boys.

One wall of the shack was covered in dozens of TV monitors showing video feeds from around the casino complex. Joe's wolf-brothers Laddie and Fidaux were staring intently at the screens; part of their security detail, I supposed. Laddie pointed excitedly at one of the monitors and Fidaux rescued a remote control from the clutter on a nearby coffee table and zoomed in on the image of a willowy blonde woman playing blackjack. They sniggered and Laddie shouted, 'Here I go, it's happening again, get ready, baby!'

Joe looked embarrassed and grabbed my arm, trying to lead me away from the screens. 'What the heck is wrong with Laddie?' I asked.

'Oh, nothing, not a big deal, just Laddie being a doofus, nothing weird going on there at all, nuh uh.'

Joe tried to block my view of his pack mates and tugged at my elbow insistently. I felt sure that some secret werewolf stuff was happening and, dammit, it's not a proper secret unless Heffa Lump knows about it. Laddie howled, and I craned my neck to be greeted with the sight of him rubbing himself enthusiastically against the arm of the couch. He looked back at the blonde in the monitor, howled again, and rushed stiffly out through the door. 'Go get her, bro!' Fidaux shouted encouragingly. I'd known the werewolves for some time and they weren't exactly what you'd call sophisticates, but this behavior was pretty gross even for them.

'Something funny *is* going on, Joe. You'd better tell me what it is or I'll be out of here faster than you can say "pathetic unrequited love".'

Joe's arms fell to his side. His sensitive brow creased and he looked at Fidaux, then back at me. He nodded, gestured for me to follow him and hurried into the kitchen. The room was brightly lit, and the piles of dirty dishes in the sink and the empty tins that covered every surface made me glad that the main room was so dingy; lord only knows what was lurking in the shadows.

'Sorry about the mess. Laika should have cleaned; she's so unreliable.'

I fixed him with my most interrogative gaze, partly so he knew not to change the subject, but mostly to avoid looking at whatever was scuttling around behind that stack of pizza boxes.

'You already know a lot about us werewolves, Heffa, compared to most ordinary humans.'

I wasn't too happy about 'ordinary', but I nodded.

'And you know from our relationship how moody and passionate we can be?'

I nodded again, eagerly.

'Those passions come from deep within us. The Utensil elders tell legends about their origins. I always found the stories pretty dronesome myself, so I don't know the details, but whatever gives us the power to transform physically into wolves affects our emotions just as powerfully. These feelings come without warning, maybe in response to seeing a certain person, or smelling a certain perfume, or any number of other things. When they strike, they take over completely, and we'll do anything to possess whatever the target is. The legends call it "Inflicting".'

Joe looked at me imploringly as he finished his speech, clearly worried that this new information might sicken me. Like the state of the kitchen wasn't bad enough. It did all sound a bit far-fetched, not to mention rather sleazy, but I supposed that some people might find my relationship with Teddy somewhat odd too, so who was I to judge? I'd keep an open mind, and find out more. Joe Cahontas and his perverted gang of emotionally unstable stalkers were my closest non-dead friends after all, and I owed them that much. 'Maybe it's not as twisted as you think, Joe. I guess it's like falling in love at first sight.'

He brightened. 'Hey, yeah, maybe it is!'

'Or like the old Greek legend about people searching for the person who's the other half of their soul. And when they find them, they know instantly, and they stay together forever. That's quite romantic, when you think about it. That's all that Inflicting is, isn't it? You just have another name for it.'

Joe seemed very interested in his sneakers suddenly. 'Well, it's not exactly like that, on second thoughts. I mean, it's a powerful feeling, but I've never heard of it lasting forever. Twenty minutes or so is more common. Or a few hours. Couple of days, maybe.'

'Oh, well, the candle that burns twice as bright burns half as long.'

'And also, well, it's not always someone the same age or anything. Actually, it's quite often not a person at all. Fidaux Inflicted on a lamppost outside the 7/11 last week.'

'Eww, okay, I think that's enough werewolf lore for now. If anything else like this suddenly gets added to your backstory several hundred pages after we met, there's no need to mention it unless it becomes relevant to the plot.'

'Well, we do have other stuff to discuss, don't we?'

I felt myself shiver as if the temperature had suddenly dropped fifty degrees. Joe obviously wanted to get down to business. I'd better be straight with him in return. I held his hands in mine. 'Oh Joe, you glorious stupid wolf-man. Of course I want to be with you, absolutely definitely I do. You're my best friend, like a brother to me. A brother who is very, very attractive, who could, maybe, one day, perhaps very soon (even later on today), be more than just a hot best friend. You could be the one person in the world I give myself to entirely.'

Joe beamed. It seemed to be going really well so I continued, 'That is, if it wasn't for Teddy, who, as you must surely remember, is my soulmate, the one person in the world I would give myself to entirely. He's also my best friend too, by the way.'

Joe growled and pulled away from me as if I'd poured hot oil over him. 'Damn it, Heffa, why can't you just say what you mean? You know I love you, why can't you just choose between Teddy and me? By which I mean, choose me, of course, because I'm tall and warm and buff and handsome, and he's all dead and stuff.'

The feelings flying around in here were pretty intense, but I'd come this far, it was no time to back out now. 'Joe, I have chosen, my love, I've chosen you, you're my best friend who I also love and I want to be with you forever!'

He regarded me with an entirely unjustified expression of skepticism. 'Okay, anything else to add to that...?'

'No, of course not, except to mention that we can never be together because my love for Teddy is eternal, and unbreakable, and I hate you for trying to come between us!'

'So you love Teddy, then?'

'Yes, Teddy, absolutely.'

His lips curled back over his teeth in what I knew was his special 'Heffa smile'.

'And you. A bit. Sometimes.'

I know that not everyone appreciates plain speaking, but I'd thought that Joe would want to know where he stood, once and for all. I must have got him wrong, though. He seemed – what's the phrase? – 'enraged beyond reason' by my kind words of love, and the next thing I knew he was dashing for the door, gnashing his teeth and tearing his T-shirt from his rippling torso as he shifted to his wolf form.

I was always amazed by the suddenness of the transformation. One second there was a big cute guy standing there, and then there was a cheap-looking puff of smoke and he was replaced by an eight-foot-tall CGI wolf. I always assumed that the red eyes and slavering jaws were supposed to be terrifying, but there was something so cute and fluffy-looking about them, it just wasn't possible to be scared. Truth be told, the Utensil werewolf pack were more Angela Lansbury than Angela Carter. A second later, Joe was gone.

I shrugged. It must be time for his security patrol. He was certainly in a hurry. Usually the pack carefully removed and neatly folded their clothes before transforming, but the shredded remains of Joe's shirt remained as evidence of his haste. He hadn't made me anything to eat either, what a lousy host.

Back in the main room of The Doghouse, Fidaux was passed out on the couch, and a young girl I didn't recognize was busy sweeping the empty candy wrappers, tissues and other items that covered the floor into a neat pile. She had the same prominent brow and long dark hair that was the mark of the Utensil werewolves, but that must have been a coincidence – who'd ever heard of a female werewolf? Hearing me come in, she looked up from her tidying and eyed me suspiciously. 'Thanks for upsetting Joe, now he'll be more unbearable than ever.'

Shocked by this less than friendly greeting, I mumbled some sort of incoherent denial, but I needn't have bothered. She obviously wasn't the listening type.

'It's bad enough that they lounge around here all day when they should be working, and that they expect me to cook and clean and follow them around with little plastic baggies for when they go toilet, but at least it's a routine. We're a pack: brothers – and one feisty outspoken sister – and we don't need you disrupting the harmony of the group, you get me?'

'You mean you *are* a werewolf? Not just an annoying girlfriend or the maid or something?'

'I'm Laika, and I'm just as big and hairy as any of these scrawny pups, whatever Joe says about me.'

'Um, he's never mentioned you at all, actually.'

'Typical,' she snarled. 'We women are always getting written out of history by the patriarchal hegemony.' She gripped the broom tighter, and twisted it in her hands.

This Laika seemed like a very bitter person. I did all the cooking and cleaning for my dad, and I never complained about it even though the stupid oaf never showed any appreciation for my homemaking skills. One day I'd drop that precious TV of his right on his fat head. She was being awful mean about Joe, too. Who did she think she was, badmouthing my best friend like that?

'Joe's got a lot on his mind. It can't be easy being the Top Dog of a werewolf pack. Maybe you just need to try a bit harder to please him? When my boyfriend is angry with me, I just do whatever he tells me to until he calms down.'

Tiny wisps of smoke had started to curl out from between Laika's fingers where they clenched the broom handle.

'Top Dog? Try harder to please him? I think you should go, Heffa, it's about to get very violent in here.'

Her face contorted with anger and the broom handle burst apart in a shower of splinters. I realized that as a younger member of the pack she must still be having trouble controlling her transformations.

I glanced at my watch; it was nearly five. 'Gosh, you're right. I need to get home and put the casserole on for dinner. Thanks, Laika!' I waved to her as I left, but she was busy kicking Fidaux between the legs.

Outside, I hopped into Joe's van. The keys were still in the ignition and I was sure he wouldn't mind me driving it home. Friendship shouldn't be all 'take, take, take', but 'borrow, borrow, borrow' ought to be fine. As I drove along the coast road back towards Spatula, I thought about everything Joe had said. He claimed to be in love with me, but if he was, why didn't he 'Inflict' on me? Surely that proved that he was just leading me on? And he had other chicks around too; that Laika was clearly very jealous of me. There were lots of reasons why she should be, of course – my educational achievements, my elegant posture, my easy way with people – but most likely it was because she was worried I'd take Joe away from her. And maybe I would, but not until he had proved that he was worthy of me – and better than Teddy, my current soulmate. I knew I faced some tough choices ahead. And on top of that, I was unemployed again.

I passed the boundary that marked the edge of Utensil Indian territory. Long ago the vampires and the werewolves had divided up the area around Spatula between them, and if either one strayed into the other's territory (which they did all the time with no consequences) then there were terrifying consequences. In my rear-view mirror, I saw the warning sign by the side of the road. It read 'TUO PEEK SERIPMAV' and below was the image of a fanged mouth with a cross through it. Next to it was another sign that promised a picnic site, 2 miles.

My drive back to Spatula passed in a blur – Joe's van was faster than it looked – but as I headed through the town center I looked closely at the shops and businesses that lined Main Street. The simple one-story brick buildings spoke of a simpler age of small-town hospitality and good honest American values, when a girl was just told by her parents who she had to marry and she didn't have to have her soul torn in two by a horny dilemma. There was the musty old hardware store, the desolate-looking video rental place, and the modish glass-fronted apple store. Surely one of them had an opening for a spunky young go-getter called Heffa Lump?

It was the end of the day and the simple shopkeepers were drawing down their shutters and waving goodbye to their staff. Except at the apple store, where they were open late for a seminar on making the perfect strudel. Spatula was closing up for the evening and the sidewalks were filled with people heading home. They stopped to talk to each other, exchanging pleasantries and apples. How happy they looked, without a care in their simple mule-like heads.

I was so caught up in my thoughts that I almost didn't notice the large silver coach that was parked across the road up ahead until it was too late. I slammed on the brakes and closed my eyes. There was an almighty screeching sound as the van skidded to a stop. I heard a familiar voice outside, and I shivered as if I'd been hurled through the windscreen and into a bath of ice-cold honey.

'Precisely where do you think you've been?' Teddy said.

I opened my eyes and saw my darling of the damned standing in front of the coach with his arms folded and legs wide apart. He was resplendent in his simple outfit of blue jeans and powder blue sports jacket. It had been two days since I had seen him, and I thought this time apart was a good excuse to describe his face all over again, for the gazillionth time. His luminous white skin was as perfect as ever and his flashing red eyes were set beneath his noble brow like precious stones on an ivory necklace. His nostrils were flared, though that did not disrupt the elegant proportions of his simple nose. Although for obvious reasons there was no color in his face, his anger was plain to me, and the look he gave me filled my heart with fear. He pointed to the coach windows with a threatening gesture and I saw the passengers peering out, all with the same simple black outfits and terrified expressions on their faces. One of them adjusted his dog collar, and gulped. Not priests again!

Teddy clenched and unclenched his fists, but said nothing more. I had an inkling that he might know I'd been to see Joe. The fact that I was in his van was a bit of a clue, after all. But so what if I had? Joe was my friend, and probable future lover. I had nothing to be ashamed of, and I was sure we could talk about our problems like sensible young people.

I got out of the van and walked briskly towards Teddy. He and I were alone in the street, but people regarded us from the sidewalk. Teddy spoke again: 'I told you what would happen if you didn't stay away from those filthy stinking animals, Heffa. Unless you want to be wading home through the blessed entrails of fifty brand new Catholic martyrs, you'd better have a dashed good explanation of your recent whereabouts.'

His voice was loud, almost a shout, and a few passers-by slowed down, no doubt eager to see how I calmly handled my enraged vampire boyfriend. I smiled and held my hands open in a conciliatory gesture. 'Explain what, my darling? I'm only on my way home to make a casserole for dinner, there's no reason for you to get all cranky and murderous.'

'You must be under the impression that I was reborn yesterday! I know you were absent from your place of employment all afternoon, and I've been beside myself with fear.'

'Work was difficult and boring, so I quit. Then I went for a walk and thought about how much I love you.'

'I know you are lying. Your father gave me access to the town CCTV system, and you didn't appear on any of the cameras.

Although I did learn some very surprising information about 'Mrs.' Doubtfire from the kindergarten, so it wasn't a total waste of time. What have I done to make you hurt me like this?'

The crowd of people on the sidewalk was quite large by this time, and their eager murmuring suggested that they weren't going anywhere until this was over. I felt awkward suddenly, and Teddy's plaintive words had stung me. I didn't know exactly what I was feeling right now, but I had to be honest with him.

'If you can't figure it out for yourself, you must be even stupider than you look, you pasty-faced dolt. I'm driving Joe Cahontas's van, coming from the direction of the Utensil reservation, and I smell like I've spent the last week hanging out with Scooby-Doo's drug-dealing brother. Where do you think I've been?'

Teddy's expression changed from anger to shock, and then to horror. 'You mean... you've been with Joe Cahontas?'

'Well, not "been with", not yet, but been to see, yes.'

There was a collective gasp from the crowd of onlookers.

'But I specifically forbade you from going to see him. You know that the Kelledys and the Utensil werewolves are sworn enemies. Even leaving aside the fact that they're an inferior form of supernatural being, that casino of theirs is a big part of the reason why we find ourselves lacking in finances. Their slots are rigged, and I'm pretty sure the blackjack guy is bottom-dealing. The cabaret is appalling; the lions never eat the magicians. And their dress sense, ugh. They are simply awful, Heffa, and Joe Cahontas is worst of all.'

'You can't tell me what to do! I'm an independent young woman with a wide social circle, and if I want to see my friends I will, whether they're human, werewolf, or any other sort of sexy monster. You get me, fang-face?'

Teddy staggered backwards as if he'd been slapped. There was a smattering of applause and a shout of 'you go, girl' from the crowd. The tension in Teddy's powerful shoulders threatened the continued survival of his jacket. I knew Teddy better than anyone had ever known anyone else, and I could read his emotions in his perfect marble face. First came confusion, which was something of a default expression, actually. That was followed in rapid succession by fear, rage and, hmm, not sure about that last one. Wistfulness perhaps? For a moment, I felt a pang of guilt for putting my probable soulmate through this torment, but I reassured myself that I was worth suffering for. Or because of.

After a few moments, he spoke once more, his voice calm now. 'You are my everything, but we need to be able to trust each other or our relationship will probably not endure for eternity like I planned. You refuse to listen to reason, so I'm afraid you leave me no choice. I'm going to kidnap you and lock you up in my house.'

'I'm sorry, you're what?'

'I'm going to kidnap you, Heffa. Kidnap you and lock you up in my house. Don't worry, it's for your own good, and I shall ensure Bobbi keeps you entertained and feeds you and so forth. You'll probably quite enjoy it, actually; it'll be like a little holiday.'

Now I was the one reeling with shock. I'd known all along that Teddy loved me, and wanted to protect me, and I was all in favor of that as a rule, accident-prone as I was. But kidnapping?

Before I could say anything more, Teddy rushed at me, and grabbed my arms. I'd forgotten how strong he was, and as he threw me into the back of Joe's van, I felt my skin tingling from his icy touch. It was dark in the van and although I was still in shock at Teddy's sudden boldness, I also felt strangely safe and protected. As he started the engine and sped away, I could hear the reaction of the crowd who had watched our confrontation. Some people were booing while others applauded loudly; they'd clearly been hanging on our every word. Spatula was such a sleepy town; I wouldn't be surprised if it made the paper. In fact, I was sure it would. The town's palest and most interesting girl caught in a love triangle between two totally different but equally pretty boys? That had front page written all over it. *Front page.* And where there were headlines, there was money to be made.

This was it: this was the path to fame and fortune I'd been looking for! The public had an appetite for Heffa Lump, and

I was going to make sure they got regular feedings. First I had to keep Joe and Teddy guessing about which one of them I preferred, which would be easy because I seemed to change my mind every five minutes. To make sure they stayed motivated, I would keep score and let them know where they stood. Next, I had to make sure that I staged frequent public arguments, which the media could report. And then I'd just lie back and watch the talk-show requests and endorsement offers roll in. It was so simple, why hadn't I thought of it before?

I felt as if I had turned a corner in my life. I hadn't solved any of my problems, but at least I'd worked out how to turn them into cash. As Teddy drove Joe's stolen van back to his house in the woods where he would lock me up for an unspecified period, I lay warm and cozy in the van dreaming of the bright future I could see stretching out before me.

And – who knew? – maybe this kidnapping thing would be fun. After all, it's important to try new things in a relationship.

chapter 5

heffa scores

Teddy sped home in Joe's stolen van at his usual steady speed of thirty miles an hour. I sat slumped in the back practicing my most disapproving expressions to use on Teddy when (if) he finally let me out. We bumped along the back roads that led to the Kelledys' home deep in the woods and eventually pulled to a stop.

My senses buzzed, desperate for some clue to Teddy's mental state. It was dark in the van so sight wasn't much help, but the deep mulchy smell of the forest filled my nostrils, and the deep mulchy pile of the van's carpet filled my hands. I could hear Teddy pretending to breathe on the other side of the van doors. At first, his pretend breathing was rapid and angry-sounding, but then I heard him make an effort to calm himself, pretending to take several long deep breaths amid mumbled reassurances.

I stood up, composed my face into the vengeful scowl that I had recently perfected, and waited for Teddy to open the doors. When he did, I huffed loudly to attract his attention to my annoyed expression. To my amazement, he didn't even look at me, but simply grabbed me roughly and threw me over his shoulder. I caught the merest glimpse of his deep green eyes, but the blazing anger I saw in them thrilled me to my toes. Teddy was really jealous; my plan was working!

My angry undead amour marched through the main gate of his family's majestic fiberglass castle and headed into its maze of passages. It was dark inside, due to the energy-saving light bulbs that the newly thrifty Teddy had insisted on installing. Slung over his shoulder as I was, I couldn't tell where we were going, but I consoled myself with the sight of Teddy's rock-hard buns straining against the denim of his designer jeans.

The next thing I knew, I was roughly deposited on the sofa in Teddy's vast bedroom. He stood in front of me, and the rage in his face had become the weary expression of tired indulgence that he so often wore in my presence. It must be exhausting looking after someone so incredible, the poor dear. I waited for him to say something, but he remained silent. Bored by his pensiveness, my attention wandered, and glancing around the familiar room I spotted a large and alarming addition to the furnishings.

'What the heck is that thing?' I asked, pointing to the item in question.

'It's a bed. I had it specially crafted for us, although at present I wish I had not bothered. Do you... like it?'

My mouth opened to reply, but as Teddy stood aside to let me examine the bed in detail, the words died in my throat. I took in every aspect of its design and was astonished by its complex beauty. I struggled to compose myself, overcome with love for Teddy at this latest display of his compassionate thoughtfulness. After a few seconds, I managed to speak. 'It's incredible, my love.' Teddy smiled as I attempted to express my admiration: 'I didn't even know that you could get king-size hospital beds!'

He proudly flicked a switch on the wall. On either side of the bed, an impressive array of medical machinery flickered, whirred and beeped into life. Teddy waved his arm in an expansive gesture.

'It's not just a bed, Heffa, it's also a state-of-the-art medical facility. Defibrillator, ventilator, morphine drip, automated blood-transfusion system... it's got everything, and I have a ready supply of O-positive chained up patiently in the dungeon. This equipment can keep the occupant safe and healthy almost indefinitely.' He hopped up onto the bed and lay on his chest looking towards me. 'And the red leather sheets are a delightfully decadent touch, aren't they? Won't you join me?'

I wanted nothing more than to lie next to Teddy while he hooked me up to his incredible instruments, and I took a step towards him, craving the safety and security he offered. Then I stopped. He had already kidnapped me this evening, and now he wanted to put me into a coma to keep me out of trouble. I liked a nice long nap well enough, but I couldn't get Joe and Teddy mad at each other if I was unconscious.

I decided to decline politely. 'Get out of here, you psycho! I should be at home cooking Dad's casserole, not locked up as a prisoner. Joe's right about you, you are very slightly controlling sometimes. I'm not saying I don't like the attention, but I'm not in the mood.'

'But Heffa, I must keep you safe, if you were to fall into the wrong hands it would. . .'

'Just go, Teddy. We'll talk in the morning, but right now I need to be alone with my thoughts.'

I pointed at the door, and after hesitating for a moment he withdrew. The confrontation had left me feeling drained, and I collapsed back onto the sofa. Teddy had to know that he couldn't take my love for granted. It was a two-horse race now. It was only fair that he and Joe both knew exactly where they stood. My lovers were incomparable in many ways, like chalk and cheese, fire and ice, sea and forest, magnet and. . . slightly different sort of magnet. This was what made my decision so agonizing: how was I ever going to choose between them when they were so utterly unique and special? Wait a second, though; Teddy had already shown me the way! The other evening, when he'd demanded that I tell him about our top ten times together. Everything made more sense in a nice organized list!

I sprang from the sofa, and after a moment rummaging in Teddy's desk I dug out a pad of paper and some colored pens, and set to work. A few minutes later, I had drawn up a chart with Teddy and Joe's names across the top. Down the side were various categories such as 'Hotness', 'Richness' and 'Deadness'. This simple handy scorecard would help me to keep track of my competing suitors' efforts to woo me. Now they would know *exactly* where they stood. So far they were about even, although after this evening Teddy wasn't doing so well on 'Trustfulness'.

I crossed back to the magnificent, horrifying bed. It was a thoughtful gesture on Teddy's part, and testing the mattress with my hand confirmed that it was delightfully soft and comfortable too. Pausing only to switch off the machinery, I climbed in and was soon drifting off to sleep. I heard a plaintive howling from somewhere close by, and I knew that Joe was watching me from the woods. I made a mental note to award him an extra point for 'Stalkiness', and then I slept.

I was woken the next morning by the light that streamed through the floor-to-ceiling glass window that dominated the far wall of Teddy's room. Teddy himself stood in front of it. He had his back to me, but I could tell from his slumped shoulders that he was feeling bad about the way we had argued last night. I didn't mind if he was feeling a bit guilty about kidnapping me, but I couldn't remember the last time I had slept as well as I had in Teddy's creepy bed, so I was in too good a mood to renew the row. And anyway, there was no need for petty verbal point-scoring; I had my card to keep track now.

'Isn't the sun meant to be shining out of your ass?' I asked, to let him know I was awake.

He turned, and shrugged. 'It doesn't seem to be so much of a problem these days; I think Stephfordy lost interest in that particular aspect of vampirism. The bed's built-in monitors assure me that you slept well, my love. I trust you are feeling refreshed?'

I nodded, and Teddy sat beside me. He held my hand and looked at me with his icy blue eyes. 'I'm sorry I abducted you, my darling; it was foolish of me. I am so terrified of losing you. Oh, how I wish you would consent to let me drink you dry and turn you into a vampire, only then will I be assured that you will be safe from harm. And from werewolves with busy paws.'

This was a conversation that Teddy and I had had many times before, and I was about to explain yet again that I wasn't sure I was ready to give up my human life. As a living resident of Spatula, I knew I was better than everyone else, but if I became a vampire, who knew where I would be in the undead pecking order? And I had this pink top I was really attached to; I'd never be able to wear that again once I turned into an inhuman fiend. But Teddy wasn't finished. 'There's no danger, darling, I promise. One quick bite from me, and then the bed can take over, it's got all the equipment right here. Just lie back and think of eternity.'

Before I could react to Teddy's alarmingly eager offer, the bedroom door burst open and his sister Bobbi hopped into the room waving the morning paper.

'I can't believe it, have you seen this?' she exclaimed, throwing the paper onto the bed between us. The headline read 'Showdown on Main Street', and below that there was a picture of Teddy and me during yesterday's confrontation. I couldn't believe it; we'd made the front page. My plan was working! Teddy grabbed the paper and paced the room as he read the story, while Bobbi came and sat on the bed, bouncing enthusiastically.

'And that's not all!' she cried, handing me her trendy wireless tablet computing device. 'Look at what's been posted on supernatural gossip blog Stawker this morning!'

I glanced at the headline: 'Obama declares Bon Temps STI epidemic a federal emergency, sexy.'

'No, below that – "Furry Fiend Stakes Claim to Vampire's Territory",' Bobbi said, but before I could read it, Teddy snatched the trendy wireless tablet computing device from me. He retired to the sofa muttering angrily, his fangs protruding from his snarling lips. I picked up the paper again, and noticed the sub-headline for the first time: 'Local Hunks at Odds Over Some Girl'. Gah, honestly! How dare they, lousy two-bit scribblers; it was supposed to be 'Local Beauty Torn Between Two Boys'. Still, it was a good start. I'd just have to offer to do an exclusive interview or two and the media was sure to realize that I was the heart of this story.

Teddy was suddenly waving Bobbi's gizmo in my face. 'Have you heard what that stinking pooch says here? "No creepy preppy vampire is going to steal my girl, she might be with him for now, but I know it's me she loves because— "' and here Teddy shouted for emphasis, '"SHE TOLD ME SO!"' He grabbed me by the throat and lifted me effortlessly into the air. 'Is this true, Heffa?'

I looked into Teddy's maroon eyes, those deep maelstroms of anger and despair, and croakingly reassured him. 'No, my love, it's not true.'

He put me down and mimed breathing a sigh of relief. I picked up my scorecard from the bedside table and showed it to him tenderly. 'Look here, my darling, as of now it's you that I love, eternally and unequivocally. By a clear three points.'

Teddy stared at the chart, struggling to take in the details. 'I see from this that your emotions are torn between him and me. We are two very different creatures; I can understand your dilemma. He may very well score ten points for "Shirtlessness", but I shall never give up, Heffa. You are my one and only love, for now and all time, and rest assured I will do whatever it takes to have you for myself!'

He paused for effect, his nostrils flaring with earnest resolve, and I quickly adjusted his score in the 'Determinedness' column. 'Get dressed, Heffa, it's time I showed you how much I love you.' He strode purposefully towards the door. 'I'm taking you shopping!' Bobbi snatched the paper from me and rushed out of the room behind him, leaving me alone with my thoughts, and the slightly disturbing bed.

I showered and changed as quickly as I could, and just an hour and a half later I entered the Kelledys' lavishly decorated kitchen. Bobbi and Teddy were sitting at the breakfast counter. The newspaper was laid out on the counter, and Bobbi was prodding it with one of her elegantly manicured fingers. Teddy shook his head and tried to push the paper away. The special shopping outfit I had selected showed off my oh-so-ordinary curves to devastating effect, so I struck a dramatic pose in the doorway and waited for the sinister squabbling siblings to notice me.

'You can't take Heffa shopping in Port D'Angerous; it's a crazy idea. Look here!'

'I've already seen it. "Perilous Plot Development Approaching Rapidly: Fatalities Forecast." But I do not have a choice, sister. She's been seeing entirely too much of that ghastly Joe Cahontas creature, and if I'm to stop him from stealing her away from me, I need to do something to show her how I feel, and quickly.'

'I get that, but can't you just make her another compilation CD or something? Why the sudden urge for a shopping spree?'

'Simple, Bobbi. Even in our current impecunious state, the funds we have at our disposal are vastly superior to those of that hairy hobo of a werewolf. He may be able to woo my Heffa with his warm embrace and constant bare-chestedness, but I can retaliate in a way that he could never match. I intend to buy her love.'

So that was it. Teddy was really starting to worry about Joe coming up behind him in the rear-view mirror of romance, and he thought that hauling me around the boutiques and jewelry stores of the state's most upscale shopping district would be enough to enable him to pull away and leave Joe eating dust. Well, I wasn't as easy to buy as all that. I'm not saying that it couldn't be done, but it wasn't going to be cheap.

In the meantime my arms were starting to ache, thrust out dramatically as they were, and the two stupid bickering vampires still hadn't noticed me. So much for their super-senses. I stamped my foot on the stylish granite flooring, and kicked over a cast-iron planter for good measure. They looked around, and Teddy hastily scrunched the newspaper up behind his back. 'Here I am, my darling,' I cooed. 'You may escort me to the diamond necklaces now if you please.'

'You look quite presentable, my darling. Is that a new pair of sweatpants?'

I grabbed Teddy by the arm and led him gently towards the door. 'Stow the compliments, mister, let's get to the shopping.'

'Yes, of course, anything you want, love of mine. We shall head forthwith to the consumer paradise of Port D'Angerous, where I shall indulge your every whim, no matter how trivial or selfish, and where nothing bad, and certainly nothing in any way fatal, will befall us.'

Bobbi shook her head at this last comment, but before I had time to ask her why, Teddy had bundled me out of the door and into the passenger seat of his sports car.

Seven hours later, I sat at a table outside 'Qaddaffi's Caffeine Compound', slurping my quadruple mocha-mint frappuccino and surveying the teetering pile of bags, packages and parcels that surrounded me. Teddy knelt in front of me, gently massaging my aching feet. He looked at me with a concerned expression. 'How are you feeling now, my love?'

'I can't believe you made me walk all that way. I thought my feet were going to drop off!'

'I'm sorry, my darling, it just became difficult to carry all our purchases, and the tray of coffee and cake, and you, at the same time. And it really wasn't that far from the front door to the table, was it?'

My eyes narrowed at this last comment. I didn't care for the hint of sarcasm in Teddy's voice. We had had the most wonderful afternoon, sauntering down the elegant boulevards of Port D'Angerous, me pointing at things in the windows of the stores and Teddy rushing off to acquire them for me. He was the perfect shopping companion, just as he was perfect in every other way. It seemed like months since we'd spent any quality time together, just the two of us, and I had been reminded once more how much I loved him. From the tips of his impeccably coiffured hair to the tips of his impossibly pointy shoes, I loved every part of him, in a way that was utterly impossible to quantify. I had to try, though, to make sure I could keep score of who was winning my love, so I had decided that the shopping trip and the associated romantic emotions had been worth five points. But if he was going to get peevish with me that could easily change. I frowned, and Teddy leapt to his feet.

'What's wrong, my love? Did I hurt your foot? Are you hungry? Thirsty? Too hot? Too cold? Too human? Shall I buy you some more things? Shall I kill that shop girl who was rude to you?'

I smiled to hear him sound so desperately attentive. It would be five points after all.

'What's all this crap, Heff?' said a familiar voice. Teddy hissed and bared his fangs, his eyes flashing red like brake lights on a snaking mountain road. Turning my head as far as my shopping-weakened state would allow, I saw Joe grinning at me.

'We've been shopping, you cur. I've been buying presents for Heffa. Designer clothes, fabulous jewelry, a Swarovski-encrusted casserole ladle, anything she wanted, money no object.' Teddy jumped nimbly over the pile of packages and landed right in front of Joe. He thrust his face close enough that Joe recoiled slightly, and grinned. 'How do you like them apples, dog-breath?'

Joe shrugged. 'Hey, your choice, suck-boy. I guess store-bought stuff is okay, but I prefer something a bit more creative.'

Teddy stepped back, puzzled. Joe smiled broadly and waved the shopping bag he was holding from the carpentry-supply boutique Got Wood. 'I just came into town to buy some mahogany and some chisels, and now I'm going to head home and carve Heffa a bracelet in the shape of two wolves screw—'

Teddy screamed and dived at Joe, who nimbly sidestepped, sending Teddy careening into the table behind us, and the coffee and coffee-drinkers tumbling to the ground. Teddy quickly hopped to his feet and wiped latte froth from his face with his sleeve. I had never seen him so angry before, and I was suddenly afraid that he would try to deal with Joe in the way he dealt with most of his problems: by biting them repeatedly until they stopped twitching.

Joe was a picture of calm, standing patiently with his arms folded. His muscles had none of the tension that wracked Teddy's twisted form. With a wide smirk on his face, he said, 'Whatsamatter, Ted, lost your receipt? Well, guess what, you're gonna lose more than that when I'm through. Just give me a second to get undressed and fold my clothes, then I'll change shape and we can settle this like men.'

The food court had been busy, but the other patrons had fled at the sudden outbreak of violence, and now Joe and Teddy circled each other warily among the empty tables and half-eaten food. I stood by our table, desperately hoping that my bags of new clothes wouldn't get damaged in the fight that threatened to be fatal to one of the two loves of my life. I couldn't let that happen; there was no point in having a bunch of fancy outfits to wear on TV if the romantic conflict that was supposed to make me a media celebrity ended here and now. Bravely leaving my packages undefended, I stepped between Teddy and Joe. 'Stop it, there's no reason for you to fight like this over me!'

My interjection was enough to make them pause for a moment, long enough for me to reach into my purse and pull out my scorecard. 'We've got this, remember? You two just have to keep smothering me with attention and gifts – homemade or store-bought, both are fine – and then eventually I'll tot up the totals and tell you who I love.'

Teddy waved his hand dismissively. 'This is about me and him, Heffa, and we'll settle it our own way, right, boy?'

Joe growled in response and shifted so that he could see his rival clearly.

'No, no, it's about me,' I clarified. 'You're fighting over *me*; your relationship is only narratively significant insofar as it affects my feelings towards you. Otherwise, it's entirely superficial and trivial.'

Joe glanced in my direction. 'Maybe so, Heffa, but we want this thing settled so the survivor can get on with getting down. Neither Teddy, or me, or the reader, has got the patience to drag this trite love-triangle plot line out for several hundred pages.'

'But I don't want either of you to die! Yet. I'm still not famous, and that's the whole point of the feud. Oh look, a camera crew has arrived; don't start fighting until they're ready.'

Silence fell on the abandoned food court as Teddy and Joe circled each other. Chairs and tables had been upended in their initial scuffle and trays of discarded food were strewn all across the terracotta-style floor. I busied myself moving tables and chairs out of the way and checking the spare food for re-usability while the tiny lumpy-faced reporter woman was encouraging her cameraman to hurry up by waving her microphone in his face. As a fellow career woman, I applauded her determination to get things done in the most shrewish way possible. She turned to acknowledge my applause and I saw her clearly for the first time. I let out an involuntary

'ZOMG!' She was Kumquat Karloff, the intrepid investigative reporter/presenter of *ZOMG! With Kumquat Karloff*. Watching her show 'Which is better – shoes or cake?' had been life-changing for me.

Teddy waited as her cameraman finished setting up his camera, then scowled at me. 'Your plan is going to take too long, and you know how fickle the media can be.'

'Wait a minute, I think I have an idea,' Joe said. He grabbed the microphone from the startled Kumquat and shook his fist in Teddy's face. 'Hear this, you lousy vampire puke. Next week is La Trine Fest, the Pacific Northwest's premier festival of Native American culture and competitive drinking. Me and my band are playing there and we are going to rock the freakin' joint.'

Teddy rolled his eyes. 'I sincerely doubt that. I've heard your sub-grunge caterwauling. You'll never be as good as the inspiring and talented Muse, whom I promised Stephfordy I would mention at some point. It is my contention that the "freaking joint" will remain decidedly un-rocked.'

'You think you can do better, fang-face?' Joe was strutting up and down in front of Kumquat Karloff now, his words directed at the watching audience as much as at Teddy.

'I fancy myself a passable musician, you ghastly oaf. I would certainly be ready to pit my harpsichord arpeggios against your ham-fisted guitar torturing, any time.'

Joe looked directly into the camera. 'All right then, you heard him, folks. It's on! Werewolf brawn versus vampire whatever, in the mother of all rock battles, only at La Trine Fest, next Friday! The prize: the hand in marriage of the county's most eligible feminina – her!' He pointed at me, and the cameraman raced over to get my reaction.

I felt queasy. I wasn't sure I wanted to stake my whole future on this, especially after I'd spent so much time on my scorecard, but Joe's stunt was a triumphant media coup, so for now I had to go along with it. Kumquat Karloff asked me a question, but I didn't hear it, or my mumbled reply, my head was spinning so fast. She rushed off to grab Teddy. 'Wow! Amazing! Mr. Kelledy, your reaction please?'

I collapsed onto a nearby seat, chomping absent-mindedly on a discarded taco while Teddy laid down some serious trash-talk in Joe's direction. I gazed around at the devastated food court. All things considered, it had been a lovely afternoon. My darling Teddy had bought me lots of new stuff and Joe had also been trying, in his simple blue-collar way, to win my affection. And now it seemed as though my plan to gain my rightful place at the celebrity top table was going to work out, just like I'd decided it should.

Teddy and Joe were filling Kumquat's camera with TV gold, but I needed to make sure that the simple folk of Spatula were getting the message. Time to head home and watch Kumquat's show. I politely indicated the end of Teddy's interview by shoving the cameraman to the ground, and led Teddy briskly back towards the parking lot so that he could chauffeur me home. I had a date, with my loving fans out there in TV-land.

chapter 6

coming together

That evening, Dad and I watched the TV coverage of what the excitable Channel 7 news team dubbed 'The Shopping Mall Showdown'. My uncharacteristic incoherence in front of the camera meant, annoyingly, that I hardly featured at all, except for when I stood behind the reporter waving as she interviewed Teddy. Both Teddy and Joe had made quite an impression on the viewers, as became clear during the phone-in that Kumquat hosted after the news bulletin.

The theme of the show was 'Feuding Fiends: Taking the Ruff or the Smooth?' and the callers were split right down the middle. Half of them thought that Joe was clearly a decent working-class hunk and that Teddy was a pencil-necked pretty boy who wasn't fit to polish his pecs, while the others thought that Teddy was suave and romantic, and would treat a lady like what she done ought to be treated. All were agreed that one of them needed to be 'kicked to the curb' or 'given his marching papers' or otherwise told to drop dead with a colorful metaphor.

I was about to phone in myself and explain that being in love with both of them and refusing to pick was a perfectly valid choice with no negative consequences, when the phone rang. I went into the kitchen to answer it, and Dad switched channels to watch the game as soon as I got off the sofa. I gave him an angry look but he was already engrossed.

It was Bobbi on the phone, and I hardly got a word in before she was telling me about how the online coverage of the afternoon's boyfriend-off had gone completely crazy. 'You won't believe it, Heffa, there are already dozens of fansites for Teddy and Joe; Kanye West has said dreadful things about both

of them on his Witter feed; and the YouTube video of the fight
has been watched hundreds of times.'

'That was mostly me, I think. On that important topic, what
about *me*, Bobbi, how many fansites have I got?'

I heard Bobbi typing at the other end of the phone. 'Hold
on, I'll just pop your name into Ghoolgle and see what comes
up. Okay. Um, someone called wolfgirl69 has started an online
petition called "please dump Heffa Lump" that's got 60,000
signatures already, wow. And there's a game here where you
get apples thrown at your head, and every time one hits you,
you say something annoying. Hah, got you!'

I could just make out a strangely familiar whiny voice at
the other end of the line over the sound of Bobbi's cackling.
'I think you must be looking at the wrong Internet. Can I talk
to Teddy please?'

'Ooh, missed. Sorry, what? Oh, no, he's in seclusion,
working on his performance for La Trine Fest; he said he
couldn't be disturbed under any circumstances.'

My spine tingled at this news. Teddy was clearly getting into
the spirit of the competition. I couldn't wait to find out more
about the piece he would be unveiling for me in front of all
those people. 'What's he going to do, did he drop any hints?'

'No, not really. He came back this afternoon with a big stack
of music paper and the string section of the Seattle
Philharmonic Orchestra. He shouted something about his
"song cycle" and how sorry they would be if they hadn't
mastered the adagio section by nightfall, then he marched
them off into the west wing and I haven't seen him since. I did
hear some loud screaming just after sunset, but that's often a
good sign with Teddy, and it's all quiet now.'

After I got off the phone with Bobbi, I thought I'd better
ring Joe to check he was going at it as hard as Teddy. Laddie
answered, and told me that Joe was off helping with the festival
set-up. Two stages, food stalls, a poetry tent... it was a very
significant erection, and he was going to be drilling and
banging non-stop for the next few days.

The next morning, I still couldn't get in touch with either
Joe or Teddy. I missed Teddy first because he was usually

looming over me lovingly when I woke up, ready to carry me to the bathroom and pick out my clothes. Puzzled by his absence, I lay there patiently for a couple of hours shouting, 'Teddy, help!' every twenty seconds or so.

Eventually, I remembered that he was busy working on his 'song cycle', whatever that was, and so with a superhuman effort I fell out of bed and staggered feebly towards my bathroom. I leant on the doorframe to catch my breath, reflecting that if I did give in to Teddy's urges and become a vampire, I would at least have more energy for this sort of strenuous activity. I wouldn't actually need to breathe either, although constantly pretending to do so for the benefit of any passing humans would probably be just as tiring as the real thing.

After dressing, I tried to call Joe again, but without success. Feeling at a bit of a loose end without anyone around for me to make demands of willfully, I sat at the kitchen table idly flicking through the pages of my favorite cookbook, *1001 Casseroles For Every Occasion*. I was consoled by the knowledge that both of my beaus were off doing things that were, in the end, for my happiness, but I wanted one or both of them here to make me happy *right now*. That was the worst thing about delayed gratification, the waiting.

I slammed the cookbook shut in frustration and just sat at the table, my mood becoming blacker by the second. This wasn't like me; I'd always been so self-reliant. Ever since kindergarten, when I had first realized that I was more mature, intelligent, and just downright better than the other kids, I'd been happiest in my own company. Which was convenient since those first schoolmates had seemed to resent the presence of a late-starting eight-year-old in their playgroup. But now I was sitting here pining over some dumb boys. Well, no more. I was Heffa Lump, independent young woman, and if Joe and Teddy didn't want to spend their every waking moment abasing themselves before me, then that was their loss. I didn't need a man to define me. Scooping the cookbook off the table, I resolved to drive down to the sheriff's office in town and see what sort of casserole Dad wanted me to make for his dinner.

My visit with Dad turned out to be a brief one, as he was in the middle of coordinating the statewide search for a busload of missing musicians, or some such nonsense. He shooed me out the door with a terse 'Pick whichever you like, darling, they all taste the same to me.'

The sheriff's office faced straight down Main Street, and as I stood on the steps I noticed some sort of commotion outside a store towards its far end. I couldn't make out which one it was from such a distance, but as it was a nice day by Spatula standards – with only a light rain falling and just the merest hints of a lightning storm playing over the distant hills – I figured I'd stroll on down there and see what had got the hicks' knickers in such a twist.

Getting closer, I saw that the crowd was gathered around what had until recently been a vacant store. For years a fixture of Main Street, 'The Umbrellas of Spatula' had gone out of business a few months ago, brought down by the financial crisis and the freak two-week dry spell we'd experienced in the spring. But there must have been thirty people outside now. There was no name painted above the store, so I pushed my way through the men and women who stood in front of the window to see what incredible new retail experience had got everyone so excited.

A hastily scrawled paper banner hanging in the window announced 'La Trine Fest: Official Merchandise' and below that was a crude display of posters, lurid multicolored hats – which I understood were commonly used at festivals to identify the mentally deficient – and T-shirts. I knew that La Trine Fest was the cultural highlight of the season, more so than ever now it looked like the symphony orchestra had split up, but all this excitement over a bunch of shoddy clothing? Come on, Spatula, have a bit of self-respect. People seemed to be lapping it up though.

As I puzzled over the window, a thirty-something old woman came out of the store waving a T-shirt triumphantly over her head. There were loud cheers from some members of the crowd, swiftly followed by booing from the others. When the woman turned in my direction and I saw the familiar face emblazoned across her prized new T-shirt, my confusion turned to horrified understanding. I shoved her out of the way and entered the shop. Determined to confront the proprietor, I elbowed my way to the front of the queue with practiced speed, slammed my fists on the counter and demanded calmly, 'Who the heck is in charge here?'

'Oh, hi, Heffa, fancy seeing you here,' replied Bobbi Kelledy. She stood behind the register holding a thick wad of dollar bills. There was a sound from the doorway behind her and Joe Cahontas's wolf-brother Laddie emerged from what must have been the stockroom carrying several large boxes.

'I've got some more of the XL size 'Team Teddy' tees, Bobbi, where shall I put them?' Noticing me, he dropped the boxes in alarm and stood there, sheepish in wolf's clothing.

'"Team Teddy" T-shirts, Bobbi? *What* is going on?' I demanded.

Bobbi stuck out her chin and answered defiantly, 'We're selling merchandise, isn't it obvious?' She indicated the display of T-shirts hanging all round the inside of the store. Teddy Kelledy and Joe Cahontas pouted, scowled and glared moodily at me from at least a dozen different designs. Shrugging, she added, 'They're quite low quality, but these rubes will buy anything as long as it's got Joe or Teddy's face on it. It's amazing, isn't it, Laddie?'

'But vampires and werewolves hate each other, what are you two doing working together?'

'Well, I was out patrolling in the woods last night, and I came across Bobbi reading the gossip blogs on her hand-held tablet device,' Laddie said.

'I'd gone out there to get away from the noise of Teddy's rehearsals,' Bobbi continued. 'When I saw Laddie, I dropped my hand-held device and went straight into a defensive posture, like I'd been taught, you know.'

'And I did the same. But then, instead of attacking and tearing the filthy bloodsucking leech's throat out like I meant to, I started to read the headlines on Bobbi's device.'

'And I made some sort of comment about how crazy it was that everyone was suddenly in love with my goofy brother, and Laddie said the same about Joe.'

'Then we got chatting, and after a while I came up with the idea of making T-shirts to cash in on the whole Teddy vs. Joe phenomenon.'

Bobbi snarled at this last comment. 'I think you'll find it was my idea, you pup.'

'No, I'm pretty sure it was mine,' Laddie retorted, flexing his shoulders and backing off a couple of steps.

Feeling that we were about to get away from the point, I reached over the counter and grabbed Bobbi by the lapel of her designer blouse. 'But this isn't supposed to be about Teddy and Joe! It's about me, it's me that they're fighting over, where are the Team Heffa T-shirts?'

'Relax, Heffa, we haven't forgotten about you. They're over there.' Bobbi gestured to a dark corner of the store where a wire bin lurked, filled with creased and unloved clothing. A sign above it read 'SALE .99c! Help us out and buy one!'

I let go of Bobbi and slumped onto the counter. It wasn't fair. All I wanted was for the whole world to love me and be jealous of me, but everything I did just seemed to make Joe and Teddy more famous, while I languished in the bargain bin of history. I sobbed quietly, and Bobbi patted me on the shoulder.

'Don't worry, Heffa, it's not you. It's just one of those crazy short-lived pop-culture fads, like Jedward or the Liberal Democrats. People have gone mad for Joe and Teddy. You can't explain it; all you can do is exploit it by creating more and more junk with their faces on. If it makes you feel any better, we've hardly sold any Wanda Mensional merch either, and she's headlining La Trine Fest.'

That didn't make me feel a whole lot better, but it did give me an idea. Wanda was just like me in many ways, a strong independent woman who had taken on the male-dominated media and carved herself out a star-shaped niche in the musical firmament. If I could get close to her, then maybe I could learn from her, and steal her place in the spotlight somehow. At the very least, I could become a member of her entourage; that had to be worth a few headlines. And it should be easy, too. We were old school friends after all, and I was sure she would have forgotten about how I'd upstaged her at the *Worrying Heights* audition by now. I would head to her house in Port D'Angerous right away and explain that I was going to be her new best friend.

I had one last thing to do here first, though. I raised my head from the counter and fixed Bobbi with my steeliest glare. 'You can sell your T-shirts, Bobbi. And your buttons, mugs, playing cards, boardgames, tea cosies, marital aids, and anything else you like.' I snatched the wad of bills from her hand. 'But I'm your partner from now on, you get me? Dad will be round each week to collect my cut; don't make him hurt you. Okay, see you soon, buh bye!' I waved and blew a kiss to my beloved 'sister', then trotted back to my armored vehicle, eager to commence the next phase of operation 'Heffa Gets Famous'.

An hour later, I was standing on the front porch of my old friend Wanda's palatial mansion in Port D'Angerous's toniest suburb. I probably should have announced myself at the front gate, but I wanted to give my visit an extra bit of zing by surprising her, so I'd hopped over the wall and dodged through the extensive grounds from bush to bush, arriving unnoticed at the door.

I pressed the buzzer and Wanda opened the door a few moments later. I smiled at her and opened my arms wide, waiting to give her the joyful hug she would no doubt want. Wanda brushed a stray strand of hair from her forehead and regarded me with the doubtful look I remembered fondly from our schooldays. After looking me up and down for a further second or so she said, 'Sorry, I don't want to join Weight Watchers, thanks.'

'Oh Wanda, you're just as funny as ever I see!' I said, complimenting her on what was a rather weak joke, there being no way that Weight Watchers would let me join. It would be too demotivating for the others to have to gaze upon my sleek form every week. Wanda still looked unsure so I threw my arms around her and exclaimed, 'It's me, Heffa

Lump from school, I've come to be your best friend again.'

To get a better look at me, she wrestled herself from my vice-like grasp and pushed me back onto the porch. 'Yeah, I remember you from the audition. You're the girl from school who never used to talk to anyone except when she wanted something, right?'

'That's me – didn't we have fun that evening when I followed you all around town until you let me copy your Trigonometry homework?' I chuckled at the happy memory, just one of many similar evenings we had spent enjoying each other's company. And homework.

'I don't need any new friends like you, Heffa. I already had to divorce my parents because they wanted a piece of me, and my accountant is doing twenty in federal prison for attempted fraud. I only hang out with non-human bloodsuckers now. And besides, I have the love of my millions of fans; that's more precious to me than your pathetic wheedling sycophancy could ever be!'

What was she talking about? I wasn't sick or fancy, I was just plain old friendly Heffa Lump. She had started to close the door on me, so I squealed one last charming compliment through the narrowing crack between us. 'You're so popular, Wanda. I need you to show me how, before Teddy and Joe become too famous to care about me anymore!'

Wanda threw the door open. 'Teddy? Teddy Kelledy? He's that pathetic excuse for a vampire that you go out with, isn't he?'

I got off my knees and nodded enthusiastically. 'My passionate preening prince of the undead, that's him.'

'And Joe is?'

She was interested in me after all, excellent. 'That's Joe Cahontas, of the Utensil Indian werewolf clan. He's my other boyfriend. I'm a modern woman but I still believe in being faithful and monogamous, so instead of two-timing them I turned them against each other and now I'm making them have a competition to decide who gets to be with me.'

'Classy,' Wanda said with an approving sneer. 'And this competition, does it have a... musical element?'

'Oh yes, they're both going to perform for me at La Trine Fest, and whoever rocks the crowd the most will win my love.' I smiled with pleasure at sharing my ingenious plan with my best friend Wanda. Every time I thought about it, the musical face-off idea seemed more and more rational.

'My manager said that merchandise revenue in Spatula is falling way short of his projections; would you know anything about that?'

'It's crazy – everyone in town wants Teddy and Joe stuff. None of the other crummy acts that are appearing are selling anything. Even *my* T-shirts aren't selling!'

I could tell Wanda was as horrified by this last piece of news as I had been. She clawed the doorframe with her razor-sharp talons, sending long spirals of wood curling down towards the floor. I tried to reassure her that I didn't mind about the T-shirts. 'It doesn't matter. I know that it's me they're fighting about, and that's what's important. Why, if I wasn't around anymore, they'd have nothing left to prove; they probably wouldn't even bother to perform at the festival if I wasn't there to impress. It's all about me, Wanda, it really is.'

Wanda nodded, and smiled widely, revealing a surprisingly large number of perfect white teeth, several of them very pointy indeed. 'Is that so?' She tapped my shoulder with sisterly affection. 'Could you wait here for a while, Heffa? I'm sure you'll be dying... to catch up with me some more, I mean. I just have to make a quick phone call. Okay, girlfriend?'

'Oh sure, I'll be right here, no problem at all!'

Wanda smiled again and closed the door gently. I couldn't believe my plan had worked out so perfectly. Here I was on Wanda Mensional's porch, and she was going to be my best friend and help me get the attention I deserved. Joe and Teddy would soon be back in their proper positions as satellites orbiting the glorious Planet Heffa, and then we'd see whose face looked best on a set of coasters. Thank goodness for Port D'Angerous, where dreams came true and nothing bad ever happened, despite what the ominous newspaper headlines foretold.

It had been late in the afternoon when I'd arrived at Wanda's mansion, and as I waited for her to come back, the sun set and the porch lights flickered on. The sounds of the neighborhood were my only company. A dog barked in the distance and somewhere a few houses over a pool party was in full swing. Closer by, I heard the whirr of automated gates being opened, followed by an untold number of rage-filled screams, which did nothing for the mellow evening mood.

I looked up in alarm to see a large mob of people heading up the drive towards the house. As they got closer, I saw that they were mostly young girls, and that many of them had the exact same brown bobbed haircut as Wanda Mensional. Some of them carried flaming wooden torches while others wielded pitchforks aggressively. Where the hell do you even buy a pitchfork? These kids obviously had storecards there, wherever it was.

My first thought was that this angry gang of youths was here for Wanda, probably because they didn't dig her new musical direction. Twenty-minute-long harp songs weren't for everyone, it's true, but she was an artist; let her have her head. Then I noticed that the eyes of everyone in the front rank were fixed on me, and I started to get worried. A girl at the front shouted, 'Get her, the power of Wanda compels you!'

I ran to the end of the porch and hopped over the railing. My stupid foot caught the top of the railing and I fell face first onto the lawn. Standing, I felt my ankle twist agonizingly as I put weight on it, and I collapsed onto my backside. The angry mob was getting close now and I shuffled away backwards as quickly as I could, which was not quick enough. I felt the stone wall that surrounded Wanda's property behind me, and hauled myself to my feet. I had climbed over it easily enough on my way in, but there was no way I was going to be able to climb out again. I turned to face the approaching mob. Wanda's face smiled out from dozens of T-shirts, and in the torchlight her eyes seemed to have an evil glint that I had never noticed before. What kind of a way is this to treat your new best friend? I reflected, as her crazed fans came ever nearer.

All hope seemed lost and I closed my eyes in accordance with tradition. Then I heard a growling rumble from the other side of the wall and I was thrown to the ground by some sort of shockwave. There was a screech of brakes and I heard something that sounded like dozens of ripe melons exploding, followed by plenty of panicked screaming. I opened my eyes to see that the wall next to me had been demolished; presumably by the jet-black armored car that now sat threateningly on Wanda's lawn. The mob of murderous fans had scattered and the girls were cowering by the house, or running back the way they had come. A door opened in the side of the armored car and my beloved Teddy Kelledy's head popped out.

'Darn it, Heffa, I warned you Port D'Angerous was unsafe; don't you read the paper? Get in, before they regroup and return.' I hobbled into the safety of his arms, and collapsed. 'Get us out of here, Bobbi,' yelled Teddy, glaring at me. I could sense that if we spoke now it would turn into an argument, so I thought it would be best if I fainted for a bit.

When I decided to come round, we were back at the Kelledys' house, with the whole family gathered around the kitchen table. They were looking at me with a mixture of concern, anger and deep resignation. Teddy spoke first. 'We managed to save your foot, my darling.'

'It's only a sprain; what do you mean you "saved" it?'

Teddy's father Joseph grinned. 'I thought we should amputate, just to be safe.'

'We saved it from Father, is what I mean,' Teddy sighed. I nodded.

'Not to worry, another time,' Joseph said reassuringly.

Teddy stood up and crossed his arms in a gesture I recognized only too well. It meant that I was about to be subjected to one of his frequent and interminable personal safety lectures. He would kill himself if anything happened to me, I was too clumsy to be out on my own, blah blah, I had a habit of making people want to murder me, yadda yadda. . .

I sat back in my chair and stared into the distance, prepared to let his words wash over me, like a shower taken reluctantly after a lazy week in bed, but before he began, Bobbi was on her feet too. 'Don't bother, Teddy. This chapter has already gone on long enough without us having to listen to your "Heffa, please be more careful" speech again. We know it backwards by now, and it never does any good. Let's get down to business.' She turned to me. 'While you were pretending to be unconscious, I got a text message from Wanda Mensional. She says that she's still going to kill you, and since you want to be famous so bad, she's going to do it where everyone can see, at La Trine Fest. And she's going to summon every one of her fans to make sure we can't stop her. It was a very thorough text.'

Teddy slammed his fists on the table. 'And she's right, dash it all. If it was just Wanda, we could easily defeat her. She's a vampire too, but four of us against her would present no significant challenge. But with her fans too, I don't know.'

'But they're only human, my love. And you love killing humans, don't you?'

'You saw them this evening, my one and only, they were as numerous as they were implacable. I have no doubt that I could tear through them like a cat shredding an unread Sunday paper, but while I was bathing in the river of their blood and feasting on their sweet offal, Wanda might be able to get to you.'

'But all four of you together?'

Teddy sat down at the table shaking his head. 'It wouldn't be enough. I'm afraid Wanda is definitely going to kill you at La Trine Fest.'

'Wrong again, paleface,' said Joe Cahontas from the kitchen doorway. The vampires span as one to face him, hissing with the hatred born of a feud that stretched back to the dawn of time.

'Joe, where did you come from? Do you have some sort of psychic connection with me that tells you when I'm in danger? Is that it?'

'Nah, my guitar tutor lives nearby, I was just passing.' He jabbed a thumb at the instrument case slung across his back.

Teddy stopped furiously hissing for long enough to ask, 'What do you mean "wrong again"? There's no way that we will be able to fight Wanda and her army of rabid fans; I've done the math a dozen times, and Heffa is doomed. Dead as disco. Brown bread. It's just a plain fact, fuzzball.'

I understood that Teddy was sticking up for his position, but he didn't have to be quite so certain about my death. It was very demotivating.

'Your math is screwy, Kelledy. Here's mine. Vampires plus werewolves equals a right royal ass-kicking. You dig?'

'You mean work together?' Teddy paced furiously. 'Never! You shaggy devils are our eternal enemies; there is no cause that could possibly bring us together were the universe to last a million years!'

'Gee, thanks,' I interjected.

Teddy looked at me apologetically. 'Sorry, love, but it is the simple truth.'

Bobbi walked to her brother and took his hand. 'I'm not sure it is. Laddie and I have been working together in our merchandise store for a whole day now, and we haven't murdered each other once.'

'You haven't?' he said with amazement. Bobbi shook her head. 'Oh, okay then. I guess we could work together after all. Let's give it a shot.' Teddy turned to me once more. 'You probably will still die, though, just to be clear.'

Although he wasn't always the most encouraging boyfriend, I was proud of Teddy for overcoming his deep-seated prejudice against werewolves, and I loved him for it. Joe was also very clever to have suggested the alliance in the first place, and if I was still alive after La Trine Fest, I would have him to thank. Joe gave me a satisfied wink and nodded with approval at Teddy. Teddy returned this gesture of friendship warily. My two men: working together at last with the righteous goal of keeping Wanda Mensional from tearing me apart. It was a beautiful moment, but I didn't want them to lose sight of the ultimate goal of their efforts. I walked over to Joe and planted a big kiss right on his lips, then walked out into the night air. Behind me I heard a plaintive 'That's not fair!' from Teddy, and a satisfied bark from Joe. Gotta keep 'em on their toes.

chapter 7

getting physical

The arena is still and quiet as the warriors approach, their sinews and muscles glistening in the moonlight – four shining pale as the moon itself, the others' fur gleaming silver. What a match this is: old enemies now united against a common foe; deadly beasts pitting themselves against one another to see who is the stronger. Will this friendly sparring match turn deadly? Can these inhuman fiends resist the urge to let their tempers get the better of them?

First into the ring, it's Joe Cahontas versus Bobbi Kelledy! What a fight, ladies and gentlemen... Just to remind you of their stats, Cahontas weighs in at 500 pounds (wolf) and 200 pounds (human), making him the heavyweight in this encounter; Kelledy is only 160 pounds but has vampiric super-strength and super-reflexes to aid her.

Well, this is an exciting encounter and no mistake. Cahontas is preparing to leap, front paws flexing, hair standing on end... WHAMMY! Has he made a kill...? No! Bobbi Kelledy has jumped clear, she's circling, she's coming at the wolf from the rear. Will he be able to spot her, will he...? Yes! Yes, he's turned, he's coming at her, the tension is rising—

'HEFFA!'

I put down the microphone. 'What?'

'What on earth are you doing here?'

I gestured around me – microphone, notebook, earphones, binoculars, a copy of *VWWE: vampires vs. werewolves 2011–12 season*. 'What does it look like? I'm commentating.'

Teddy paused. 'I did specifically tell you not to come, remember? It's far too perilous. I thought I made that very clear when I imprisoned you in the basement.'

'Well, the basement was boring,' I said. 'Besides, if I'm not here to narrate, how will anyone know what's going on? After all the games Chump's made me sit through over the years, I thought I'd be brilliant at a bit of claw-by-claw commentary.'

'It is somewhat distracting, though,' Teddy said, 'not to mention if you're announcing when people sneak up on each other that does rather remove the element of surprise.'

Honestly, everyone was a critic. I gathered my things together and climbed out of the bush that I'd chosen as a commentary box, brushing the leaves out of my hair. In the clearing, Joe and Bobbi were waiting to resume their fight: Bobbi texting merrily away on her cellphone; Joe engaging in more doggy activities, one leg cocked against a tree.

'Oh my,' I murmured. 'Do you think those proportions stay the same when he's human?'

Teddy frowned. 'That's it, back to the basement with you,' he said.

'I'll sit and watch quietly,' I promised, fixing him with my best beseeching stare. 'I won't even ask why you're training at all as long as you take your shirt off at some point.'

'We're training to protect you, Heffa,' Teddy reminded me, looking so earnest that I didn't point out that both the vampires and the werewolves had amply demonstrated their martial abilities in the previous book. Who was I to stop them if they wanted to indulge in a bit of rough and tumble? At least it would keep them busy.

The werewolf–vampire alliance was going surprisingly well, all things considered. No one had killed anyone yet, and Bobbi and Laddie between them were managing to keep Teddy and Joe apart. But this was the first time they'd engaged in full battle training, and anything could happen. I looked around the nondescript clearing where all the important outdoor scenes took place, and felt my mind flood with memories of previous events... over there was where Teddy had single-handedly defeated a ravenous zombie horde... by the bush was where Bobbi had gracefully caught a high-flung frisbee... up that tree was where Teddy and I first 'went all the way' to use his coy term. He was so eager that we nearly fell off the branch. I smiled at the memory; someday soon I would need to explain what came after holding hands.

My reverie was interrupted as someone swaggered into the clearing. It was the third Kelledy sibling, the one who didn't talk much. Jack, that was it. He was wearing a black satin shirt with a thin tie and a white cream suit, sporting a trilby on his auburn locks. This was a most unusual outfit, and the most description I could remember ever giving him – perhaps he was about to have a reason to exist at long last! I leaned forward, eager to find out how he was going to contribute to my safety.

'Right, team!' Jack declared. 'La Trine Fest is tomorrow, so we've got a lot to fit in. Is everyone ready? I've drawn up a schedule and tactics for you to study, which I'll be handing out in a moment. Any questions?'

I stuck my hand up. 'I have one! How come you're in charge, when Teddy is clearly the best of all the Kelledys, and why do you suddenly have a New Jersey accent? I thought you were from Texas.'

Jack looked off into the distance. 'I had hoped the answers to those questions would remain lost forever, but now I must expose my deepest secret.'

That was also the longest speech I'd ever heard from Jack; he usually sat in a corner and drooled at his steak. What had he been hiding? I would not have to wait long to find out, as he ripped off his shirt to expose red scars all over his torso and arms. I squinted at them. 'Are those... *lipstick* marks?'

'Indeed,' Jack said. 'For as I must now explain, in great detail and over many pages, I have a terrible secret in my past.

'I was born in Hoboken, in 1928. My mother, Alice, worked as a waitress in a cocktail bar. She had red hair, green eyes and a beautiful smile. My father, Pietro, had recently arrived from Sardinia – yes, Heffa, what is it?'

I stopped waving my arms frantically. 'Um, are you going to tell us your whole life story? Because it's only been four sentences and I'm kind of bored already. I snuck out here to watch some vamp-on-wolf action, not to sit through an extended flashback sequence. What say you give us the Cliff Notes version of your terrible past and we can get the plot moving along?'

Jack looked a little sulky – he had clearly been looking forward to this big speech – but I wasn't about to let anyone else muscle in on my narrative turf, no sirree! I was sure whatever he had to say couldn't be that interesting anyway, since it wasn't about me.

'Oh, fine,' he snarled. 'Long story short, I used to be a lounge singer in the sixties. Ol' Red Eyes, they called me. My big hit was "Come Die With Me". I played all the famous venues: Slay Stadium, Heebee Geebee's. I lived the dream, I had it all... but as you see, there was a terrible price to pay.'

'Are all those lipstick scars from groupies?'

'It's the most important lesson,' Jack said solemnly, raising his voice so that the whole crowd of wolves and vampires could hear. 'Signing autographs gives you carpal tunnel syndrome, singing three sets a day ruins your voice, but what you have most to fear from feverish fans is the moment they get their mouths on you. Lipstick is a bugger to get out of diamond-hard vampire skin.'

'But how did you manage to escape that life of never-ending touring and screaming devotees?' I inquired.

'Bobbi found me at the Madison Torture Garden,' Jack recalled fondly. 'I knew she was the fan for me after she ripped apart eight of the people in the signing queue in her haste to get to me. She explained there was so much more to life – deer to stalk, lions to kill, high schools to attend over and over again. Platinum-selling albums and a lifetime supply of willing victims wasn't going to make it compared to that!'

I decided Jack was just as dumb when he was speaking as when he wasn't and waved an impatient hand. 'Okay, fine, don't let Wanda's fans kiss you, check. Now get back to the fighting part!'

'First we must talk strategy,' Jack declared. 'Teddy, how are the comms?'

'I will interpret what the werewolves want to say with my finely honed perceptive abilities,' Teddy said proudly. 'Joe, would you care to demonstrate this with me?'

Wolf-Joe yawned loudly and then shrugged; both of which actions were highly impressive in his lupine state. I fanned myself with the stats book as he stuck one paw in the air.

'One word,' Teddy said, frowning as he struggled to disentangle the meaning from the werewolf's actions. 'Sounds like... er...' Joe was limping on one leg, and moaning piteously, then started to rub his right forepaw with his left. 'Broken leg. Twisted ankle.' Joe nodded enthusiastically, spittle flying over the clearing. 'Ooh, I have it! Cramp! Sounds like "cramp" – oh, *vamp*!'

Joe howled in appreciation and Teddy beamed at me. I couldn't help but wonder whether the vamp in question might have attacked by the time they'd finished their game of charades, but then I wasn't a military strategist. I was sure it'd be fine.

'Good work, team!' Jack said. 'Sleepover at the Kelledy castle, everyone? We've got to get our strength up before the big day tomorrow.'

The four wolves sped off into the bushes. After some rustling noises, Laddie, Joe, Fidaux and Laika emerged. Laika was wearing hot pants and a sports bra, and looked deeply unhappy about it. I guessed figuring out what to wear as a lady-wolf was more difficult than it was for the man-wolves. Poor her.

'Hey, you, put some clothes on!' I said sympathetically, throwing my hoodie at her. 'You can't go around flashing when there are all these men around, they might forget who they're meant to be fighting over – I mean, for.'

'Why are we fighting for her anyway?' Laika asked, scowling at me. 'Just cos Joe's got a thing for her vamp-baity self, why do the rest of us have to protect her?'

'She's, like, our friend, Laika,' Laddie said patiently.

'Why?'

'Er. Well. Um.' Laddie scratched his head, obviously at a loss for words to explain how my humility and awesomeness meant that everyone in the world naturally fell over themselves to look after me. 'Because I said so, all right? And you have to do what I say.'

'Huh,' Laika said, and stalked off in disgust. '*Men.*'

I began to see why Joe and the others had such trouble with her. She clearly didn't understand the wolf hierarchy, if she was going to complain about me being at the top of it.

We made our way back to the Kelledy castle. Bobbi, in typical perky fashion, ran ahead to get the dining room ready for guests. She rather considered herself the family's social secretary; she was the only Kelledy who'd ever attempted to make friends during our time at high school, though I'd swiftly stopped her trying to talk to any of the no-hopers once I started hanging out at the Kelledy table. No way was I going to let any regular kid bring down the general level of fabulousness of the Kelledys plus Heffa by hanging about and breathing and so on. Bobbi had persisted with her invites to ballroom dances, graduation parties and all-u-can-eat slaughter buffets, but somehow no one ever received the invites. It was as if a strange person with a shredder somehow managed to get rid of them all. Mysterious.

True to form, by the time the rest of us arrived at the castle Bobbi had used her super-swift vampire skills to re-paint and re-upholster the main room. She'd also laid on some Pedigree Chum canapés and changed into a silver ball gown. 'Welcome! Welcome!' she cried cheerily as we entered. 'I'm sorry I didn't have time to varnish the floor but I hope you enjoy my party!'

'Yeah, whatever,' Joe said, sharpening his claws on the Louis XIV chaise longue.

'It looks lovely,' I told Bobbi briefly, and then quickly proceeded with the constructive criticism I knew she craved from an honest friend such as I. 'Of course, the red-on-black color scheme's kind of sinister, and I would have had fewer of the Halloween decorations over by the table – but well done anyway!'

'I couldn't make my last guests leave,' Bobbi said, shocked. 'Not when they're having such a lovely time!'

I looked again at the long table. In the middle, a dessicated birthday cake sagged under the weight of moldy icing. Above it, a banner read 'Happy 50th Birthday Jack'. The people seated around the table were grinning under their party hats and streamers, but then, being skeletons, they didn't have much choice.

'That's great,' I said encouragingly. 'You really are the hostess with the mostest.' The end of that sentence would have been 'the mostest insanity', but since I needed Bobbi on my side the following day, I decided not to critique her interior design skills further right now. It could easily wait till later.

'Hey, Heff,' Jack said, juggling a frisbee, 'me and Laddie and Fidaux are going outside to play Extreme Fetch, you want to join in?'

'Thanks, but I'd rather stab out my eyes. I mean, yaaaaawn, I'm so tired I think I'll just catch some shut-eye. Have fun though!'

I made my way over to the sofa, thinking I could catch forty winks. As soon as I lay down, Joe and Teddy took up guard, one at each armrest. I could feel their glares clashing over my head. I yawned again, louder.

'Oh my, I am *so* tired. I think I'll fall asleep right here, so that if anyone wanted to talk privately about me, I wouldn't be able to hear it at all. Being asleep. Which I am.'

There was silence. I snored ostentatiously.

Teddy cleared his throat. 'So, now that it is clear I am the victor in the competition for Heffa's affections, I would hope that you would accept defeat like a gentleman and leave us to our happiness.'

Joe didn't answer. In the way of dreams – for I was asleep, after all, and couldn't hear a thing – I somehow sensed through my half-open eyes that his response was simply to stick a finger up at Teddy, the brute.

'Please do not persist in being so childish,' Teddy said. 'Heffa belongs to me, and only I can cherish, bite and love her as she desires.'

Joe mimed vomiting. I wouldn't have believed they could communicate so effectively when only one of them was speaking, but clearly the battle practice had gone better than I'd assumed.

'If you want to be vulgar, then so be it,' Teddy said. 'The more you continue your uncouth horribleness, the more obvious it will become to Heffa that only I have the gentlemanly abilities to treat her as the lady she so longs to be. And only I can turn her into a vampire, and give her the grace and poise she needs to become the lady she so longs to be. Accept it, Joe, I have won the fight, and there is nothing you can do about it.'

I snuggled deeper into the cushions. He was so noble, so fair-minded and handsome. Wrong about me needing any extra poise and grace, of course, I had that in spades, but he was utterly perfect in every other way apart from his occasional idiocy. Sometimes I had to pinch myself to remind myself that I wasn't dreaming. Except at that moment, when I was. Dreaming. Honest. Not eavesdropping at all.

I blinked, and in my slumber seemed to see Joe miming a crude but clearly interpretable scene in which he tore Teddy's throat out, jumped up and down on his remains, and then had his wolfish way with me. Even asleep, I blushed.

'You will never have her,' Teddy hissed. 'Heffa is beautiful, witty, intelligent, sparkling, well dressed, pale and wonderful. She's out of your league, dog.'

'Oh, keep talking,' I murmured. 'I mean, zzzzzzzzzzzzzzzzz.'

Joe clenched his fists, and waved them threateningly.

'Do you think you could best me in a fight?' Teddy asked, amused. 'I'd rip you into tiny shreds. I'd do it right now, actually, but Heffa would frown at me. So I will not. But that's the only reason why I am holding my rage in check!'

It was amazing, I reflected, the things you could hear as narrator even when you were fast asleep; Stephfordy was very clever like that. Why, in the morning I would probably believe that this detailed conversation between the two rivals had been nothing but a dream... I'd have to get them to fight all over again just so I could be sure of who'd won.

But that could wait for the morning. In the meantime, as Joe and Teddy seemed to have lapsed into quiet sulking, I decided I could drift off into a deeper sleep without missing any critical emotional developments.

chapter 8

performance anxiety

The next day dawned pretty fair, for Spatula — the clouds overhead were a pale white, offering occasional glimpses of the blue sky somewhere behind them, but not enough to make any ass-rays break out. La Trine Fest was due to start at midday.

At around eleven, I roused Joe and the other werewolves from their stinking sleeping bags in the garage (Bobbi wouldn't hear of them sleeping in the castle, in case they brought in lice), and reminded them that they were meant to be saving my life, not lazing around sleeping all day. Once they had all taken turns to go into the bathroom to fold their clothes and transform discreetly into their animal forms, they ran off through the forest, making their way to the La Trine lands.

Teddy, Bobbi, Jack and I followed at a more sedate pace in the armored car, with the werewolves' clothes carefully stowed in the trunk, ready for when the wolves (as humans) needed to perform on stage later. Joseph Kelledy had been invited too, but had claimed a prior engagement with an old friend and a new bacon slicer. He was the wisest of the Kelledys, and a fearsome warrior, but I could tell the others were relieved by his absence; there's nothing more horrifying than the sight of your parents at a festival, snapping their fingers and pretending that they're really into that hot new band's 'records'.

Our mood was tense. I could tell Jack was having painful flashbacks to his musical days, from the way he kept shuddering. 'The harmonicas. . .' he murmured to Bobbi. 'You have never heard the music of the damned till you have heard the harmonicas!' She patted him soothingly, and went back to flipping through her latest fashion guide, 'Top Ten Outfits to Wear at a Funeral'. I didn't find this choice of reading matter particularly encouraging. I'd hoped Teddy would be on hand to offer some words of support, but one of his violinists had managed to escape, and he was too busy re-writing the score to notice the general atmosphere of dread.

I steered the armored car past the cheery sign that marked the edge of vampire territory: 'You are now leaving West Spatula, home of the friendly vampires, please come again!' The population count had not been updated recently, and was woefully over-optimistic. That was it, then... no turning back now. Whether we triumphed or lost today, one thing was certain: people were going to die. I just needed to make darn sure none of them was me.

La Trine Fest had been set up on scrubland near the beach. The ocean's swells crashed in the distance, reminding us all that we were as tiny specks in the eyes of infinity, or something like that, and also that I really needed to pee. I left Teddy, his siblings, and his captive orchestra at the car, and headed off to find the Portapottys. On my way, I passed the main stage, a smaller music tent, a tiny poetry stage, an incredibly dangerous-looking fire, and about eighteen cider and burger stalls. As with any music festival, the music was clearly the least important part – La Trine Fest was all about booze, botulism, and trying not to fall into any bonfires.

It was a shame they hadn't got any corporate sponsorship or big-name acts – aside from Wanda – but thanks to the excitement about Joe and Teddy's musical face-off, there was a buzz in the air. I couldn't spot any media presence, but they must be here somewhere. Perhaps I should focus on surviving the day and worry about finding good places to be papped later.

I quickly freshened up in one of the Portapottys – always good to get in early before the crowds turned them into stinking hellholes – and then decided to have a quick look around. If we were right about Wanda's plan (and her text had been very specific), then later on today was going to be bloody and dangerous, and if being a narrator had taught me anything, it was that you often got useful foreshadowing before fights. It was just as well; how would I know what to do if it weren't for helpful narrative pointers?

The first tent I peered into was dark and homely. Someone had built a campfire; the smoke was meant to exit via a hole in the roof, but due to pervasive Spatula drizzle it was wafting around atmospherically instead. This definitely seemed like the kind of setting in which significant thematic hints might be dropped, so I wandered in further.

Amidst the haze of smoke, I could just make out several old men sitting in a circle round the fire. They were propped up in camping chairs, each with a can of the fearsome local cider 'Olde Yeller'. One of the men appeared to be holding court, while the others sat and listened, and as I came closer I recognized the speaker as Joe's great-uncle, Moe Cahontas, one of the tribal elders. This was very promising: Joe always complained about what an old bore his great-uncle was, all 'werewolf legends' this and 'where are my teeth now' that. I was sure whatever story he was telling was bound to give me some clues about how to make sure that, however many corpses stacked up over the course of the fighting, mine would not be one of them.

'Right,' Moe said, belching, 'are you ready for this? This is the tale of the First Wife.'

I pulled up a nearby beanbag and settled down. Outside, I could just about hear Teddy wailing my name, clearly worried that I'd wandered off and got myself killed, but I figured he could wait a while. Served him right for not paying enough attention earlier.

'Beautiful, she was,' Moe said mournfully. 'Green eyes, black hair, figure to die for. All the men of the tribe competed for her from the day she came to town, but only one was handsome enough to catch her eye. And so they were married, and settled down in a trailer by the lake.

'But all was not well at that time. Jobs were scarce, and the salad-tong factories laid off many workers. The First Wife began to grow restless, as the money for her clothes and jewelry dried up. No doubt her husband didn't help matters; he was more interested in the bottom of a bottle than in noticing what was going on under his nose. Soon she began to look elsewhere for love, comfort, and a steady supply of cash. For women are fickle and disloyal and stray easily when the mood takes them.

'So it went on, till one day the husband came back from the bar earlier than usual, and caught the First Wife in bed with her lover.

'"Don't harm him!" she pleaded. "For you were gone, and I was lonely, and no one can resist the urge to be loved." Her green eyes welled up with tears. But the husband was jealous, and he raised his fist and struck her.

'Her lover was an angry man, and could not bear to see his lady hurt so. He climbed naked from the bed and he and the husband began to fight. The First Wife begged them both to desist, but they would not. So in desperation she found the pistol her husband kept in a drawer and aimed it with her shaking hands.

'"I swear to God I'll shoot if you don't stop!" she screamed, but neither man would ever know which one of them she most wanted to protect, for as her hand shook, her finger brushed against the trigger, and the gun, which was an old one, fired...'

Moe stopped speaking. I was listening, rapt; the story was so pertinent. A beautiful woman, forced to choose between two men, using violence herself to try to keep them from killing each other... It was just like my situation! I wasn't quite sure what lesson I was meant to draw from the tragic tale, but I decided to get hold of Chump's gun in case of emergencies.

'Anyway, that's how come my first wife ended up in prison for murder,' Moe said. 'Best thing that ever happened to me, I'm telling ya, cos my Second Wife, whoo-ee was she a stunner.'

I blinked tears from my eyes. How the poor First Wife must have felt, killing one of the men that meant so much to her. Surely that wasn't going to happen to me... if the choice had to be made between letting Teddy or Joe die, I had no idea who I'd choose. Perhaps I'd toss a coin or something; I couldn't see any other way to resolve the terrible dilemma.

Moe appeared to have fallen into an alcoholic slumber. I contemplated kicking him or one of the other old men in case they had any other legends to share, but time was getting on. I'd have to hope I'd gleaned all the hints I'd need. Honestly, you may think I just sit around and wait for other people to sort out my problems, but being a narrator is no easy ride; there's all kinds of stuff you have to focus on... scenery, remembering long bits of dialogue, people's names.

I could have done with a nap, but as I left the tent I found the Fest was filling up with the local townsfolk. Too late for a sleep: there was peril on its way. Hopefully my father had been fooled by the fake announcement I'd planted on the kitchen table about a special play-off game, and was still trying to find it on TV. I was sure he wouldn't be able to resist New England Patriots vs. Toronto Bluejays. I couldn't bear to think of him coming to the festival; he might try to dance, or pretend he knew who the acts were, and then I'd die of embarrassment. Plus there was the possibility that he might die of Wanda. Either way, I was glad he was out of it.

I checked my watch again – 2.30 p.m. – time for Teddy's set! He was booked to appear at the poetry stage, which he'd chosen because it afforded a good view of the entrance and he could keep an eye out for Wanda while presenting his arts to the world.

My beautiful black-souled white-faced minstrel shuffled nervously onstage, holding a mandolin in one hand and the end of a thick iron chain in the other. The chain was attached to several sets of manacles, designed to prevent the other musicians in Teddy's ensemble escaping. They started to tune their instruments with shaking hands while Teddy hissed and flashed his fangs at them encouragingly. When it seemed like they were calm enough to play without making everything vibrato, I waved furiously at him to make sure he knew I was there being supportive. 'Teddy! Look, I'm over here! Woo-hoo! Go, Teddy, go! Remember, our future happiness depends on you not messing up! That's my boyfriend, isn't he a stud?' I asked the two other audience members.

'Man, could you, like, be quiet?' asked one of them, wearily. I made a mental note to tell Teddy that he was one of Wanda's minions. Anyone who failed to rejoice in my dulcet tones or recognize my centrality to everything deserved to get torn apart by werewolves later.

Teddy cleared his throat and plucked a note on his custom double-neck mandolin. The string section joined in and a wave of pure melody washed over me. 'Shall I compare thee to a Heffa Lump?' he recited. 'Thou aren't as pretty, nor as divine; you're less likely to cause supernatural wars, unlike dear Heffa, who is all mine.'

I let his golden, musical voice envelop me. The rehearsal time and death threats seemed to have inspired the orchestra, as they sawed, plucked and beat away at their instruments. But I only had eyes for Teddy and his mighty organ, and his tuneful mouth organ too, of course. I had heard many of his compositions before, as he liked to sing me to sleep with them: 'Song for Heffa', 'Heffa Sonnet 132', 'Ode to Heffa's Puncturable Neck', 'Why I Like Blood and Heffa, In That Order', and my personal favorite, 'Perhaps It's Time for the Chloroform'. Still, I could never tire of listening to his ditties. He was so talented. His epic song cycle 'Don Heffa' was particularly brilliant; I had never realized how many words there were to rhyme with 'Lump':

Oh my plump Lump, your hair like sump
Oil, you bring me to earth with a bump,
Recoil, for I wish to pump
You with my fangs and dump
You in a grave and never let you get
Mumps or whumped or Klumped
Like in that terrible Eddie Murphy film
Which marked his late career slump.

Well, you get the idea, and that was only one verse.

It seemed, however, that Teddy's odes to my untouchable, almost indescribable brilliance were too much for the plebeian audience, both of whom wandered off shortly after he began 'Naked Heffa', his thirty-minute homage to the beat poets. To be honest, I didn't completely blame them; it was rather obscene in places. Still, I looked forward to recreating some of the more anatomically unlikely passages, if vampires could indeed bend that way.

Moments later, my rapt attention was distracted as the first power chord from Joe's guitar ripped across the field, and the feedback yowled. Teddy stopped, perturbed and angry at this blatant attempt to disrupt his set. I decided to cheer him up with my customary good-natured banter. 'Sorry, Teddy, Joe's gig is starting now! I love you, but I have to be fair to the other guy who I also love even if not quite as much as you! Byeee!'

My diplomacy was astounding, all things considered. I was keeping completely neutral; I was the UN of inter-species relationships. But there was no time to contemplate my awesomeness; I had a competition to judge. I made my way over to the main stage to catch The Protection Racket's set, ignoring the yelps of terror and pain and the sound of tortured metal behind me; no doubt Teddy had got onto the prog rock bit of his journey through the twentieth century.

Joe, Laddie and Fidaux were naturals onstage; their testosterone, leather jackets and teenage grease creating a miasma of hormones that even the most hardened groupie would have been swayed by. I pushed my way through the crowd, barely noticing the unnatural stillness of the audience around me. Clearly they had been stunned by the magnificence of the pheromones and the ear-splitting volume emanating from The Protection Racket. I congratulated myself on remembering to bring earplugs.

The band opened with a stirring rendition of 'Oh Heffa, You're So Fine', followed by 'My Heffa Lumps'. It was true that Joe didn't quite have Teddy's versatility with rhymes, but the suggestive way he fondled the curves of his guitar more than made up for it. I bopped merrily about to the pounding beat, which was so loud you could barely hear Teddy's agonized screeching. I glanced over nonetheless; Bobbi and Jack's attempts to hold Teddy back from storming the stage looked increasingly desperate, but they were just about hanging in there. I gave them a thumbs-up for their efforts. The whole point of the day was for the boys to sort out their little rivalry in a grown-up and mature way, by posturing on stage, and I didn't want Teddy to get carried away and violent; he had to save his energy to defeat Wanda.

The second song ended. I whooped, but my cheers fell into a stony silence. Surely I couldn't be the only one who loved a bit of death metal? I glanced around to figure out what was wrong with the idiots surrounding me, and felt my heart clench. I was in the midst of a crowd of eerily silent teens. They were all wearing Wanda Mensional T-shirts, and many of them had also cut their hair like her. It was just like my near-death experience at her mansion. I knew the fans were waiting only for Wanda's word before killing me. I caught Joe's eye in an attempt to telegraph 'bit of rescuing right now please!' and felt an icy chill shudder down my spine.

'Teddy, please stop breathing down my neck!' I hissed, turning to him. 'We're in real danger here – look at all the fans. How can we hope to defeat so many?'

'You're right,' Teddy frowned. The crowd around us turned as one to the La Trine Fest entrance and started chanting Wanda's name. The noise started softly but increased slowly in volume and intensity. I had already seen that these obsessive fans worshipped Wanda Mensional to the point of dying for her. From the way they were behaving, it was obvious they sensed her imminent arrival; once she got here, I knew we were in real trouble. We stood no chance against their fervent idolatry. It was infuriating – why couldn't I have a fan base like that, for heaven's sake? All I had were three vampires and four werewolves.

Joe had jumped down from the stage, panting, the deadly rivalry between him and Teddy set easily aside once again now that there were more important things to consider. The three of us edged slowly away from the wide-eyed, staring children, carefully trying not to attract their attention. We crept to the side of the stage to confer.

'Wanda must be on her way,' Joe said. 'Once she starts singing, we're screwed; the crowd will crush us. What are we gonna do?'

I thought fast. Surely there was something that had happened recently that could inspire me? Suddenly I remembered Moe

Cahontas's tale of the First Wife. Maybe I could shoot someone! No, that probably wouldn't help. Unless... the First Wife had been doomed because she'd tried to choose between her two lovers. What if I didn't have to choose?

I didn't realize I'd been speaking aloud till I saw Joe and Teddy's twin expressions of disgust. 'Don't be silly, I don't mean a threesome!' I explained. 'I just mean that apart you're both pretty hot, so together you'd be smoking! I bet if you combined Teddy's beautiful poetic lyrics with The Protection Racket's raw rock energy, you'd have the crowd eating out of your hand. We can't fight them, so we'll have to entertain them.'

'But who's going to stop Wanda getting on stage?' Joe asked.

'Leave that to me!'

'But Heffa, the whole point was to protect you, not put you in danger,' Teddy said with concern, his lower lip wobbling at the thought of me in peril. I patted his cheek.

'Don't worry – if all goes to plan, it'll only be a brief moment of peril and then you can kill her, it'll be awesome. Now get up on stage and play like you've never played before!'

Joe and Teddy exchanged nervous glances, but my plan was clearly the only workable one, and obviously the best, because I had thought of it. I left them to sneak back on stage and ran off to put my (though I say it myself) unbeatably brilliant idea into action. There was just one thought in my mind: I had to get Wanda as far as possible from the stage until Joe and Teddy crashed it. I ran, searching desperately for Laika. She was my only hope if the plan was to work.

As agreed, she was standing guard by the ladies' Portapottys in case Wanda needed to visit the bathroom. As I ran, I fumbled in my pocket for the crude knife Joe had made me in shop class. It wasn't very sharp, but enough for my purpose.

Laika looked up as I approached. 'Heffa, what the hell—'

'No time!' I shouted, and stabbed wildly at her arm with the knife. 'We need a diversion; someone must sacrifice themselves!'

'Yeah, but shouldn't it be you?' Laika scowled. 'That really hurt.'

'I'm the heroine, I can't endanger myself – who would tell the story?' I said. Honestly, some people had no idea of how hard it was to narrate all these action sequences. I certainly couldn't participate and maintain attention to detail, all sorts of things would just never get described at all, and where would that leave us – all the important stuff happening off-stage and no blood and gore at all. 'By the way, if I were you, I'd start running.'

'What?' Laika said. 'Why?'

Over at the entrance, a long white limousine had pulled up. My timing was impeccable. As Wanda emerged from the back seat, I drew air into my lungs and screamed: 'Smell that, you vampire tramp? Yes, that's right – *blood!* Come and get it!'

Laika looked down at the blood seeping from the cut in her arm, and then at the enraged vampire racing towards us, now driven even more insane by the combination of the sight of me and her bloodlust.

'Jeez, Heffa, so much for the sisterhood,' she said, but demonstrated a faint amount of sense by moving fast. She nipped into the Portapotty, swiftly shed her clothes, and re-emerged as a fluffy golden beast, racing off into the woods a scant few seconds before Wanda reached us. The crazed vampire teen idol picked up the scent of werewolf blood in the air, licked her fangs with anticipation, and followed Laika into the trees. I was a bit worried about Laika; she seemed so much smaller than the male werewolves, and I was yet to be convinced that she had the kind of ferocity she'd need if she was to escape Wanda unscathed. Oh well, never mind. The important thing was that my plan had totally worked! I was a strategic genius.

From the stage I heard Joe shout 'a–one–a–two, a–one–two–three–four' as The Protection Racket (feat. Teddy) swung into their debut performance. I ran back to witness the world's first supernatural supergroup.

The initial reaction of the pre-teen audience was puzzlement. They had been expecting bland pop trills and uncontroversial lyrics; the combination of Teddy's impenetrable but profound-sounding lyrics and the werewolves' insane backing beats was opening up a whole new world to them.

'This isn't Wanda,' one of the spotty youths complained, 'but... they're kind of... um...'

I could tell that Joe's shirtlessness and Teddy's sculpted abs beneath his cardigan were bringing on some faint stirrings of teenage lust – brilliant!

'I... think I like the dark one,' a twelve-year-old girl muttered. 'He's kind of... sexy?'

'I'd like to spend some time with him holding hands or... something,' her friend agreed.

Yes! The raw power of Joe and Teddy's combined attractiveness was spreading through the crowd. As I pushed my way to the front, I had to force my way through several scuffles beginning to break out about which of them was hotter, and by the time I'd got to the barriers, several groups had begun to scream with the crazed enthusiasm of kids who had never before encountered musicians whose voices had broken.

'Ace work, Heffa!' Bobbi whispered in my ear as the band continued to work its magic on the crowd. 'I'll sell loads of my Joe and Teddy merchandise after this!'

Huh. Once again my talent for planning and inspirational leadership was being overshadowed. It just wasn't fair. I had to get on stage. I scrambled over the barrier, and up the side of the stage.

'Look, it's me, the third key component of the band's sound!' I told the crowd, though I don't think they heard me over Joe's caterwauling. Teddy shot me a bemused smile and then went back to sliding suggestively up and down the mike stand. I rummaged in the wooden crate of instruments at the side of the stage, frantically searching for the one that I knew I could play. Seeing it at the bottom, I grabbed it and rushed back to the front of the stage, where Joe and Teddy were engrossed in the mandolin/guitar duel that brought the song to its climax. The last notes faded away and I raised my triangle high above my head, wrapping the set up with a triumphant 'ding'.

The audience went wild. I stood beside Teddy and Joe, and accepted their adulatory applause. They loved us! They really loved me!

The moment of triumph was interrupted by a high-pitched wailing sound. At first I thought the screaming was just a particularly rapturous fan, but as it got closer I recognized Wanda's high C. She must have killed Laika already! She could have tried to put up a decent fight. Worst werewolf ever!

My vampire nemesis emerged at a run from the forest. Her wholesome school uniform stage outfit was ripped in several places and spattered with mud. Her former fans recoiled from her, for the first time seeing her as she really was without the benefit of hair stylists, make-up artists, and Photoshop. Her bright red eyes, gleaming fangs, and the way she was literally tearing her way through the crowd might have freaked them out too. She arrived at the stage dripping with entrails and gore, and turned to confront her once-loyal audience.

'You're *my* fans!' she shrieked. 'I brought you here. Kill her! Kill them all!'

The fans shuffled nervously. Most of them had already abandoned their Wanda Mensional backpacks, pencil cases and lunchboxes; others were hiding 'Marry me, Teddy!' posters behind their backs.

'It's too late, Wanda,' I said, standing tall and proud on the stage where I was hiding behind Laddie and Fidaux. 'They belong to me now. You're nobody!' I struck Teddy on the arm with my triangle. 'C'mon, then, what are you waiting for? Get her.'

Teddy frowned. 'But won't you be frightened of me if I display my penchant for ultra-violence? And also, I am not sure tearing a vampire limb from limb really fits with our new demographic, you know.'

'Well, slaying my mortal enemy would actually be a total turn-on, and if you don't do it for me, I bet Joe will,' I said, fluttering my eyelashes.

'One dead vampire, coming up!' Teddy vowed and leaped from the stage. 'Heffa, do not watch, this is liable to be R-rated!'

Pshaw, I could handle a bit of violence, and there'd been a sad lack of it up till now. I was hardly going to close my eyes or faint at the most interesting moment so far. I hurried to the front of the stage to get a proper view. Teddy was almost balletic in his approach, and he and Wanda were a blur as they confronted each other, feinting and parrying as they circled, each looking for a weakness they could exploit. Wanda grabbed a hapless fan as a shield, reckoning without Teddy's mindless rage when his dander was up. He simply wrenched the poor human in two, keeping hold of the torso to beat Wanda with. I sighed. He made it look so easy, graceful almost. Distracted by the hammer blows of the bloody midriff upon her head and neck, Wanda stumbled. It was all the opening Teddy needed. He pounced, his long musiciany fingers burrowing deep into Wanda's neck. With a superhuman heave, and a crimson spray of blood, it was all over. Wanda's head went flying through the air to impale itself on the microphone stand. I guess she got to headline the festival after all.

The crowd went wild at this terrific display of macho exuberance, so I thought I'd better get close to Teddy in case anyone got any ideas. I was wise to do so. As I reached him, an earnest teen had already sidled up to him. She was skinny, drenched in blood, and wearing a T-shirt with the slogan 'Wanda's number-one fan!'

'Please understand,' she was saying, clinging to Teddy's shirt. 'We were misguided! It was the Disney Channel's fault, they played her records all day every day; we totally thought she was telling the truth! I thought I owed everything to her, but I realize the error of my ways now. It's a really sad story, actually; I had all these friends and a boyfriend, but they put our lives in danger; they made us fight over who was better, Wanda or Justin Bieber... so many lives were lost. My name's Breef Novella, by the way. If you like, I can recount how I came to see that Wanda was a bad role model and fell for you instead; it's a short and dull tale, but I bet loads of people would be really interested...'

'Get lost, footnote,' I told her, shoving her out of the way. Perhaps if I glanced into her eyes I would wonder about everything that had happened to bring her here, but that would slow down the story far too much, and also I didn't really give a stuff. 'Oh darling, you were so awesome,' I said as I embraced my Teddy, 'the singing, the decapitation, what more could a girl wish for?'

'What indeeeed?' a low voice hissed. Teddy and I turned round to see three cloaked figures emerge from the backstage area like ghosts. Teddy flinched and held me tighter.

'What is it, my love? Who are they?'

'Oh, cool,' Bobbi said as she came to stand beside us. There was no sign of Jack. I supposed that now the fighting was over, Stephfordy had forgotten all about him again. 'Don't you recognize them, Heffa? It's the Vindicti!'

The *Undead's Got Talent* judges continued their approach. 'But what are they doing here?' I asked. Had word of my amazing talents with the triangle already reached them?

The first of the dread figures drew back his hood to reveal the smarmy features of D'Arcy D'Acula. 'Daaaarlings,' he greeted us. 'This is a surprise. We came to persuade Wanda Mensional to sign a contract with Psycho Records – but you! You and the smelly dog, you were amazing, my goodness, that was sensational stuff, boys. Tell me – how would you like to make an album?'

I backed away from his fetid breath and camp enthusiasm. 'Hands off, D'Acula. These are my boys, they belong to *me*, not you.'

Joe scratched his forehead. 'Are you sure, Heffa? This could be the deal of a lifetime, I wouldn't mind the chance to have a life outside of my dad's scooter repair shop. . .'

'Don't be silly, you love the simple, blue-collar life. You don't want to take what they're offering, no matter how much it is. If we want to be stars, we can do it on our own terms, right guys?'

'But think what we could offer you,' the second figure said. Cowl. He was every bit as creepy in the flesh as he seemed on TV, from his unnatural hairline to the ghoulish orange of his skin. His nipples strained against the confines of his tight black T-shirt as he gestured wildly with his hands. 'A number-one hit! A platinum-selling album! Then a couple more top-hundred hits, somewhere around the mid-sixties probably, followed by a rapid slide back into obscurity and a lifetime of emotional issues. How could you pass up such an opportunity?'

'It's tempting,' I allowed. 'But as the self-appointed spokesperson and manager of The Protection Racket (feat. Teddy), I must decline.'

'Must you?' whispered Teddy. 'I thought you craved fame?'

'But I have to do it on my own merits, not yours,' I insisted. 'It's only fair.'

'That makes sense. I think,' Teddy said.

I patted his hand. 'Trust me, darling, I know what's best for us.' I turned to the Vindicti. 'Begone, foul fiends. We're not signing anything.'

The third figure laughed, the sound of her madness echoing around the festival site. A long, wizened finger tipped with bright green nail varnish extended from beneath the cloak. 'We will return,' Lady CooCoo moaned. 'The Vindicti are patient, but not that patient. Sooner or later, we will come back for you. Independent acts do not survive long in this harsh business environment without the permission of the Vindicti!'

'Yeah, yeah,' I said. 'Bring it on. We'll be ready for you, won't we, guys?'

'Oh great,' Laika said, limping into the group. She'd survived after all. Figures. Stephfordy never allowed anyone on what she considered the 'right' side to die; it was very undramatic. 'Fighting another battle for Heffa, are we? Swell.'

'Be quiet, you bitter harpy,' I smiled at her. 'Everything clear?'

The three Vindicti conferred in low voices for a time, then bowed as one and began to drift away as silently and mysteriously as they'd come.

'Um, excuse me?' said a small voice. We all turned. It was the irritating fan who'd tried to speak to Teddy earlier; I couldn't remember her name.

'It's me, Breef Novella again,' she said. 'Sorry to interrupt, but Stephfordy said I had to establish my presence in case she ever wanted to use it for something else, hope that's okay...'

'You are annoying,' whispered Lady CooCoo. She whipped off her cloak, exposing twin machine guns where her breasts should have been. I gasped and looked closer – she was some kind of weird alien robot! I hadn't been expecting that.

'Avert your gaze!' Teddy commanded, and clutched me to him, so that I only heard the harsh rattle of gunfire and Breef Novella's dying cries, rather than witnessing them. Possibly that added pathos, but I didn't really care about what happened to her, since she'd tried to muscle in on my story. I was Teddy and Joe's number-one fan, I wasn't going to have anyone else hanging around and confusing things.

Lady CooCoo covered herself with her cloak again, and the Vindicti departed, leaving a fearful hush in their wake.

'Well,' I said, looking around. Very little of La Trine Fest had escaped unscathed. The traumatized audience members were picking their way through the piles of flesh of their peers, helped by the stall owners who were taking advantage of their weakened state to convince them to buy overpriced burgers and organic cider. Breef Novella's broken body lay slumped by the stage next to the bloody mess that had once been Wanda, before she'd foolishly attempted to pick a fight with me. In an unconnected incident, someone appeared to have ripped the poetry stage apart; there were broken violins and bits of tuxedo-clad musicians all over the place. All in all, it looked like a festival where shit had got real, and what more could anyone possibly ask for? 'I think we did what we came to do – good work everyone! All back to the Kelledys' for the afterparty.'

chapter 9

popping the ~~cherry~~ question

Our victory party was in full swing. In the mayhem earlier, Laddie had 'liberated' the decks and records from the La Trine Fest DJ booth and transferred them here. Bobbi had impressed everyone with her latest lightning-fast redecoration of the Kelledy home. The seventies-style light-up dancefloor that she had installed in the living room was now the scene of some serious rump-shaking, thanks to DJ Laddie's subtle blend of classic R 'n' B and big horror movie themes. So why did I still feel an overwhelming sense of dread?

It was a night to remember, a celebration of life after our narrow victory that afternoon. The drink flowed: blood for the vampires, Mountain Dew for the werewolves and a sensitive floral tea for *moi*. So why did my tisane taste like the bitter leaves of defeat?

The atmosphere was buzzing, and everyone was getting along famously. So why was I sitting alone in the dark while Joe and Teddy danced together to the theme from *Halloween*? Maybe they were getting along a bit too well, actually; reconciliation is one thing, but they'd be no good to me if they went off girls altogether. That reminded me: I still hadn't tallied up their scores from La Trine Fest. Wasn't I supposed to be deciding which of them got to spend the rest of his life with me?

Suddenly, I felt crushed by the awesome weight of all the problems I had been wrestling with these past few days. The others here were my friends, lovers, hangers-on… but they were just intoxicated capering fools; they could never truly understand how difficult it was to be Heffa Lump. Especially if they ignored me because they were too busy having a good time, instead of paying attention when I was telling them how difficult it was to be me. Honestly, no one was even listening.

If I was destined to be alone, then so be it; I would leave them to their shallow amusements and wander the halls of Castle Kelledy like a lonely specter, my once-lovely face gaunt in the eternal gloom of those winding stone corridors, desperately searching, searching for the room that had the TV in it.

As I left the raucous din of the party behind me, I thought more about the events of La Trine Fest. I remembered Joe and Teddy on stage together, and the powerful reaction that Wanda's fans had had to their music. All those confused young girls – they had started the day modeling their every life choice on Wanda, but before the first chorus of 'Midnight Train to Heffa' had finished, they'd forgotten all about her. The chemistry of The Protection Racket (feat. Teddy) was that powerful.

Too powerful, I realized suddenly. All that female attention would be disastrous for Joe and Teddy; they would never be able to handle it. There was real danger here: danger that they might get their heads turned by one of those nubile groupies and – I felt queasy at the very thought of it – forget about me! That could never be allowed to happen. Steadying myself against the cool stone wall of the passage, I summoned my strength. This was a serious situation, and required serious thought. A second later I had resolved that, for the good of all concerned, I was going to have to break up the band. It was a bitter blow, but I knew I'd get over it. Someone else would probably turn up to revolutionize popular music for ever one day, so there was no big loss in the long run.

Teddy's family had exiled their TV to a distant antechamber of the castle so they could 'talk to each other at mealtimes' or some other such quaint old-timey guff. When I finally found it, it must have been five o'clock in the morning. I flopped exhausted into the nearest armchair and began idly flicking through the channels of their basic cable package. My mind was still in turmoil. Breaking up the band might deal with the problem of unwanted female attention, but I still had to choose which one of them was going to get the wanted female attention they'd been fighting for. I looked over my scorecard in case that helped, but Joe and Teddy were evenly matched in every way. How stupid I had been to think it could help; it clearly wasn't up to the job. I tossed it away in frustration, lousy double-crossing piece of card.

I racked my brains for something, anything, that would make one of my perfect suitors seem imperfect enough to ditch, and I remembered a peculiar incident with Joe from earlier that evening. Laddie had been busily arranging his record collection when Joe had started to Inflict on a Wolfmother CD he was holding. We all recognized the signs of the preposterous hormonal werewolf curse well enough by now, and if it hadn't been for Bobbi swiftly distracting Joe with a chewy rubber bone, the CD would have been rendered completely unplayable. I had to face facts. Despite his tall, bronzed, muscular perfection, Joe's werewolf nature made him unreliable. He was too emotionally unstable. He could never be a one-woman man, or even a one-object man. For all his total lack of faults, at least Teddy could be relied upon not to run off with a lamppost.

And there it was. After months of agonizing uncertainty for Joe and Teddy, and for you, the readers, my decision was made, just like that. Teddy would have the honor of being my soulmate after all. Glad we got that sorted. Now, what's on TV?

I flicked through several channels but they all seemed to be showing the same thing. A black car sat outside a dilapidated building, possibly a hotel. Then she emerged, and suddenly I was watching a vision of my future on screen, as if the TV had sensed my romantic resolution and had decided to show me the logical next step. The bride stepped out onto the sidewalk, and I squealed with excitement. Her white dress was ravishing, the most beautiful thing I'd ever seen, after myself and Teddy, in that order. Shy and unused to being part of such a huge spectacle, the bride waved to the crowd and brushed a strand of rich dark hair from her eyes before climbing into the car. I was utterly transported by this vision of perfect loveliness, and my thoughts turned to my wedding to Teddy, which I had decided would take place as soon as possible.

I watched with rapt attention as her car drove through the historic British streets towards the church where the wedding of the century would take place. Each moment was more wonderful than the last. Her husband-to-be looked majestic in his outlandish uniform. His family might be more closely related than is healthy from a genetic point of view, but they certainly knew how to dress for big occasions; their many-coloured outfits were memorably garish. His grandmother was the exception; with regal aloofness, she wore a simple blue suit.

I shivered with pleasure as I sat alone in the dark room, soaking up every trivial detail and reveling in their outlandish traditions. The temperature had dropped several degrees, which could only mean that Teddy had come to find me. He didn't speak but stood beside me, gently stroking my hair, entranced as the couple exchanged their simple vows. Wiping a joyful tear from the corner of my eye, I said, 'Isn't it beautiful, darling?' He nodded, never taking his eyes from the screen.

Their vows exchanged, the happy couple turned to walk back along the aisle past their beaming friends and family. It was at this point that the groom's gran punched the bride's father in the face, and soon the traditional post-wedding riot was well underway.

'I do love an episode of *My Big Fat Gypsy Wedding*,' Teddy said, finally finding his voice. 'But you are missing a most excellent party. Laddie has turned into a wolf and Bobbi is riding him around the sitting room, and Jack is mixing very bloody Bloody Marys. I fear I am a little tiddly.'

'That sounds delightful, but I came up here to think about our future. And I know now what I want, having just seen it on TV.'

'Heffa, do you mean...'

'Yes, Teddy, yes, after twelve hundred pages, I have decided. I do want to be your dark lady of the night, for all eternity.'

'You mean...'

'Frickin' hell, I mean, you get to make me a vampire! Darling. It won't... it won't hurt too much, will it?'

Teddy frowned. 'Do you want me to tell you that it burns more fiercely than the fires of hell, till your soul quails in pain, or do you want me to unveil the full horror?'

'Actually, let's leave it altogether for now. Maybe you could surprise me one day so I won't have to worry about it?'

'I do love surprises!' Teddy said joyfully. 'And speaking of which...' He dug into his pocket and drew out a long white box. I gasped. 'Heffa, will you marry me?'

'NO!' I said. He blanched, stricken to the core, so I hastily added, 'Not till you propose properly.'

He nodded, smoothing his clothes and straightening his hair. Then he knelt on one knee before me, and proffered the box. 'Heffa, you are the morning to my evening, the Britney to my Justin, the angel to my devil, the hot water bottle to my frozen skin. Will you do me the honor of becoming my wife, to be joined in holy matrimony, and shortly thereafter unholy eternity?'

'Sure thing, baby!' I said. 'I bet we can sell the wedding pictures for a fortune, that'll set us up nicely till my super-special vampire powers kick in and I become the most famous person in the world.'

'I love you too,' Teddy said, and proudly opened the box. I looked in. 'Do you like it? I studied all the gossip magazines until I decided on the perfect ring to get for you.'

'It's lovely,' I said, slightly faintly. It was lovely, a platinum gold band with a deep blue sapphire in the middle surrounded by rubies and diamonds, and I could imagine the officially licensed imitations selling at a good twenty dollars, if not more. 'It's only... well... usually you just get the ring, not the finger it's on.'

'Forgive me,' Teddy said, ripping the ring from the finger of its previous owner and tossing the cadaverous digit carelessly aside. 'In my haste to give it to you, I forgot to remove it from its home. Still, I understand that it's important to have a family heirloom, and I made sure the family in question was a very noble one. Also, I thought that by leaving the finger, I'd already covered all the "something old, something new, something borrowed, something blue" requirements.'

'Yes, that is... true...' He looked so pleased with himself that I didn't quite have the heart to scold him. I figured there'd be plenty of time for that after we married, and made a mental note to start writing down things that I could hold against him for the next few centuries.

'Come, Heffa, let us tell the rest of the family the happy news,' Teddy said, and he stood and picked me up in his strong encircling frosty arms. He swept down the hall. I thought I could get used to this, and wondered if he'd carry me everywhere till the wedding ceremony.

'Brother, sister, assorted until-recently-enemies,' he called out when he reached the sitting room. 'Heffa and I have tidings of great joy.'

The assorted siblings and until-recently-enemies looked up from their game of half-man half-beast twister – Laddie's left foreleg was contorted most effectively – and variously looked attentive or sat on their haunches, panting excitedly.

'We're getting married!' I announced. 'Isn't it awesome, isn't it the most awesome news you ever heard? Even though I totally hate the limelight and the anti-feminist nature of the whole enterprise, I've got this blinging ring and all of Teddy's potential future wealth, so screw it. Everyone, isn't that the best news you've heard ever?'

Jack shrugged. 'Ring-a-ding! I hope you're going to stick the fang in her on the wedding night.'

Bobbi squealed. 'Oh, Heffa, can I choose your outfit and do your hair and wash you carefully and shave you all over?'

I thought about that: 'Yes, yes, no, EW!'

'Aw,' she pouted, but no way was I letting a makeover-and-blood-crazed vampire get anywhere near me with a razor; you never knew what they might decide you didn't need anymore.

'Laddie, Laika, Fidaux, Joe, what do you think?'

Laddie and Fidaux rolled their shoulders in the doggy equivalent of a shrug; Laika burst into tears. 'How come Heffa gets a husband? Where's my husband? Why will no one ever love meeeee?'

I did my best to ignore her selfish attempt to ruin my newfound happiness and looked at the one member of our alliance who had yet to speak up, my best friend and close runner-up as groom. 'Joe? Please say you're happy for me even though I've crushed your heart and ruined your life for ever?'

Joe drew himself up to his full, impressive height, and pushed out his full, impressive chest. 'If this is what you want, Heffa, I will no longer stand in your way. I've played fair, I've played dirty, and I'm all played out. Now, if you'll excuse me, I'm off to run to Canada, crying all the way.'

'Okay, Joe, but remember, be back for the wedding!' I said and waved him a cheery goodbye as he flung himself through the window, transformed into a wolf, and disappeared with a bloodcurdling cry of desolation. I was so glad there were no hard feelings.

We started planning that afternoon. The day needed to be the high-profile media event of the season, as well as a romantic celebration of our eternal love. Bobbi and I sat around the kitchen table, she taking notes while I blurted out my every childish whim. Soon we had compiled an epic list of my terrifyingly precise requirements. With an eye on the budget, Bobbi read it back to me to confirm the absolute necessity of each item.

'To do list (page eight of thirty-seven): design dress; book horse and carriage (elephant if poss); carve champagne luge from glacial ice; book bubble machine; confirm Celine Dion's availability for afterparty; buy gold for gold-edged invites; sew dress; re-landscape gardens of Castle Kelledy; install gazebo; more lace on dress; weather – arrange sun. . .'

Hearing it all out loud made me realize how difficult it would be to get everything just right. It would require forensic attention to detail, absolute tenacity and superhuman levels of resolve. There was only one thing to do.

'Bobbi, you're in charge of everything. I'll see you on the day, okay, sis?'

'Oh right, I didn't see that coming,' she said, clearly surprised, but thrilled that I trusted her with such a critical level of responsibility. It could be overwhelming even for someone as talented as her, so I went all out to encourage her.

114

'Just remember, Teddy's musical career has been tragically cut short. If I'm ever going to become as famous as I deserve to be, then this wedding has to be the most spectacular event that Spatula has ever seen, with me right at the heart of it.'

'You and Teddy.'

'Yeah, sure, whatever. Anyway, if you run out of things to do come find me, I might have further willful demands to make. In the meantime, I'll work on the guest list and the media circus. Okay, go team!'

Pep talk over, I held out my palm so that Bobbi could give me the high-five that my inspiring words deserved, but she was so eager to get on with the arrangements that she walked off without a word. Bless her perky black satanic heart.

Now Bobbi wasn't monopolizing my attention with her trivial nonsense, I could focus on compiling a guest list that represented the crème de la crème of contemporary society. If I was going to be famous, I had to think famous, and make sure only to invite people befitting the stellar new world I was about to enter. But I had to be careful; I'd heard that a lot of these celebs were a bit wayward – crazy, even – and I didn't want any loopy behavior to derail my special media event. I started scribbling names. Mel Gibson, Charlie Sheen, Silvio Berlusconi, Sarah Palin. Oh, what a party it was sure to be with such looninaries in attendance!

Once I was finished, I hollered for Teddy, who I knew would be lurking in loving proximity. I wasn't convinced he'd have any useful suggestions to make, but I understood the importance of sharing one's plans with one's betrothed.

Teddy appeared gracefully from behind the door and perused the list attentively. 'I love it, Heffa, so many exciting people, but I do wonder whether perchance you have forgotten anyone?'

'Like who?'

'Well, Bobbi, Jack and my father appear to be absent, as do any of our former schoolmates. Then there's the werewolves, your mother and her new husband, your father. . .'

I glowered at him; why was he trying to stink up my star-studded wedding with the regular crowd of hicks? Obviously

I'd have to explain the whole point of the wedding again – to leave behind the mundane Spatulan world forever. Nonetheless, a little compromise was a good thing, and if our family and friends were put on an obscure table at the back and promised not to cause any problems, I supposed I could tolerate their presence. I wasn't going to invite my mother, though; she'd only disgrace me by being all happy and stuff. Besides, I'd more or less ignored her existence for the last year, and it seemed like far too much effort to try to turn her into a realistic character at this late stage. 'Oh, all right then, but that's the last time: after we're hitched, they're ditched.'

Teddy grabbed my hands, and a look of somber contemplation passed across his face, like a cloud of soot in front of a snowy Himalayan crag. 'Don't joke about such things, my darling, it is more true than you know.'

'What do you mean? I wasn't joking anyway. What do you mean?' I asked, my giddy sense of anticipation momentarily sobered.

'Our wedding is merely the necessary first step towards your final terrifying fate, you are aware of that, are you not?'

'You mean me becoming a perfect immortal superbeing like you?'

'Yes, for once we are wed, I shall deign to have you join the ranks of the unliving, and once you have become as I, you will be cursed forever to live in the outer darkness, shunned by all decent folk.'

'Uh huh, yeah, looking forward to that, what's your point?'

Teddy shook his head in response to my innocent questioning. His world-weary sigh spoke of wisdom gained through painful experience, and I was reminded how ancient a being Teddy was: more than a decade older than me.

'Your father, Heffa. Once you have crossed into the land from whence no traveler returns, you will never see him again.'

'Wow, this deal gets better all the time!' I said. 'I'm going to go tell him about the wedding right now.' I kissed Teddy on the cheek and rushed out. 'And while I'm gone, you need to start thinking honeymoons, mister.'

Soon I was parked outside the simple family home where I had lived with Chump these last few years. I looked up at the simple wooden house, and was assailed by a flood of pleasant memories. I had changed so much since I'd moved to Spatula to get away from my controlling witch of a mother, but Chump's house had remained a comforting shabby presence throughout. Some might say it was modest compared to the glamorous fake castle that was to be my new home, little more than a shack, really. Maybe it would be a kindness to demolish it, before the rats and the termites did. I gunned the accelerator of the armored car and took hold of the gearstick, but then something stopped me. Maybe it was the thought of all the incredible times Teddy and I had spent in this house; maybe it was my father looking at me strangely from the kitchen window. I just wasn't ready to grind my human past into the dirt. How I longed for the sweet kiss of death that Teddy had promised, maybe then I would find the strength of character that I lacked now, and be able to obliterate this last trace of my old existence with a smile on my face.

Turning the engine off, I headed inside to tell Dad the incredible news. He was waiting for me just inside the door, keen to give me a warm fatherly hug. I sidestepped him and went into the kitchen.

'Welcome home, kiddo. Is it time for casserole?' he greeted me. I sat down at the table, worried that his tiny brain would not be able to deal with what I was about to tell him. But he must know the truth, even if it killed him; my happiness demanded it. I gestured for him to sit next to me.

'I'm afraid I have shocking news for you. Soon I will no longer be here to cook your casseroles or wash your smalls. Teddy and I are getting married! Squee! And immediately after the wedding we will disappear from your life forever, with no forwarding address, for sinister reasons we cannot share. Don't worry about us, though, we'll be blissfully happy.'

There was a long pause, as my announcement percolated through his sluggish thoughts. 'You're getting hitched? And you won't live here anymore?'

117

'That's about the size of it.' It was going very well, but he had better start blubbing soon; it was supposed to be a happy occasion, and I wanted to see tears, either voluntarily or the hard way. He hugged me tight, and I wasn't fast enough to dodge him this time.

'Aw, Heffa. My little girl! I'll miss you, darling. Still, on the plus side, I guess I'll get to move in with Lassie now.'

'WHAT?'

'Lassie, Laddie's mom? We've been dating for a while, and she's a dab hand with a stew; she always says something about having learned to cook from feeding ravenous boys. . . I didn't want to upset you, and she didn't think she could cope with being a stepmom, but now you're going, I'm sure she'll be happy to shack up with me. Say, when's the wedding? Is it soon?'

I looked at his homely, hangdog, eager face, and felt a sudden rush of loving pity for him. He'd raised me into the plain, perfect, humble superstar I was about to become, and it was only fair he got a reward in the shape of a convenient new housewife; God forbid he might try learning to cook for himself. I thought if he got a shave and a nice new suit, I might even let him walk me down the aisle. I'd been considering borrowing Joseph Kelledy – he was much more photogenic – but that suddenly seemed unfair; besides, he wouldn't actually show up in the photos. Nor would Teddy, of course, but that just meant more exposure for me, so it would all work out in the end.

'It's in a week or so, Dad, following which you will not see me ever again.' He looked like he was about to ask why he couldn't see me again, and if I was honest I wasn't too clear on that myself. We would still be here in Spatula, and Teddy would probably insist on us enrolling in high school *again*, so the disappearing act, although convenient, didn't seem entirely necessary. I didn't want to get into a long debate, however, so to deflect Chump's attention I glanced at my watch and idly remarked, 'Isn't it time for the start of the baseball season?' Chump leapt from his chair and dashed off to check the schedules, and I left my old home for the last time.

When I got back to Castle Kelledy, Bobbi grabbed me as soon as I walked through the door. Time to be measured for my wedding gown. This took much longer than I thought it would, firstly because there was something wrong with Bobbi's tape measure – there was no way that my waist was more than 16 inches; I don't care what the tape said – and secondly because Bobbi insisted on measuring *everything*. She was quite intrusive, actually; I wanted my dress to be nice, of course, but did she really need my inside leg measurement? Sometimes I found Teddy's adorable sister a bit creepy.

After she had her way with me, I had a long and very thorough shower, and then went looking for my wonderful husband-to-be. I found him on the balcony of his room, gazing out at the forest with ineffable sadness. I touched his hand and he turned to me solemnly. 'How went the conversation with your father?'

'Who?' I replied.

He clutched my hands to his chest. 'You are so brave, my darling. If I ever doubted your love, your willingness – nay, eagerness – to jettison your old life is the surest proof I could require. But there can be no going back, for either of us. Marriage, honeymoon, vampiric transformation – we are climbing aboard a veritable switchback ride of life-changing experiences.'

'You... you're not having doubts, are you?' I whimpered. The caterers' fee was non-refundable.

'Not about you, my love, never about you. It is just that... I am just not sure I am quite ready for the adult nature of the commitment.'

I kissed him gently on the lips. 'Teddy, my love, just learn your vows and practice your biting, leave the adult stuff to me.'

He nodded, and managed a thin smile. 'On the subject of biting, it would be for the best if we secluded ourselves following your transformation, for the aftermath is a difficult one.'

'Will we be making love like vampire bunnies?'

'I fear not, Heffa, for when a person is newly a vampire there is a period of great torment, when the vampire is rageful, bitter, flouncy and hateful of the whole world.'

'You mean—'

'Yes, Heffa – the hormones and lack of blood create a terrible result: adolescence. You will be overweight, moody, selfish, incommunicative, and spotty.'

I gasped. 'How long does this time last?'

'Oh, you know, a few years, same as the human one.'

I weighed up this staggering new information. I'd thought being a vampire was going to be pretty swell, and then Teddy hit me with this. I simply couldn't picture how life would feel during that time of transition – thinking only of myself, tetchy, constantly changing my mind and railing at an unfair and unloving universe... I shuddered at the image of it, so far from my gentle and saintly nature.

'But you will love me regardless, won't you, Teddy? And stay with me throughout, and make sure I don't hurt anyone even when I want to dismember the whole world?'

Teddy wrapped me in his marble-cold arms. 'Heffa, my darling,' he swore passionately, 'I promise I won't even notice the difference.'

My heart swelled in my chest as I pushed myself closer to him. I'd definitely chosen the right one to wed; I bet Joe wouldn't have been half so noble. 'Teddy, ravish me!'

'No, my dearest,' he admonished. 'Not till after the wedding; I'm saving both my fangs and my other pointy-outy parts for when our union is sanctified. Well, as far as it can be given the circumstances.'

Curse his pointless nobility! Still, the wedding was only a week away and there was an awful lot to be done before then; I would just have to hold on, before I could let myself go... forever.

chapter 10

up the aisle

The following morning, I woke bright and early and started ringing round America's premier style magazines. Bewilderingly, the first four affected not to have heard of me; a fact I found most confusing. Surely they'd seen all those editions of the *Spatula Gazette* that I'd either contributed to or been featured in; and wasn't my love triangle and face-off with Wanda world-famous by now?

Then it slowly dawned on me — they must all be respecting my desire to stay out of the limelight, knowing how much I hated to be fawned over and made a fuss of and placed in center stage. It was very sweet of them, though not, at this point, particularly helpful. I would have to email them all to let them know that it was really all right this one time, for a girl's wedding is the one day she is allowed to shine, even if she is a blushing withdrawn kitchen-chained flower the rest of her days.

I was midway through composing a diplomatic way to let them off the hook, when I had a stunning idea of how to preserve my shy anonymity *and* make a bucket of dough from flogging an exclusive interview and snaps. Heffa Lump, you are a genius, I thought, and picked up the phone once more. By three o'clock that afternoon, the auction was over, and *Scream!* was the proud winner of an exclusive peek at the secret nuptials of Prince Harry and Pippa Middleton. After all, when they arrived to find little ol' me, I knew they'd be just as thrilled — and in the meantime, I now had over a million dollars waiting to be spent on a wedding breakfast.

The rest of the week was a whirlwind of activity as the wedding plans fell into place, with me as the quiet, motionless eye of the storm. Before I knew it, it was the night before the wedding. Everything had been done that could be done. I was gazing mournfully at my super color-coded wedding spreadsheet, regretting afresh the lines colored taupe for 'unobtainable'... why were dolphins so hard to get hold of anyway? They would have looked perfect jumping merrily in the fountain.

Almost as bad, there was still no word from Joe Cahontas. The other werewolves had been out looking for him for days, ranging far and wide all across the Pacific Northwest. Laddie had caught his scent a few times, and Fidaux had found his spoor, whatever that was, but there was no sign of a completed RSVP anywhere. I could hardly imagine getting married without my best friend by my side to support me, and bother me to change my mind at the last minute. His absence would bring a bitter note of sadness to the otherwise joyful occasion. He was so selfish. I would have to rise above his childishness, though, so yah boo sucks to you, Joe Cahontas.

I had barely seen Teddy since our passionate balcony scene a few pages earlier. Bobbi said he was spending most of his time struggling to write his vows. I understood – I'd tried so hard to express in words the true beauty of my and Teddy's love, but I knew they were only a pale imitation of the reality. So I was overjoyed when he peeked warily round the door late on this final evening.

'TEDDY! What are you doing? Don't you know it's bad luck to see the bride in her wedding dress?'

'But you're not wearing the wedding dress,' Teddy pointed out.

'BUT I MIGHT HAVE BEEN,' I said, using my special reasonable wedding voice.

'I just came to let you know that Jack and Father are taking me off for my stag night. There are going to be actual stags!'

'FINE!' I said. 'I'll be here SLAVING AWAY to make the last few things PERFECT, but you go and have FUN. It's FINE.'

Teddy frowned. 'Are you sure you are all right, Heffa? You seem to be using copious amounts of capital letters.'

'I'm just a little stressed. After all, tomorrow is going to be THE MOST SPECIALEST PERFECTEST DAY OF MY LIFE. It's nothing, don't worry about it.'

He nodded understandingly, backing away from the door. 'I will send Bobbi to help you get ready,' he promised. 'And I shall see you tomorrow, my love. And after that we will never be apart, ever ever again.'

I sighed as he left. A life of constant, eternal attention. It was what every girl wanted... and yet why did I feel so apprehensive? Was I having cold feet? How I wished my ever-so-warm friend Joe could have been there, to rub against me in an entirely platonic way, he was so hot...

'Heffa?' Bobbi asked. She looked concerned. She was already changed into her maid of honor outfit, and was brushing a few stray feathers off her shoulder. I was glad I'd ordered an extra 80 doves; Bobbi kept setting them free as a practice for the day, or at least that was what she said, though her bloody lips made me question that explanation.

'I'M FINE,' I said. 'I was just lost in a reverie, thinking of everything I'm giving up in order to marry Teddy IN THE MOST SPECIAL CEREMONY THERE WILL EVER BE EVER. Children... body heat... food that isn't just blood... Oh, Bobbi, am I doing the right thing?'

'Beats me,' Bobbi said with her tender maniacal cheerfulness. 'Still, too late for nerves now. C'mon, it's only ten hours till the wedding; we'd better get started on your makeover. Teddy thinks I can work miracles, but we're cutting it fine!'

Bobbi tenderly painted my nails, then she waxed, buffed, cleansed, moisturized and made-up my face with several layers of foundation, followed by what felt like a lake of eyeliner. She lovingly fixed my hair in a loose bun with tendrils draped artfully round my face, then fastened me into a corset, and sewed up the dress as tight as it would go. I only had to remind her once that I did, in fact, still need to breathe. Next, she carefully added the finishing touches: various diamonds in my ears, a tiara, and a magnificent necklace that I vaguely remembered Nicole Kidman wearing in an advert once.

I let my mind wander. It was best not to think about the scene too closely because if I actually paid attention to what was going on, I thought I would freak out at the weird homoerotic undertones, especially since Bobbi and I were about to become sisters. Instead, I thought about all the different turns of fate that had brought me to this moment, and wondered if any of them might have come out differently. If Teddy had managed to kill either himself, or me, in one of his homicidal rages. If Wanda had succeeded in her mystifying plot to kill me. If I'd run away with Joe...

I'd nearly died so many times since getting together with Teddy. Some would say that made our relationship a little on the troubling side. But I knew that when I died for real, it would be at the hands of someone I loved, and *that* wasn't insane at all. It was perfect romance.

Dawn came and went. I watched through a crack in the curtains for the bachelor party's return. Only two hours until showtime and they STILL WEREN'T BACK! I began to pace wildly in my wedding gown, only tripping over my heels and the train once or twice. The gamboling lambs outside could not lift my spirits. The sound of the string quartet tuning up and the synchronized roller-skating waiters practicing did nothing to abate my fear. Why wasn't Teddy back yet? Almost anything could have happened to him out there in the forest. I knew that he hadn't got mixed up in some sort of hilarious comedy situation featuring a tiger and Mike Tyson. They were both downstairs enjoying the champagne breakfast, good as gold. But what if one of the stags had gotten ugly? What if Teddy had been GORED? Even if he wasn't late, a gushing chest wound would STAIN his tuxedo terribly. WHY WAS EVERYONE TRYING TO RUIN MY WEDDING?

My heart pounded in my chest as the minutes ticked by. How I wished Teddy would come back and stop it beating forever. After what seemed an eternity, I heard the sound of raucous singing from somewhere off in the woods, and then Teddy, Jack and Joseph staggered into view. Leaning on one another, they zig-zagged uncertainly across the manicured lawn, still singing. As they approached, I recognized the tune as another of Jack's ancient hits, 'The Lady is a Corpse'. Teddy stumbled, dropping his whisky glass, and the three of them collapsed with laughter. They were drunk! How TYPICAL

124

that other people were having a GOOD TIME when there was so much still to get READY.

At least they were already wearing their tuxedos. I sent Bobbi out to them with fresh, less bloody, shirts, and returned to checking myself in the mirror for microscopic last-minute imperfections. (As if.) Laika had arrived and was hovering unpleasantly in my peripheral vision, in the way as always; she kept pleading for me to toss her the wedding bouquet. I sent her off to check whether the champagne was sufficiently bubbly before she covered my gown with her horrid fur. Honestly, I had to keep an eye on EVERYTHING.

Bobbi returned, clutching her wedding planning master file and looking flustered. 'Heffa, the people from *Scream!* want to know when they'll get their exclusive interview with some Prince or other. Did we hire Prince? Can he play "U Got the Look"? That's my favorite.'

'Go away, Bobbi. Can't you see that everything is TERRIBLE now? The canapés will be soggy. Chump looks like a chimp, and the chimps look like chumps. Teddy is going to embarrass me by doing some awful dated gyrating on the ice rink. I know the performing monkeys will mess up the final pyramid. The wedding is CANCELED.'

'Right, I'll just get rid of them then,' Bobbi said, licking her lips. 'No problem. They won't complain at all about not getting their interview. In fact, no one will ever hear from them again. Leave it to me, Heffa!'

I leant against the cool fiberglass and contemplated dying right now. This was, I knew, the pinnacle of my existence. Of all my incredible feats (list them for yourself), this day would be my greatest creation. This was the climax of Heffa Lump. All my suffering and pain had culminated in this day. If a single thing went wrong, then when I was a vampire, I was going to come back and murder whoever was responsible in the most violent way possible. Time to start a new list.

In the distance, the string quartet began to play the joyfully funereal wedding march that Teddy had composed especially for me. One of the performing monkeys stuck their head round the door and asked, 'Are you ready, darling?' Suddenly realizing that the over-familiar ape in the tuxedo was my father, I took his arm so he could lead me towards my PERFECT DESTINY.

I caught a glimpse of myself in the mirror as I hobbled towards the stairs in my nine-inch heels. Bobbi wasn't necessarily a miracle-worker — after all, who could improve on the drab perfection of my humdrum blazingly hot looks? — but I had to admit she'd done a good job. The tiara was shiny, the veil was a cloud of ivory lace, and the dress was a perfect princess-style meringue.

The assembled guests stood as I entered the Kelledys' living room, which Bobbi had turned into a makeshift chapel. I clomped gracefully down the aisle on my dad's arm, smiling at the guests in each row of pews. First I passed my school friends in the back row, they being the least important attendees. Then there were a couple of rows of local civic dignitaries, the mayor and dogcatchers and suchlike; not famous, but good people to have in your corner. As we approached the altar, the quality of guests improved. Look, there was that guy from *CSI: Miami*; and over there, the runner-up from the third season of *Hell's Kitchen*. It was all working out like I had dreamed. I passed Mike Tyson's tiger in the second row and I wasn't sure who was purring most happily, me or the big cat. I waved cheerily in response to Sarah Palin's imbecilic thumbs-up gesture and then I was at the altar. It had all flashed by so quickly. I thought about making my dad turn round and doing it again, but I knew I could enjoy the 3D movie of the day any time I wanted.

Jack stood next to the priest, who I thought was brandishing his crucifix in a rather over-dramatic way, but my senses were overwhelmed and I struggled to take in all these minor details. I only had eyes for Teddy. All my doubts, all my fears, vanished in a rush of love and desire when I saw his brown crushed-velvet flared suit. Who cared if his style as well as his social attitudes were stuck in decades past? He was mine, and I loved him.

We gazed deep into each other's eyes as the final notes of the wedding march died away. Teddy's deep silver eyes swallowed me up, and I hardly heard the minister's words as he started the service. 'We are gathered here today in the sight of. . .' he began, his voice shaking. Jack whispered something in his ear and the poor man gulped nervously. It was reassuring to know that people besides us blushing brides got the jitters, but he'd better not SCREW UP AGAIN.

He continued, 'I've been advised to skip that part. Let's see . . . Uh, if anyone kn-knows of any reason why this union should not take place, l-let him sp-speak now or forever hold his peace.'

The world trembled in the hush. Then came a low despairing cry: 'HEEEFFFFFFFFFFFFFFFAAAAAAAAAAAAA AAAAAA!'

JOE! It was Joe Cahontas, pounding his fists against the closed doors, crying my name. 'HEFFFFFFFFAAAA! Come to me! It's me! I'm the one you want! PLEEEEEEEEASE?'

I looked at his sweet, shaggy face; felt Teddy's stiff rage (and stiff other things, but there'd be plenty of time for that later); and reached inside myself for all the sympathy and understanding I could muster.

'JOE CAHONTAS YOU ARE RUINING MY WEDDING THE MOST IMPORTANT SPECIAL SHINY SUPER SPECIAL DAY OF ANYONE'S LIFE AND I WILL STICK RED HOT POKERS IN YOUR EYES IF YOU DISTURB ANOTHER SECOND OF THIS MOST PERFECT BEAUTIFUL SONG-FILLED SPARKLING BETTER THAN ANYTHING EVER DAY IN WHICH I AM THE MOST PRETTY AND ENVIED GIRL IN *THE WHOLE ENTIRE WORLD*.'

There was a long pause.

'Yeah. On second thoughts, Teddy, she's all yours. Sorry to butt in. I think I'm gonna date sane people from now on. Where's Sarah Palin sitting?'

I turned back to Teddy. It was time for our vows. There had been some controversy about these. Ever the traditionalist, Teddy had initially insisted that I promise to love, honor and obey him. I wasn't keen on such a restrictive form of words and besides, as Bobbi had explained to him, 'As if!' And so, eventually, we had decided that we would just express whatever was in our hearts.

'Heffa, I love you more than life itself,' Teddy began. 'Life and I have been somewhat estranged for a while, and I have often felt that I would be better off burning in hell than walking the earth. But you made me see that being an inhuman, occasionally murderous freak is actually something to aspire to. Heffa, it makes no sense to anyone, including me sometimes, but I love you. It's like I am forced to by a greater power than I can understand. Maybe it's God. Maybe it's the author. Either way, I know it's real. You complete me. I can't imagine life or death without you. Heffa – be mine.'

'Oh, I will! I do! I am! Take me!'

I'd planned a much more eloquent response, but that seemed to satisfy Teddy. As the priest quavered, 'I now pronounce you man and wife, may you both return to the evil dimension that spawned you, holy God what have I witnessed this day, the horror,' Teddy lifted me in the air, and kissed me till spots swam before my eyes and I fainted, overcome by emotion, lust, and the lack of air. My last coherent thought before I swam into the darkness was of him. Well, I also wondered whether the wedding photographer had captured the perfect majesty of our kiss, but mostly I was thinking of him.

chapter 11

meta-phwoar

Teddy had kept very quiet about his honeymoon plans, and no amount of pleading, tickling, snubbing or refusing to kiss him had swayed him – at times I suspected that he had not organized anything at all. But then I reminded myself that while he was occasionally single-minded – especially when it came to his desire to drink my blood – he was usually fairly focused on my happiness, so I was sure he hadn't done anything so foolish.

When I came round from my unfortunate wedding faint, I found that Bobbi had taken care of changing my clothes while I was unconscious (I was beginning to find this habit more than a little creepy). I climbed down from the altar where I lay and went to check on the party. The guests had completely ignored my carefully arranged seating plan but were dancing with great enthusiasm while Laddie stood between the wheels of steel, pulling the triggers on the 45s. Seeing me, Laddie waved and reached for the record Teddy and I had decided on for our first dance. The music started and the misshapen crowd began to lurch from side to side to 'Islands in the Bloodstream'. I went to find Teddy; he was a key component of this part of the evening.

He was in the kitchen helping with the dishes in his modestly perfect way. Suddenly alone with my husband (SQUEE!), I had no desire to spend the rest of the evening making small talk with my Aunt May or Teddy's Uncle Fester. It was totally time for us to get out of here. 'Darling! Let's leave this crude and awful party and get some. . . alone time. Where are you sweeping me off to?'

Teddy's perfect features creased ever so slightly into a heart-stoppingly gorgeous frown. 'Heffa, you know it's meant to be a surprise. Now, come with me. Bobbi's arranged your trousseau, so all we need to do is say goodbye and then—'

'Oh, saying goodbye will take forever, let's just sneak off, I'm sure they'll understand. It's romantic!'

'Very well, if that is what you desire... Mrs. Kelledy.'

I almost swooned again at the sound of my new name on his lips. Legally I was now his, owned and possessed, and hopefully by this evening that would also be true in a more (how could I put this coyly?) physical sense.

'Come on then, Teddy, let's go! Where are you taking me? Apart from to Heaven and back...' I winked and nudged him playfully in the ribs.

His lower lip wobbled. 'We will never reach Heaven, Heffa, do you not recall? We are damned, damned for all eternity—'

I sighed, and dragged him towards the waiting car, to which someone (I figured Jack and Fidaux were most likely responsible) had tied boots and cans. It was a nice nod to tradition, but some of the hiking boots looked still to be occupied; perhaps the stag night had got crazy after all. I sat in the passenger seat, ready to be whisked off to paradise.

'Heffa...?' Teddy said, plaintively. 'Shouldn't you be driving?'

'What? Why?'

'Well, we are about to leave Spatula and environs, which means a marked increase in the chances of sun. I fear that people on the freeway might become startled if they see a burst of shining ass-rays emanating from a stretch limo, and I cannot expose you to the danger of a traffic incident. My only desire is to protect you. So you drive, and I will secrete myself in the trunk.'

This seemed a rather unfortunate start to our romantic getaway, and I couldn't quite understand why Stephfordy had chosen this moment to remember his slight sunshine issue. 'But what are you going to do once we reach our five-star hotel? And how will I know which way to go?'

'Do not worry, my dearest. The place we are going is utterly deserted; there will be no one to witness my rectal luminosity. And as to the other, I have programmed our destination into the car's SWAT-Nav; all you need to do is follow its instructions.'

Reluctantly, I scooched over into the driver's seat. 'Don't you mean Sat-Nav?'

'This is a special state-of-the-art model!' Teddy exclaimed proudly. 'If the car were to be dented even slightly, the nearest police riot squad would be scrambled to come to your rescue. My father liberated it from Sarah Palin's car as a wedding gift, isn't that thoughtful?'

I smiled at Teddy, overcome once again by the amazing good fortune of marrying into such a special family as his. It was no more than I deserved, naturally, but still... it was a dream come true, and I knew that my honeymoon would be the pinnacle of all I'd ever imagined and fantasized. 'Teddy, my love, please tell me where we are going?'

'Very well, my sweet. We are going to... Rio!' With that, he swung gracefully into the trunk, and brought the lid down upon himself. I squealed with excitement and gunned the engine. RIO! With my mind full of caipirinhas, carnival party dresses and recreational macaw hunting, I began the long drive south.

The SWAT-Nav directed us down the west coast, and as the miles fell away, we left the familiar dank and tree-infested world of Spatula far behind. At first, it was strange to be back down south, where the sun rose as normal and visibility wasn't severely restricted by fog. Excited at being able to see more than twenty feet in front of me, I put the pedal to the metal. The roads were quiet at this early hour, and without too many other cars on the road, we made good time. Some sort of schoolbus tried to get in our way, taking up a whole lane with its pathetic suburban chugging, but a quick nudge of their rear fender was enough to set the SWAT-Nav alarm buzzing, and soon a police helicopter had arrived to blast their lousy tailgating asses off the road.

At midday, I was directed to turn off the freeway and head east into the interior of our great country. I tried to figure out where we could be going from the route I drove, but the SWAT-Nav's instructions were frustratingly broad, tending to be commandments like: 'Turn left... drive straight on for 3,000 miles.' Whenever I had got lost in the past, evil rapists, goths or crazed armies of teeny pop fans tried to attack me, so perhaps it was best that the route was kept simple.

As we drove further and further inland, away from the beach resorts, I started to think that it must be on the fritz. All too soon I knew I was right, because when it smugly announced that we had arrived, we were somewhere in the middle of the Nevada desert, in front of a metal gate sagging off a rusty post, which was unconnected to any fence or sign of civilization. Teddy must have only programmed the first part of the journey, the adorable idiot. This was not the Brazilian hotel facing a golden beach that I had been merrily anticipating. I got out of the car and went round the back to release my beloved from his tin coffin. 'Teddy, there's something wrong; we're in the middle of nowhere!'

'Ah, perfect,' Teddy said, his sculpted hair emerging from the trunk, 'we're here.'

'But you said Rio!'

'Yes, the Rio Bravo Dude Ranch. Horses, cows, chickens, our very own barn – Heffa, welcome to your ideal honeymoon home!'

Teddy whipped a cowboy hat from his bag and popped it on his head, grinning from ear to ear with childish excitement. So many thoughts crowded my mind, I could hardly think which to vent first. Teddy had had one thing to take care of, one thing, and this is what he came up with. A gosh-darn farm. What did that make me, a sow? A big fat sow, ready for the slaughter? Is that how he thought of me? I knew it was how he thought of other humans, but I was his wife now, and I... WANTED... MY... BEACH... RESORT! I opened my mouth to cry my rage and frustration into the unending blue sky, when something stopped me. Perhaps it was Teddy's eager expression, waiting for my favorable reaction. Perhaps it was the notion that, after all, honeymoons were for spending time with your new spouse, and not excuses for over-the-top expensive hotels and fawning staff. Perhaps it was the last fraying thread of my sanity quietly snapping. Either way,

I resolved to make the best of it. Perhaps, if I closed my eyes, it would all just drift away...

Teddy hefted me into his arms. 'Come, my love. Our boudoir awaits!'

A small dark-skinned woman stood in the barn door. She gasped when she saw me and fixed Teddy with an intense stare. She waved her arms frantically and began jabbering away at him in a language I didn't understand. Teddy asked her a question, and she replied with a shake of the head. He asked her another, and their voices became louder. Finally, the crone glared at me once more, crossed herself, stamped her foot in a definitive manner, and marched off.

'What was that about, darling?' I asked.

'That's Juanita, our feisty maid. She said that if we're happy to re-use our towels we should hang them back on the rail, but if we want new ones we should leave them on the bathroom floor.'

'That's good to know, what a helpful lady. Well, hubby, don't just stand there, carry me over the threshold...'

Our boudoir was in the hayloft of a run-down clapboard farmhouse. The floor of the barn was packed with rusting farm machinery, and mice scuttled between the stacks of hay bales that lined the walls. The air was thick with dust swirling in shafts of late afternoon sun. Teddy carried me up the simple wooden staircase. Our room was spartan to the point of emptiness. The only piece of furniture was a large wrought-iron bedstead with a disgustingly amateurish hand-made quilt. I was relieved to see that Teddy had at least remembered that we'd be needing a good solid bed, but the overall effect of this shabby hovel was brain-wrenchingly disappointing. But – if you squinted just right – it was quite easy to imagine a feathery eiderdown, sweet-smelling sheets and luxurious air-conditioning percolating a soft breeze through the room. I imagined that I could hear the sea lapping at the sides of the sleek speedboats down below our room. Rio Bravo Ranch faded away, and I was transported to my own private paradise, 'Isla Lumpa'. I took a deep breath of clear tropical air, gagged on the smell of cow dung, and collapsed onto the bed.

Forgetting my intense disappointment for a moment, I rolled over and gave Teddy a sultry look. There was plenty of time to not see the lack of sights later; this was our honeymoon, and there was something that I needed Teddy to do. Something I'd been waiting hundreds and hundreds of pages for. Something that any normal couple would have done on page 50. 'Teddy – I've been waiting so long for this moment. It's time. Take me!'

Once more, Teddy let his beautiful confused expression cross his face. I lifted an admonishing finger. 'And if you ask, "Take you where?" I will scream. You must have read the book I left you.'

'*Bedroom Dud to Super Stud* – I did,' Teddy promised. 'But some of the words were very strange.'

'Like what?'

Teddy plucked the well-thumbed volume from the pocket of his corduroy slacks. 'Um. "Orgasm", "sex", "erection", "pene—"'

I sighed. Of course, Teddy came from a more innocent time. I would have to explain things to him very slowly and in as roundabout a way as possible. 'Come to me, darling. I'm sure we'll get there eventually...'

I woke, slowly, and stretched luxuriously out on the soft bed, which was like floating on clouds of cotton... if clouds of cotton had been sticky and oddly clumpy.

I opened my eyes.

Brown feathers covered the bed, some still slightly bloody. That was, not to put too fine a point on it, a little odd. My husband was nowhere to be seen. I went to investigate.

My memories of the previous night were very hazy, and not because of that blurring effect they use to cover up people's nards on TV. I felt sure that it must have been utterly magical, and that I would never walk properly again, but when I tried to recall the details, there was just this empty white space where my filthy memories should have been. I was tired from the long drive; that must be it.

Outside on the front porch, Teddy was a whirlwind of feathers and blood. As I approached, he looked up in despair. 'I cannot get the hang of plucking!' he announced. 'All I wanted to do was make you eggs for breakfast – I know how you like eggs and nothing else all of a sudden – but the chickens are proving most un-cooperative.'

I carefully wrested the latest bloody corpse from his gore-covered fingers and led him gently inside. 'Never mind, sweetheart. Let's just pretend you made the eggs and I ate them. Yummy! Those are the best eggs I ever tasted. Mmmmmmmm.'

'Heffa?' Teddy was looking distinctly ruffled. 'Are you all right? You are being unusually uncomplaining.'

'Well, last night was so magical,' I said dreamily.

'Was it?'

'Yes, OF COURSE it was,' I said, prodding him gently. 'Don't you recall? It was like... fireworks.'

'There were fireworks? Perhaps that was when you struck your head on the floor while trying to demonstrate – what was the word? – fella—'

'Sparks flew,' I insisted.

'Yes, perhaps I shouldn't have tried to light the fire—'

'And we reached fourth base!'

'Yes, the impromptu game was rather fun, wasn't it, you make a very good catcher.'

'And the train entered the tunnel!'

'I'm sorry, I didn't realize the ranch was so near the railroad—'

'And you gave me your big pork sausage!' I screamed.

'It *was* a good campfire cook-out,' Teddy reminisced.

'And you scored...'

'I really must cut my nails, but I am sure the scratches in the floorboards will come out.'

'*And I saw stars...*'

'Yes, the night sky is spectacular hereabouts,' Teddy said. His voice sounded so far off, suddenly, as if I was slipping away from him, into a distant, quiet world.

'*And we made such sweet music...*'

'Mmm, I am so glad I brought the mandolin,' Teddy said. Then: 'Heffa? Heffa? Darling? Are you... Can you... hear me?'

But it was too late. As I struggled to think of one last coy metaphor to express our love-making, it was as if I had reached the edge of all thought, all language. There were simply no words and I was so tired of trying to make everything fit together in the face of Teddy's extreme denseness.

Perhaps it would be easier to rest a while.

Just a little while.

Just till I felt stronger...

Chapter 12

The Secret Honeymoon Diary of Teddy Kelledy, Aged 31¾

HONEYMOON: DAY TWO

People killed: 0 (hurrah!). Chickens shredded: 4 (they are surprisingly slippery). Instances of Heffa acting oddly: 47.

Strange and perturbing news to report on what should have been one of the happiest days of my unlife. My dearest Heffa seems to have become somewhat insane. And not merely with lust, or anger, as is her usual wont. No, this is something more frightening and inexplicable. Frankly, I do not think she is stable enough to recount this part of the story (for if she tried, it would seem even more ridiculous than it will from my perspective), so it falls to me to attempt to make sense of her doolalliness.

I rose early on our second day at the Rio Bravo Ranch, intending to milk the cow and extract eggs from the chickens in order to make my beloved a healthy breakfast. My attempts were less fruitful than anticipated, and I was endeavoring to clean up some of the mess when my wife (how giddy the very word makes me!) emerged onto the veranda. She was as beautiful as ever, but her perambulation was somewhat wobbly, and she was muttering unconnected and nonsensical phrases. I leapt up and placed my hand on her forehead, and even to my icy skin she felt rather overheated. 'Heffa, you are burning up!' I announced.

'Yes... hot like burning... must cool down,' she said, and wandered away. Concerned, I followed her uneven progress and watched as she clambered into the cow's drinking trough, submerging herself in the murky waters.

'Heffa? Are you sure this is a good idea?' I queried.

'You should join me,' she murmured. 'The waves are so delightful... Oh, Teddy, I can feel the fish nibbling the dead skin from my toes...'

I did not like to point out that it was one of the friendly ranch cows licking her foot. I gently helped her emerge from the trough (like Venus from the waves, only muddier) and guided her back into the farmhouse to wash.

She seemed enraptured by the way the water fell from the showerhead, lifting her hand up to dance in the spray. 'Look at the waterfall, Teddy – oh, it's the most magical thing I've ever seen, tumbling over the rocks...'

I thought it best if I agreed with her every raving word, so I merely nodded and hastened to towel her off and remove her from the tub. By this time I was beginning to understand that she thought she was in a different location entirely: 'Isla Lumpa' she called it, some sort of preposterous private honeymoon island. I had never heard of anything so ridiculous; it is incredible what fantasies the febrile female mind is capable of. Yet she seemed to recognize me, so I hoped that she might recover her wits soon.

I could not help but blame myself. Was it my fault she had disappeared into this strange fantasy world? How had I upset her? My Heffa was so delicate and sensitive; I must have displeased her somehow. But no matter how hard I tried to ascertain from her what had gone wrong, she seemed incapable of conveying her woes. I tore the bedroom apart trying to find the mysterious 'G spot' she seemed so keen

I discover, but my frantic activities appeared only to enrage her further.

DAY TWO, 10 P.M.

I am simply exhausted from trying to prevent my darling endangering herself. Among other instances of nuttiness, she has attempted to jump from the window, saying it was merely a cliff over the ocean. She has tried to feed a particularly bad-tempered turkey, claiming it was an emerald parrot, and refused to be contradicted even when it pecked her. It seems hopeless.

Eventually, I tucked her firmly into bed, and retired to call Bobbi, who was singularly unhelpful. She advised me to give Heffa a good 'seeing-to' or a good 'hiding'. But I failed to understand how seeing her could co-exist with hiding her, and anyway I saw her all the time. I am beginning to suspect that the females of the species are deliberately making life harder for us poor males.

It is now very late. I have been sitting alone, weary and upset. This is not what I had envisaged for our honeymoon at all. I had hoped to have a nice few days riding the ranch's horses, and drinking the blood of the ranch's cattle. When we first arrived, Heffa had insisted that I ride her instead. But her back was far too delicate, and she simply could not gallop in the same way. It was so confusing.

As I look over these distraught words, I can only pray that tomorrow she returns to her former self: I do so miss her beauteous indolence and ire.

HONEYMOON: DAY THREE

Hours spent in hollow misery: 12. Eggs consumed: 17. Miles walked: 13 (at least Heffa's madness is lending her some energy!).

A new day dawned as I was wondering how best to resolve

my beloved's sudden insanity, and it occurred to me that Heffa might have woken up in a more reasonable frame of mind. Alas, when I went in search of her, I realized that, if anything, she was worse! I found her at last in the stable, where she was supergluing nails to the horses' foreheads.

'What on earth are you doing?' I demanded.

'Oh, Teddy,' she cried, her eyes wild with feverish delight. 'Look at the unicorns! Do you see them?'

I nodded. I confess, dear Diary, my still, shriveled heart was breaking. 'I see them, my love,' I lied. 'Come, come away from them. Let us find something else to do, yes?'

She came to me willingly enough. 'This is the most magical place ever, Teddy. I've never been anywhere quite like it.'

I was sure that was true, and can only guess at what visions were passing through her addled mind. We have spent all day 'exploring' the 'island' together, as she earnestly described the fantastic other world that existed only for her. Clouds of mosquitoes became fairies singing sweet songs... the pigs' muddy paddock became a gorge in a magnificent jungle, and she tried to balance on the fence, which to her was a rope bridge she needed to cross. Once I had rescued her from the ditch (and the pig), she solemnly told me that it was the cutest sloth she had ever seen. She then stared enraptured at an oily puddle for over an hour, thinking it a rainbow.

Though I am, of course, deeply worried by her behavior, I cannot deny that she is being a rather more restful companion than usual. Her incomprehensible demands for strenuous physical activity have vanished altogether. She seems content for me simply to stroke her hair and hold her tightly, rather than suggesting undertakings that sound over-complicated. She is sleeping better, with none of her usual tossing and turning and no attempts to caress me in my private place. She is also eating a new and more balanced

140

diet, forgoing casserole morning, noon and night for my carefully prepared egg salads, egg soups and roast eggs.

As I sat beside her this evening, watching the sun set and listening to her rhapsodizing over pink fluffy clouds that only she could see, I even began to wonder whether it would, in fact, be a kindness to leave her as she is. I will wait to see what a new day brings.

HONEYMOON: DAY FOUR

Nervous breakdowns: 2 (mine, short-lived, and Heffa's, ongoing). Punches thrown: 1 (by me, entirely justifiably). Sheep killed: 8. Chickens killed: 1 (but not by me!). Fear for my darling: AT EVEREST PROPORTIONS.

My hands are shaking as I unwillingly recount the horrors of this day. My complacent reaction to the situation was entirely misguided. Once I returned to the ranch this morning, having slaked my thirst with some local sheep, I found the most terrifying development of all.

Heffa was sitting in a rocking chair in the farm's living room, staring thoughtfully out of the window, her eyes alight with joy and wonder. She turned to me as I entered.

'Now, Teddy, I don't want you to panic,' she began.

Naturally, I panicked. 'What is it, my darling? Are you ill? Are you cold? Hot? More insane than yesterday?'

'Hush, love. Now, I need you to stay calm.'

I sat down on a nearby armchair and gripped its arms tightly to prevent any violent reaction to whatever she was about to say. I pretended to take a deep breath.

Heffa stood up carefully from the rocking chair. 'It's a miracle, Teddy. You're going to be a father!'

My jaw dropped. For a moment, I tried to believe she had not spoken at all.

'But Heffa—'

'I know it's a shock,' she said dreamily, 'and that it's only been a few days, but I've never been so sure of anything.'

'But Heffa—'

She stroked her stomach gently. 'It's like I can hear you talking to me, my precious.'

I blinked several times, in the hope the terrible sight would go away. 'You can... hear... the sofa cushion... talking to you?'

My darling scowled at me; a sight so familiar that for a moment I let myself hope that she was back to normal. Yet this hope was soon dashed. She ran her hand lovingly over the lump of the cushion she had placed under her jumper. 'What sofa cushion? I'm talking about our baby.'

I simply did not know how to react. 'I... must call my father,' I stuttered.

'NO!' Heffa shouted. 'I won't let you! No one must know! They'll think this is monstrous, unnatural; they'll try to take my baby away from me!'

'Heffa,' I pleaded with her, 'darling, you are not well.'

'I've never felt better,' she insisted. 'I realize now, even though I've never mentioned it before, even once, that all I've ever wanted is to be a mother, and for us to have a family. It's going to be amazing, Teddy, can't you see that? We're going to have a child to sing to, and buy clothes for, and it will be the prettiest thing ever...'

I watched helplessly as she waddled away from me and out into the yard. I heard the chickens clucking – yet by the time I reached Heffa, it was too late. She had already wrung the neck of a poor defenseless bird, and sunk her teeth into its back.

'Heffa – no!' I cried, but she wrenched herself away from me.

'The baby needs blood,' she screamed, her beautiful voice cracked and strange. 'It told me so.'

I let her go, and considered the situation at hand. My new wife had had a nervous breakdown. Living with my family, I was well used to the occasional bout of insanity. Heffa's delusions had seemed peaceful enough. She wasn't hurting anyone by imagining herself on a fantasy honeymoon island. But believing she was pregnant... that was something else. Bringing a child into this dangerous world of ours: I could not countenance it. More worryingly, she seemed certain that it wanted blood. I needed to resolve this before the 'baby' demanded something unreasonable.

My mind made up, I went over to my disturbed darling. 'Heffa,' I said. 'You have made me the happiest man un-alive.' I put my hand on her stomach and stroked it gently.

She dropped the chicken and smiled at me, her mouth dotted with blood and feathers. 'Oh, Teddy, thank you—' she began, but had no time to finish her sentence as I snatched the cushion from under her shirt and hurled it into the sky with all my strength. As the 'baby' disappeared into the distant landscape of rock and sagebrush, I waved cheerily.

'Look at her go, darling! Grown up and moved out of home already; they certainly do develop fast, don't they?'

Heffa looked confused. I took advantage of her momentary distraction to punch her squarely on the jaw. Then I picked up her unconscious body carefully, lovingly carried her back to the car, and placed her delicately in the trunk. I will finish writing down this tale of horror and woe, and then commence the long drive. It is time to return to Spatula and seek help. And hopefully someone else will take over the narration, for I can feel Heffa's madness starting to take hold of me...

CHAPTER 13

Dog with a Bone

Hello? Hello, is this thing on? It is? Okay, then. Joe Cahontas here, Top Dog of your friendly neighborhood werewolf pack. I'll be your narrator for today. Not sure what kind of stuff you wanna hear about, so bear with a guy, huh? We werewolves are all about the action: burst into a scene, mess stuff up wolf-style, get the girl, run off into the woods. That sort of thing. This 'introspecting' stuff isn't what we're about, but I dig that there's no one else around to clue you in on what's going down in ol' Spatula town, so you're gonna have to put up with me. Try not to ask too many questions; I get distracted easy.

It was a dark time for your ol' pal Joe, let me tell you that. Teddy Kelledy had stolen the love of my life and, what's worse, she wanted him to. They'd headed off on honeymoon, some fancy resort or other, and I'd been left behind with a broken heart and not much else besides.

Normally, there would have been stuff that I could have done to take my mind off the situation. I was the Top Dog of a werewolf pack, remember, and those crazy hound dogs got pretty out of line sometimes. But paranormal activity had been at an all-time low since our big dust-up with Wanda Mensional. With no terrible danger in our lives, me and the pack spent the days hanging out in our shack on the reservation. I tried to assert my authority and make the others go out and patrol some nights, but without Heffa to protect my heart wasn't really in it.

Instead, I spent my days writing long letters to Heffa, explaining how she had been wrong to marry Teddy and how he was certain to bring her nothing but misery. I wasn't seriously going to mail the letters – they were almost totally illegible for one thing, what with the fact that I crossed through most sentences straight after I'd written them. But, as messed up as they were, it made me feel better

144

to get my thoughts down on paper. And I figured that you never know, one day Stephfordy might want to tell my side of the story, maybe in a novella or something, so it would be a good idea to have some notes prepared just in case.

The rest of the time I spent outdoors, mostly in my wolf form, running through the woods. Just running. It felt good switching off my brain and letting my other senses take over. Wasn't hard, either, there not being that much to switch off. I always tried to stay away from people when I was like this, but since I wasn't paying that much notice, I occasionally ran right through the center of small towns, or gave a fright to the students of a university campus, or collapsed exhausted on the putting green of a country club.

It was on one of these long aimless runs that I came across her. Her scent, anyway. I was always picking up the smell of the other woodland creatures when I was out, and I could tell from a whiff of the breeze what animals were nearby. Most common were the deer, which gave off a rich meaty smell that made my mouth water. Wolverines had a peculiar odor of sweaty spandex and desperation that usually made me gag and head in the opposite direction as fast as I could. And the musk ox that I sometimes encountered in the far north smelled, to my great surprise, exactly like Calvin Klein CK1 for men.

But this was a new scent, rich with the earthy canine tones that I recognized as similar to my own, but with a note of elegant sophistication that was unfamiliar. I slowed to a gentle lope and inhaled deeply, trying to find out the direction of the intoxicating pong's source. As I did so, my head span and I felt the customary warm red mist descend. Whatever the creature was that gave off this scent, I had just Inflicted on it.

Blood raced through my veins with an urgency I hadn't felt since the day Heffa left. Picking up the scent, I ran as fast as I could to the source. Soon I was in a quiet mountain glade. She was on the far side. I approached. Her dark brown eyes met mine, and not long after they were joined by other parts of us. Eventually, we had exhausted each other. As we lay together on the soft forest moss, I spoke tenderly to her, but she remained silent. Her collar said her name was 'Lady', but I preferred to think of her as 'Heffa II'. We lay there for what seemed eons, but thinking back was probably only about

145

five minutes. I glanced at the wristwatch that I still conveniently wore even though I was a wolf, and realizing the time I took leave of my sad-eyed lassie and raced home. I wasn't going to miss the start of *Dog: The Bounty Hunter* for no bitch.

Anyway, that gives you a picture of the sort of thing I was up to while Teddy and Heffa were out of town. Now let's get down to business. This one afternoon I was hanging out at the Doghouse. I'd just come out of the toilet after... but maybe you don't need to hear about that. I'd been thinking about Lady/Heffa II so I'd taken a few minutes of 'alone time' away from the guys, and when I came out of the john Fidaux mumbled from the sofa, 'You missed a phone call while you were in there "dancing with the table leg".'

I sat down with a shrug. There wasn't anyone I was expecting to hear from, and since Fidaux was about to spark the bong he was holding, I didn't plan on returning any calls any time soon. He put the bong on the coffee table reverently and made a 'chill out' gesture in my direction. 'You'll want this message, bro, but just remember to stay frosty, yeah?' I yawned and stretched my arms to demonstrate my immense frostification, and he said, 'They're back. Heffa and that vamp.'

I knew the rest of the pack thought I was still sweet on Heffa, despite the many repeated and definitive rejections she had sent in my direction: verbal, written and matrimonial. But it wasn't true. The long weeks without her had given me time to think, and I'd realized that we could be friends without it needing to go any further or get any deeper. After all, girls told their best friends things they'd never tell their husbands, so in a way I was going to be even closer to her than Teddy was. That would show him, the filthy scum-sucking leech. All the same, I was keen to see her, so I leapt off the couch and started a frenzied search for my jeans, which I was sure were in the room somewhere, maybe under that pile of fried chicken buckets. Fidaux watched me as I hurried to get ready, and said goodbye with a weary shake of his head.

As I steered my motorcycle down the winding forest paths that led to the Kelledys' castle, I went through a list in my head to make sure I'd brought everything I needed to welcome Heffa back from honeymoon in a true spirit of friendship. Chocolates, check. Those handmade ones she liked from the store in Port D. Flowers, check.

Gathered by me from the secret mountain meadows where they grew. Walrus tusk, check. Carved by me with a design that showed Heffa and me walking arm in arm on one side, and Teddy being torn apart by ravenous wolves on the other. That should do it.

Heffa had been acting strangely before the wedding, not least by agreeing to marry Teddy in the first place, but nothing I'd experienced before prepared me for what I saw when I got to the Kelledys'. Their stupid plastic castle stood in a large clearing, with a wide lawn running from the edge of the clearing all the way to the moat (or 'municipal waste water drainage channel no. 3' as it was more accurately known). It was mid-September, at least a month before Spatula's long winter would start, but the Kelledys' lawn was covered in snow. There was someone sitting on a large yellow skidoo right in the middle, bundled up in so much winter clothing that it took me a minute to spot Heffa's tight body hidden under the layers of insulation.

Teddy Kelledy stood a few yards away, dressed in a puffy white shirt and jodhpurs combo that I assumed was part of an attempt to set a new personal record for uncoolness. He was pointing a camcorder in Heffa's direction, and as I got off my bike and walked towards them, he shouted 'Action!' into the megaphone in his other hand. Heffa waved her arms above her head with manic enthusiasm and then pulled a huge silver pistol from somewhere inside the folds of her jacket. I heard a noise in the treeline to my left, and then Jack and Bobbi Kelledy ran out in front of me. They were dressed in ski gear too, but were missing the standard finishing touch of actual skis. Bobbi ducked into a downhill skiing crouch, tucking her poles under her arms and making 'schwish schwoosh' noises as she ran towards Heffa. Jack Kelledy was right behind her, and as they got within a few feet of Heffa's skidoo, he fired several bursts at her from a nasty-looking sub-machine gun. Heffa returned fire with her pistol, and the 'skiers' fell to the ground screaming in pain. Teddy shouted 'Cut!' sounding pleased.

The battle had kicked some of the 'snow' into the air and flurries drifted back to earth as I walked over to Teddy. I grabbed a fistful of white feathers out of the air as I passed and waved them in Teddy's stupid vampire face. 'What the hell's going on, Kelledy, and where did all these feathers come from?'

147

He smiled. 'Heffa and I have been tearing through a number of pillows of late, if you catch my drift.'

I waited just a second to let Teddy's sleazy remark wash over me, then I picked him up and snapped his head clean off, before punting it way out over the forest for an extra point. Nah, just kidding, but I tell you, it's tough to stick to the facts with this narrating business; you just want to get in there and start changing the story round to make it come out right. But real life isn't like that, is it? It's all kinds of messed up. Fresh evidence of this fact was provided when Heffa waddled up a moment later. She unzipped her hood and asked Teddy eagerly, 'Was I okay?'

He patted her on the head and told her how wonderful she had been. Bobbi and Jack came over and did the same. I grabbed Teddy's arm and led him a few feet off. 'What's going on here?' I demanded.

The smile with which he'd congratulated Heffa disappeared and his whole body sagged like someone had let all the air out of him. He shook his head and frowned. 'Heffa is... unwell, Joe.'

'You'd better not have given her any tropical diseases while you were away!'

He looked indignant. 'Heffa is my wife now, and as such I shall give her whatever diseases I see fit, but I do not mean that she is physically sick. It's her mind. Not to put too fine a point on it, she's gone proper bonkers.'

I couldn't believe what I was hearing. Heffa had always been so calm and well balanced; it didn't seem possible that she could have lost her grip on reality so quickly. 'That can't be! What's happened to her?'

'At first I thought she was tired out by the stress of the wedding. But the longer we were away, the worse her delusions became. They come in many forms, and some days she is more lucid than others, but they all have one thing in common. She is always... famous.'

Saying the last word seemed to take whatever little energy Teddy had left, and his face went blank. He was clearly at the end of his rope. I almost felt sorry for him. 'She thinks she's famous? She couldn't get people interested in her in real life, so she's retreated into some wigged-out world where she's a film star?'

'It changes from day to day. Sometimes she's a film star, sometimes an author of implausibly popular supernatural fiction, and sometimes she's a...' he lowered his voice, clearly embarrassed, 'celebrity ho, whatever that is.'

I looked over at Heffa, who was happily kicking feathers in the air and firing her pistol at Jack as he dodged and weaved to avoid the bullets. 'But what's all this crap, the skidoos and the guns?' I asked.

'We're filming Heffa's latest big-screen blockbuster, of course. *Inheffshun*, she calls it. Here's the screenplay.' He handed me a shoebox full of napkins, store receipts and other filthy scraps of paper whose origin I didn't want to know. Most were covered in tiny spidery black writing; others bore strange symbols connected in a web of wavy lines; and one was a disturbingly lifelike cartoon of a butt-naked Leonardo DiCaprio bending over while a freight train rushed towards his... anyway, it was weird stuff.

'But this is just a load of nonsense!' I said, holding the box out for Teddy. Heffa ran up and grabbed it, a defensive look on her still-sweet face.

'You're just saying that cos you're not clever enough to understand it, isn't he, darling?' She turned to Teddy, who returned her eager smile with a superhuman effort.

'That's right, it's a mind-bending masterpiece, just as you predicted, my love. I think we need some time to set up for the next shot, why don't you go and wait in your trailer?'

'Okay, Teddy, wheeeee!'

She ran off into the house with the shoebox under her arm, leaving a trail of swirling feathers in her wake. I still didn't get what Teddy was up to, so I confronted him. 'I still don't get what you're up to, Kelledy. Heffa is definitely nutso, but how is this helping? She needs proper treatment, with injections and electricity. That's how the tribal elders helped Droolin' Pete after he did that stuff to those farm animals, and he's fine now. Well, placid anyway.'

Teddy shook his head. 'No, you're wrong, that is not what she needs at all. And even if it was, hiring these skidoos and the costumes has depleted our funds almost entirely. My approach to Heffa's situation is very simple, Joe. She has lost touch with reality, would you agree?'

'And how!'

'So, all we have to do is fix reality.'

'Huh?'

'We simply alter reality to conform with Heffa's delusions, and that way, her reality will be the same as ours and she won't be insane anymore. It's so easy, don't you see? Joe? Don't you see?'

He was all in my face now, shouting and shaking me by the shoulders. I kicked him hard in the crotch to take his mind off his problems, and when he collapsed to the floor, I decided to split so I could think on everything I'd just witnessed. I started my bike and made a wide turn to get back on the road. As I passed Teddy I told him, 'That's just about the stupidest thing I ever heard,' before racing down the forest path away from Spatula's newest insane asylum.

When I got home, I realized that I'd forgotten to give Heffa the chocolates, so I knew I'd have to visit her again. When I pulled up at the Kelledys' the following lunchtime, there was no sign of the snow battle. I strolled round to the back of the house in the hope of being able to do my usual trick of announcing my arrival by interrupting a dull conversation with a snarky comment.

I looked through the picture window into the vamps' oh-so-trendy Norwegian interior, and saw Teddy and his sister sitting at the breakfast bar in silence. Teddy still wore the same glum and defeated expression as before. Perhaps it wasn't Heffa's wackiness that had got him down. He'd been there and bought the T-shirt now, so maybe he had a slight case of buyer's remorse? Could be an opening for your humble narrator there. Except that I was totally happy just to do the BFF thing with Heffa. So it's not even an issue, is it? So why did you bring it up, huh?

I slid the door aside and strolled into the kitchen, greeting the Kelledy creeps with a cheery, 'Hi there, catalogue models of the damned, why so serious?'

Teddy huffed and turned his back on me, while Bobbi acknowledged me with a grimace. 'Not so loud, please, we were up really late filming last night.' She gestured in the direction of the lounge. I knew from previous visits that the Kelledys' living room was huge, way too big for a family of four if you asked me, and decorated in the same sickeningly understated style as the kitchen diner. Could have used a few totem poles and piles of laundry to make it more homey, but it felt as hard and cold as they were, so maybe that fit. Through the doorway, I saw what looked like ropes or something dangling from the ceiling, and I went in to check out this latest bit of freakiness.

There were dozens of ropes and thin cables of different lengths attached to the ceiling. Some had gym-style rings on the ends; others had slightly perverted-looking body harnesses attached.

Teddy joined me and, seeing the look of confusion and 'eww'-ness on my face, explained: 'We were filming the zero-gravity fight scenes, you see; this is all to create the illusion of weightlessness.'

I breathed a sigh of relief. 'That explanation's actually a lot less disturbing than I thought it was going to be.'

'It's a wonderful scene, but I'm afraid it does not conceal the essential ontological emptiness of the movie's central conceit.'

'Yeah, so where's Heffa anyway?'

'I'm here, and I have wonderful news!' Looking up, I saw Heffa standing at the top of the stairs. Yesterday she'd been covered in layers and layers of thick winter clothes and I hadn't got a good look at her, but now here she was in her PJs and a robe, and she looked good – for a crazy person. Her hair was as long and black as a midnight forest path, and her eyes sparkled with, well, that might have been insanity to be fair. Married life and/or being nuts obviously suited her. She was looking a bit heavyish around the middle, though. Heffa must have read my mind because she clutched her stomach and announced with delight, 'I'm pregnant, Joe. Isn't it marvelous?'

Pregnant, wow, these newlyweds weren't wasting any time. Either that or being dead and having no bodily functions hadn't been the effective contraceptive that Teddy had hoped. I couldn't believe that she'd let that pasty-faced creep get her knocked up – the thought of him touching my Heffa... It was super-gross. That said, the look on Teddy's face certainly didn't seem like joy at the prospect of new life and carrying on the Kelledy name and that sort of guff. He was smiling, but it was the sort of forced smile he usually reserved for unexpected visits from the police missing persons squad. He whispered to me through clenched teeth, 'Play along, Joe, please.'

I had no freakin' idea what I was supposed to be playing along with, so I just stood there, grinning at Heffa with a smile that said, 'I'm very happy for you, don't come any closer.' Heffa returned my smile, although I wasn't sure she really saw me. Then she grabbed her gut and doubled over onto the floor. With an agonized scream, she yelled, 'The baby, it's kicking!' and started writhing around at the top of the stairs.

Shocked, I began to rush to her aid, but Teddy placed a restraining hand on my shoulder and said, 'Relax, she's fine.' Picking up on my puzzled look, he explained, 'She's not pregnant, she simply has a pillow thrust up her pajama top. This happens every few days. Humor her, will you?'

I shook my head. 'That's almost certainly the stupidest thing I ever heard.'

Heffa had staggered to her feet and wiped the sweat from her brow. She gave us a brave little wave as she started to come down the stairs, then suddenly went tense and arched her back. With a cry of 'Ow, right in the freakin' ovaries!' she pitched forwards and crashed down the long flight of stairs, landing in a tangled heap at our feet. I was too stunned to move, but Teddy scooped up her limp form and laid her gently on the sofa. He crouched down beside her and stroked her hair, murmuring softly into her ears. After a minute or so, she sat bolt upright and with a panicked look shouted, 'Blood! Blood! My baby needs blood!'

From the kitchen, Bobbi called, 'Okay, coming,' with the desperately weary voice of someone who's been playing peek-a-boo with an excited infant for about four years straight. She ambled into the room with a plastic bucket and set it down on the floor next to Heffa. She popped a length of rubber hose into the bucket and handed one end to Heffa, who began slurping eagerly. Walking back towards the kitchen, her chore complete, Bobbi said casually to me, 'Don't worry, it's only tomato juice.'

'Yes, we would hardly waste real blood on someone who didn't need it!' Teddy added.

I went and sat on the sofa by Heffa. I had no idea how to help her, but I knew that friends stuck close to friends at times like these. And if at any point she decided she wanted me to slide my hands up inside her jammies and whip out the pillow, then I was right here. Her gaze wandered aimlessly around the room as she sucked on the hose, then she looked at me and beamed with recognition. 'Joe, you're here.'

'Of course I am, Heffa, always.'

Her eyes went vacant for a moment and then she was back. 'The baby wants to speak to you, Joe. Put your hand on my bump. It's amazing, it can speak to you in your mind.'

I glanced at Teddy, who shrugged. I did as I was asked, and felt the bulk of the soft downy pillow that was hidden under Heffa's clothes. She screwed her face up tightly and said in a theatrically guttural voice, 'This is Heffa Lump's baby speaking to you. Can you hear me, Joe Cahontas?'

I nodded and the 'baby' said, 'I can't see you nodding, dumbass, I'm in Heffa's womb, remember?'

'Sorry, of course. Yes, I can hear you, Lump fetus, what do you want with me?'

'I have an important message for you,' Heffa rasped in the baby's childish voice. 'Inflicting on newborn babies is really, really, really wrong. And I'm not coming out of here until you promise to stay away from me, you get me?'

I pulled my hand away from the pillow and jumped to my feet. 'Jeez, Heffa, what do you take me for? You really are sick, you know that?' I turned my back on her and headed for the kitchen door, where I bumped into the Kelledys' father coming the other way, his face buried in the morning paper. I mumbled an apology and he smiled amiably; he carried on walking and sat in one of the easy chairs next to Heffa.

Teddy caught up to me. I could tell he wanted me to stay, but I'd had just about all I could take for one day. I tried to push past him. 'This is too weird for me, Kelledy, let me out of here!'

'Weird? It's the most natural thing in the world! What could be more normal than a young married woman wanting to have a baby? It is single parents and couples without children that are the social deviants, not Heffa and I.'

He was shouting too, and his father looked up from his paper. 'What's that, son?'

Teddy snapped back, 'Excuse me, Father, but I am embroiled in a rather personal conversation.'

Joseph Kelledy shrugged and started chatting to Heffa instead. I had nothing left to say, so tried again to force my way past Teddy Kelledy and away from this madhouse. We struggled for a few moments, my irresistible werewolf muscle against his immovable vampire hardness, but then we were distracted by an excited cry from Joseph Kelledy.

'Son, Heffa says she wants a child, is that right?'

'I guess so, Father; that's what she wants today, anyway. Sometimes it's a herd of miniature unicorns, or to be the ambassador to Peru, but the idea of motherhood does seem to be uppermost in her frazzled brain at present.'

'Well, why didn't you say so before?' Mr. Kelledy exclaimed, tossing the paper away and jumping to his feet. He rubbed his hands together eagerly as he looked at Heffa. 'I can make you a child just as easy as that. I've got all the equipment downstairs in my workshop of filthy creation. What kind of kid do you want?'

Heffa sat up quickly and a glint of her old self showed in her eyes as she spoke. 'Well, she'd have to be beautiful, of course; I hate ugly people. Although not as beautiful as me either.'

'Uh huh, go on.'

Heffa paused to think and I used the brief silence to ask the question on everyone's mind, 'You said "make a child", Mr. Kelledy, what do you mean?'

'And she should be talented too,' Heffa resumed, 'otherwise she would be normal and no one would like her. Music is nice, maybe she could play musical instruments?'

Mr. K waved a hand dismissively. 'No problem, we've still got loads of symphony musicians downstairs, haven't we, son?'

Teddy nodded enthusiastically and walked over to join Heffa and his father.

'What do you mean "make", Kelledy?' I asked again.

He looked over at me. 'It's simple. We just decide what kind of kid Heffa wants, gather all the various parts together: limbs, organs, brains and whatnot. I join 'em all up down there in my workshop of filthy creation, get my equipment revved up to insert the vital spark, and hey presto!'

'He's done it lots of times before,' Teddy added.

'Sure — Macauley Culkin, Dakota Fanning, Justin Bieber... They're all mine. Teddy, Heffa, get some paper. We'll need to make a shopping list.' The three of them were suddenly busy as beavers, and as I looked from one delighted face to the next, I decided that enough was finally enough.

'Forget what I said before. This is categorically, irrefutably, indubitably the stupidest thing I ever heard!' And leaving them with that food for thought, I walked out of Heffa Lump's life forever.

Later that evening, I got a message from Stephfordy, who politely but firmly reminded me that since I was narrating this chapter, I'd have to go back and keep up with what was going on. And she added that if I didn't feel like it, then maybe she would get around to writing that short story she'd been considering, entitled 'Joe Cahontas's Trip to the Vet'. Well, there was no way I was going to be cut off in my prime like that. So for the next few days, after drinking a couple of bottles of fortifying malt liquor, I would take the long ride out to the Kelledy castle to see the latest developments.

I don't have to tell you everything I saw, though, and it's a good job too cos some of it would turn your fur white just to think of. Often the house would seem deserted, though I knew everyone was most likely downstairs in Joseph's workshop, or out 'shopping for parts'. Even if I didn't see anyone, I could still spot the grisly signs of their progress. Blood trails across the living room's wooden floor, a sink full of gore-encrusted scalpels, and the dog-eared copies of *Frankenstein* that seemed to be everywhere. Sometimes Heffa and Joseph would be sitting around the kitchen table, poring over their hideous diagrams and arguing over some complex technical question like 'does the thigh bone connect to the knee bone?'

Joseph Kelledy was the town butcher in addition to his unique hobbies, so I was used to seeing him in his blood-stained white coat, but seeing Heffa dressed like that too made me feel like I'd been kicked in the nads. She was in her element, though. Now she had something to focus on wanting again, she seemed to be coming more and more back to her old self, although she still didn't seem to notice my presence. I tried to look beyond the dumpsters full of discarded limbs, the unprecedented statewide increase in missing child alerts, and the strange howling sounds that came from the room where Teddy said the 'prototypes' were kept, and think only of my sweet friend Heffa's happiness. Then I would ride home and drink some more, until it was time to be unconscious.

After several weeks of this gross routine, everything changed. I rode up to the castle one afternoon as usual and made my way to the kitchen, preparing my stomach for the sight of dozens of tiny fingers laid out in rows on the counter, or Bobbi carrying a jar of tongues under each arm or, worst of all, a good long look at Jack's ass-crack as he loaded another crate of 'leftovers' into the back of his truck. But there was nothing like that today. The kitchen was spotlessly clean; the living room floor was free of obvious blood spatter. Heffa stood by the piano, and turned as she heard me come in. She was dressed like the Heffa I knew and loved (platonically) in clean black sweatpants and a baggy pullover. Her eyes lit up and she dashed across the room to embrace me.

'Oh Joe, there you are, I've missed you so much.' I hugged her back, as hard as I could without squashing her internal organs like ripe grapes.

'I missed you too. How are you feeling?'

'Oh, simply fabulous. You won't believe what's happened since I last saw you all those weeks ago.'

'I was here yesterday. I've been here to care for you every day while you've been sick. Don't you remember?'

'No, not so much. Anyway, who cares? I'm talking about what's happened to me; just keep your trap shut and narrate.'

My heart sang to hear her snap at me in that special scornful way. Heffa Lump was back! But why was she suddenly so rational again, and what had become of her insane desire for a kid? Well, ask a stupid question...

'I'm... I'm a mother, Joe, isn't it marvelous?' she beamed. 'It took much longer than a usual birth, weeks and weeks of pushing, and twisting, and sawing, and the labor was very painful, especially for some of the other people involved. But it was worth it. I can't wait for you to meet her.'

'Well, wow, congratulations, I guess. It might surprise you to learn that 65 per cent of divorces happen after couples start a family. That old saw about children bringing couples closer together is a total myth. Just saying, in case you have any doubts about Teddy or anything.'

From the garden, I heard the sound of childish laughter, and Heffa moved to the open patio door and gently hollered, 'Honey, get your ass in here now and meet your Uncle Joe, before I whup you.'

'Yes, Mama,' replied a voice that sounded sweeter than honey dripping down a Playboy Playmate sitting on the hood of a vintage V8 Mustang. Teddy came in from the garden first, smiling and pretending to be out of breath from whatever game he'd been playing. He greeted me warmly.

156

'Joe, how are you, my old friend? I'd like you to meet the newest member of the Kelledy family: our daughter.' He embraced Heffa and they both looked on with smiles of radiant happiness as a young girl came into the living room.

She looked about seven years old, although I figured different parts were probably all different ages. Her 'parents' had done their work well; she was one well-put-together little lady. She had her mother's long black hair, her father's haughtily chiseled cheekbones, and the arms of the missing kid I'd seen on my milk carton that morning. She was dressed in a frilly ruffled knee-length dress of silky black material, black socks, and patent leather pumps.

As I looked her up and down, I instantly forgot everything I knew about her grisly origins, taken aback by the sheer perfection of the result. She smiled, displaying row upon row of sharp white teeth. My head spun, and a familiar red mist started to blur my vision. It felt like I was...

'Hey, Cahontas, knock it off.' Heffa slapped me hard across the face and the mood left me as suddenly as it had come. 'I told you before, no Inflicting on minors.'

'Sorry, Heffa. She's amazing; you must be so happy. What's your name, honey?'

Suddenly shy, the child hid behind her proud father, who patted her reassuringly on her adorable little head. 'Oh, you're going to love this part,' he said. 'You know that my mother was called Clarissa?'

'And mine is called Penelope?' added Heffa.

'Well, we thought,' Teddy continued, 'instead of just picking a name out of a baby name book, or from a TV show, like millions of normal people are perfectly happy to do every day, wouldn't it be wonderful to take both our mothers' names...'

'... and combine them to make a completely new name!' Heffa finished proudly. She beckoned the uniquely named child out from behind Teddy's legs. 'Don't be so shy, go and say hello, Penissa!'

'Sorry, it sounded like you said she was called Penissa?' I said incredulously as the child came towards me.

Heffa beamed some more. 'That's right. Penissa. Isn't it wonderful? So original and beautiful, yet also unutterably stupid at the same time.'

157

Before I could think of a response, little – excuse me – Penissa was standing in front of me, looking longingly at me with her deep brown eyes. 'Hewwo, Joe, wiw you be my fwend?' she said.

I found my voice again. 'Penissa. The kid is called Penissa. Okay, you got me. That is surely, spectacularly, with a level of certainty that I can't even begin to put into words, the *stupidest* damn thing I ever heard.'

chapter 14

neck–rophilia

Sorry about that, everybody! I hope you didn't suffer too much from Joe's rude and earthy tones. I could totally have carried on telling the story; it was just Stephfordy thought people would find the whole 'baby' plot line easier to swallow if it was told by an impartial third person. Also, Teddy and Joe were really excited about their brief moment in my spotlight, bless them.

I would be lying if I claimed to remember everything that happened while I was 'away'. I've read Joe and Teddy's accounts, but they're full of distortions and trivial stuff about how they were feeling, so we may never fully know the truth. I do know that once Penissa was finished, it was like the final piece of the jigsaw puzzle of my life fitted into place. (Note to Stephfordy: a jigsaw puzzle could make a good cover motif.) I saw her, lying there on her slab, and it was like I was jolted back to life by electricity, just as she had been a moment before. I was Heffa Lump, and I was the luckiest girl in the world. Crisis overcome.

Things had certainly changed over the last few chapters. As well as flirting with mental instability and becoming a mother, I'd believed that I was one of the planet's biggest celebrities. I'd learnt an important lesson, one that would alter my life profoundly: being famous was *really* hard work. All those interviews, scriptwriting, novel writing, dressing up, attending premieres – I'd hardly had any time to get in my regular twelve hours' sleep, four hours of casserole cooking and thirty minutes of describing my darling Teddy's features. Frankly, the famous people could keep it. I wasn't bothered anymore.

Instead, I was going to focus on being the best darn Heffa I could possibly be. Oh, and the best darn mother too, since while I'd been working through my 'personal development' issues, I'd landed myself with a kid, who was undeniably cute if you overlooked the slightly different-sized limbs and some of the stitching. I was going to take a leaf out of the A-List Moms' handbook: if you had a darling child to dress up, sell pictures of, buy from orphanages or design clothing ranges for, then you were sure to get all kinds of attention, without doing a single lick of work! You could even become a notable humanitarian, and I was definitely one of those; I liked all kinds of humans. Just look at how much time I had spent trying to help Chump keep himself clean and fed.

Luckily, the fortunes of the Kelledy family had improved while I was 'spending some time out of the public eye'. One of Jack's old songs, '(You've Got Me) Under Your Skin', had been picked as the theme tune for TV's hottest new show, *Russell Brand's Celebrity Shooting Gallery*, and the royalties were pouring in. Joseph's sausages had been picked up by Whole Foods, impressed by their 100% organic status – it was just as well that they hadn't asked, 'Organic *what*?' Bobbi had sold my stellar screenplay *Inheffshun* to a big movie company. And when leading undead fashion designer Gianni Vampsace had met Teddy at the wedding, he'd been so taken with his fragrant loveliness that he'd made him the face of a new perfume launch, *Lividity – pour vamp*.

I counted my blessings once more that I had married into such a talented, and now loaded, family. Thanks to the pre-nup I'd made Teddy sign (he thought it was an autograph for a fan, the sweetheart), I knew I'd never want for anything again. All was right with the world. It was time to give something back.

The day after I emerged from my 'much-needed vacation', I took a few minutes out of my busy schedule of trying on all my new clothes (I had insisted to Teddy that I needed a whole new wardrobe to facilitate my latest role as a mother) to compose a careful letter to the United Nations:

Dear Banking Moon,

Angelina Jolie has loads of kids of different races and is a goodwill ambassador. Ginger Spice has no discernable talent and is a goodwill ambassador. I have just the one kid, but she's made of parts from many different races. And I have many talents, but no one's ever been able to list them properly. Basically, what I'm saying is that I'd be a brilliant goodwill ambassador. I have an unerring ability to unite everyone when I'm in the room – they all want to get together and talk about how remarkable I am! Please send my certificate, a plane ticket to the next photo opportunity, and your usual fee to Castle Kelledy, Spatula, the Rainy State.

Love and hugs,
Heffa Kelledy

P.S. *Have enclosed my Granny Lump's famous 'three-dog casserole' recipe, enjoy!*

It was the first time I'd signed my married name, and just seeing the words on paper gave me a little thrill. As did the thought that I would soon be helping those less fortunate than me, of course.

Speaking of those less fortunate. . . I addressed my envelope and emerged from my boudoir to find out what the rest of the family was up to.

The halls of Castle Kelledy seemed brighter than I remembered. Maybe it was my newfound optimistic outlook, or maybe the tightwad Kelledys could finally afford proper light bulbs again. As I wandered into the lounge, the first thing I heard was the plaintive growling of my best bud Joe, who was being forced out of the front door by a powerful jet of water – the hose itself wielded by the handsomest hubby in all the world.

'And STAY OUT!' Teddy shouted, enthusiastically spraying all over the shop.

I waved cheerily at Joe. 'He doesn't really mean it! Come back whenever you want!'

'I *do* mean it,' Teddy scowled. 'It's all I can do to stop him Inflicting on Penissa; frankly there are only so many rolled-up newspapers and hoses one man can wield.'

'Don't worry, my love,' I said. 'I'll get Laddie to take him to the pound tomorrow; that always takes his mind off things. And who knows? In a few years, when Penissa has been rebuilt with grown-up bits, maybe it will all seem perfectly normal.'

'I'm afraid I must beg to differ,' Teddy said, huffily. 'No daughter of mine will ever be courted by such a foul and pungent beast.'

'But Penissa loves all creatures great and small,' I reminded him. She and Joseph were making a whole undead menagerie in the basement; it was so lovely to see how she had bonded with her grandfather over their shared love of sweet, fluffy animals. Admittedly, the 'fluffiness' was mostly due to the electricity used to reanimate them, but at least Penissa was sure to win the Science Fair if we ever decided to send her to school.

I wasn't sure that we'd bother – after all, her father, uncle and aunt had been to school so often that they could probably teach her. And now Teddy and I had a child, I couldn't see why we'd bother to continue that weird pretence of being teenagers that he'd persevered with for so long. If people got suspicious, we could always arrange for their sudden disappearance – and then everyone would have better things to worry about than whether Mr. and Mrs. Kelledy were a bit well preserved.

'Where is Penissa, anyway?' I asked, looking round for my little angel.

'I sent her to play with her skipping rope,' Teddy replied.

'Oh, Teddy, you *didn't* – last time she got all caught up in it and one of her hands fell off! You can be *so* careless.'

'I'm sorry,' Teddy said. Even though he didn't need to sleep, he still looked tired; small children will do that to you, even the most perfect and lovely ones who are quite happy looking after themselves and can be ignored until called upon to look adorable next to their doting parents.

'Never mind, dear, why don't you go and hunt something for your dinner? I'll look after Penissa. In fact, why don't I take her into town? It's been weeks since I left the house, and I can't wait to show her off to all our neighbors.'

'What a lovely idea!'Teddy said approvingly, and twirled me briefly in his arms. Becoming a father seemed to mean so much to him, even though he'd been completely ambivalent about the idea only a few pages before. It was just something about Penissa, everyone who met her fawned on her immediately. She took after her mother that way.

I hadn't been into Spatula since the wedding, and I was struck all over again by how dull and provincial it was. There wasn't even a single photographer's studio where you could get portraits of your adorable children dressed as flowers! Still, I did my best to introduce Penissa to the sights, such as they were – the library I'd been on my way to when Teddy ripped a crowd of goths apart; the church I'd been kidnapped in once; the sidewalk where Teddy and Joe had fought over me... All the memories of our thrilling courtship that had led to her unorthodox creation.

'But Mommy,' Penissa lisped – she could lisp even when there were no 's' sounds, which was an impressive feat – 'ith Thpatula dangewouth then?'

'Why no, child,' I laughed. 'All you need to do is whimper at a slightly high volume and your daddy or your inappropriate Uncle Joe will come rushing to your rescue. It's true that *other* people might find this little old town a slightly risky place to live, but they're not you or me so I wouldn't let it bother you too much.'

'I thee,' Penissa said. 'Tho I'm perfwectly thafe?'

'Yes, sweetie, of course you are,' I reassured her. 'I will always protect you, no matter what kind of evil tries to take you from me.'

Penissa seemed cheered by this, and skipped along merrily beside me. I decided to take the opportunity to do a spot of grocery shopping, since the Kelledy house was bare of anything but blood, and we were out of the charcoal briquettes that Penissa liked to nibble on. Actually, I couldn't remember if we'd fed her at all since the day we'd given her life. I wasn't even sure if she needed to eat. Oh well! I was certain if she had any problems, she would let me know about them; I was such a caring and hands-on mother.

I wandered dreamily around the supermarket, reveling in the simple ordinariness of it all. I might be married to the hottest hunk around, and be mother to the most darling child since Shirley Temple shuffled off to the good ship Lollipop in the sky, but I could still buy casserole ingredients like a normal person. I smiled kindly at my lurching Neanderthal-type fellow shoppers, and patted a few of the more desperate cases gently – I felt it would do them good to know that a near godlike being such as myself could interact on their level, and I wanted Penissa to see that one couldn't consider oneself superior, even if one clearly was. Why, I was even *thinking* like the Queen of England, I was so exalted.

I glanced down to check that my little angel was taking my example to heart. She wasn't there.

Immediately, I felt the absolute spine-wrenching terror that all new mothers feel when something might have happened to their child. Silly idiot! Where on earth had she got to? Honestly, was she simply going to be *another* burden? I'd just offloaded Dad, but the Kelledys and the werewolf clan needed my help all the time, and I'd hoped Penissa might have inherited *some* of my common sense.

'Penissa?' I trilled. 'Where aaarrre you?'

There was no answer. Slightly worried and somewhat annoyed, I began to search the aisles – to no avail. Unless she was really good at hide-and-seek, she was definitely no longer in the store.

I brushed past the manager – who was burbling something inconsequential about why had I knocked all the goods off the shelves and did I intend to pay for them – and rushed out into Main Street. Where could my baby girl be? How could I have managed to lose her on our first mother/daughter shopping trip? Oh, Teddy was going to kill me – and he might not even resurrect me afterwards.

Looking up and down the street and checking my reflection in the window to make sure I looked panicked-yet-still-pretty (I did), I ran back in the direction I'd come. 'Penissa? Peeennnisssssaaaa?' I called, desperately. A few passers-by cast odd looks in my direction, but offered no help. I knew I was probably causing a scene, but my darling baby was missing, and sometimes considerations of poise have to be abandoned.

As I approached the park just beyond the library, still wailing my daughter's uniquely amazing name, I saw that a crowd had gathered around the fountain at its center. I could hardly bear to approach. I wasn't sure if Penissa could be killed by drowning (or indeed fire or pitchforks or any other traditional remedy), but if she was as clumsy as I could be, she'd probably give it her best shot. However, once I fought my way through the press of people, I was staggered by what I found: Penissa, standing daintily on the edge of the fountain, beaming down at those around her.

'Tell us more!' one fervent townsperson cried.

Penissa paused in thought. The light caught her black hair and made it shine, almost as magical an effect as what happened to her father in sunlight. 'If life giveth oo lemonth,' she said solemnly, 'make lemonade.'

The crowd sighed in appreciation of this piece of homespun wisdom. She walked along the rim of the fountain, touching each yearning outstretched hand as she passed. It was a warm afternoon, and Penissa was beginning to suppurate in the heat. A young woman offered her a handkerchief and Penissa daintily dabbed the ichor from her face before returning it. The beaming girl fainted with ecstasy, clutching the cloth to her bosom. She disappeared as the crowd pressed forward, reaching out to touch the hem of Penissa's garment.

She continued, 'Thingth are eathy come, eathy go. Alwayth let go of what you cannot hold. Birdth in the bush are worth two in the hand, though they are not ath eathy to eat.'

'It's like she can see right through to the truth of everything,' a woman next to me whispered in awe. My heart swelled with pride. That was *my* daughter whose every word they were hanging on. The overwhelming power of her incredible cuteness had turned even these hard-bitten Spatulans to mush.

'Hi Mommy!' Penissa cried joyfully when she saw me. 'Fank oo all for coming to lithen to me,' she told her audience. 'Jutht remember to wuv your neighbor as you would wuv yourthelf, and all will be well.' She smiled beatifically. The crowd sighed in collective rapture.

'And speaking of wuv – I mean love,' I said briskly, 'Penissa here has very kindly shared her lovely guidelines for a better life for at least five minutes, please form an orderly queue and I'll collect her fee.'

In no time at all, Penissa's new devotees had pressed what looked like a hundred dollars into my hands, and since I'd remembered to take the shopping with me when I'd rushed out of the market in a panic, all in all we'd done rather well out of the day. 'Thanks folks!' I said, pocketing the last sweaty banknote. 'We'll be here every Sunday! Now come, Penissa, we must be getting home.'

I grabbed my little demagogue's hand, and set off at a fast pace in case anyone followed us; I couldn't bear the thought of a bunch of small-town losers setting up camp around Castle Kelledy in the hope that we would bring meaning to their shabby little lives.

'Are you angwy, Mommy?' Penissa asked. I slowed down, fearing that I might literally pull her arm from its socket.

'No, my sweet, but do remember: nothing in life is free.'

'They jutht wanted to hear my pwetty wordth,' Penissa said.

'I know, darling. It's lovely, and with your amazing talent for oral you could make a million, or become a cult leader, or both, but for now, just listen to Mommy, okay? You don't want to draw too much attention to yourself, or people will start wondering where you come from and who you're made of. There are people with labs out there who aren't nice like Grandpa Joseph, all right?'

'I'll be good!' Penissa promised, wide-eyed. I made a note to get Teddy to look at her eyelids; something wasn't quite right there.

On our return to Castle Kelledy, I sent Penissa off to force Bobbi to make her something to eat, and retreated to my boudoir. I sat on the leather-sheeted bed, stroking the IV drips and heart monitors thoughtfully. It was wonderful that my little lovely was such a natural star; I could see her providing a significant income stream. But once again, it felt like the story – *my* story, the one *I* was doing all the hard work narrating – was about someone else entirely. First it was pages and pages of descriptions of Teddy, then it was pages of angsting about Joe, then there was a whole lot of obsessing about babies. Surely it was time I stepped into the limelight? Surely it was time for *my* specialness to shine?

Teddy came into the room. 'Are you well, beloved? You haven't shouted or demanded anything for ten whole minutes; I was becoming concerned.'

I turned to him. 'I'm ready now. I'm ready to be as special as you are. Probably more special since I'm sure I'll be much better at it than you.' His face lit up with excitement and hope and a little bit of confusion. 'Yes, Teddy. I'm ready to be a vampire.'

'Oh, Heffa,' he breathed. 'I have been preparing for this moment all my unlife, it feels like. Look, I went and got you all the literature—' He opened a drawer in our dresser, and pulled out a bunch of leaflets: 'So You Want to Be a Vampire?', 'Feeling Positive About O-Negative', 'Bloodsucking – the Basics' and 'Today Is the First Day of the Rest of Your Death'.

I yanked them all roughly from his grasp. 'Teddy, I want this to be passionate! Leave the leaflets alone – bite me! *BITE ME!*' I grabbed his head in my hands, and thrust my neck eagerly towards his mouth. I had waited so long, but the time for waiting was over. I forced his teeth closer, closer to my lily-white neck, totally taken over by my lust for transformation. At first, he resisted, but then I felt his will melt away, as if I had hypnotized him. At last, he was all mine.

He bit me. His fangs entered my neck. I felt my life – my blood – ebb rapidly away. I collapsed into his arms.

'Harder, Teddy, harder!'

'I don't want to hurt you,' he cried, his voice muffled by my neck.

'It doesn't hurt at all,' I pointed out. 'I was certain this would be a really significant moment of searing agony, but it barely tickles. Are you sure you're doing it right?'

Teddy stopped sucking at my neck. With one hand staunching my blood, he looked down at me and frowned.

167

'Don't you feel the terrible, aching, appalling eternal knowledge that you are one of the damned?'

I didn't, really, but he seemed so disappointed that this beautiful shared moment wasn't quite going as he'd anticipated that I decided to do what any good wife would. I faked it.

'Oooarraghhh, Teddy, now I feel it, ooooh, it burns, oh, how all goodness is being ripped from me, ah, how shall I ever recover from this pain, this dreadful pain. . .'

Looking encouraged by my shrieking, Teddy bent back to his work. Darkness began to filter into the edges of my consciousness. 'My soul. . .' I moaned, in the best mournful tones I could muster; I was beginning to feel rather lightheaded. 'Noooooooooooooooooooooooo. . .'

And then I died.

And then I was reborn. I lay on the floor where Teddy had dropped me. The smooth marble felt warm pressed against my flesh – then I realized with a start that I was lying on my own arm, that it wasn't marble at all I could feel; it was my rock-hard vampire skin. Cool. I took a moment to check everything was working correctly. Heart? Stopped. Blood pressure? 0 over 0. Lungs? Still as the grave. Spleen? I never knew what that did in the first place, so who'd miss it? It was incredible: my body was cold and dead, and yet I lived! I felt so strong. My head was spinning, dizzy with power. This might have been because no blood was reaching my brain. I was a vampire. This was going to be so frickin' sweet!

I opened my eyes. The first thing I saw was Teddy peering at me, a worried expression on his divine features. I blinked and refocused. Divine features? Something didn't seem quite right. I squinted carefully at the pale chiseled planes of his beautiful face. In close-up, their marble whiteness was marred by pockmarks, blackheads, scraggly stubble where his razor hadn't shaved close enough, a dent like a crater above his left eye, and disturbing bright red veins around his nose. I jumped out of his arms in revulsion.

'Teddy – you're hideous!' I shrieked. He advanced towards me, reeking of fear, confusion, and never having taken a shower, not once, in all the time our love story had gone on. I stumbled backwards into the bed, which went skidding at high speed into the wall. The plaster splintered and a great cloud of dust covered everything.

'Heffa?' Teddy cried plaintively. 'Heffa, my love?'

I gazed around me. The glamorous Kelledy lifestyle was crumbling as surely as the wall had. The glass windows were streaky and unwashed, rainbow smears covering every inch of them. The ceiling was cracked in a hundred places, almost gray with dust and cobwebs. And the floor. . . I shuddered. I could see the shriveled remains of every fly, spider and cat that had crept into corners to die, and there were lots of them. It was like the whole world had gone into high-definition.

'I can see so clearly. . .' I murmured in horror.

'Ah, yes, vampiric super-vision,' Teddy said cheerfully. 'It does take some getting used to, doesn't it?'

I was a vampire! I'd been so preoccupied with the disgusting details my new eyes were showing me, I'd totally forgotten that I'd died only a few scant minutes ago. I closed my mouth and didn't breathe for a while, just to check.

'Heffa?' Teddy came towards me, smiling a smile of crooked yellow teeth.

'Yeurgh!' I cried. Then, realizing that might seem a little unappreciative, added, 'I don't need to breathe anymore! I'm a vampire!'

'Isn't it wonderful?' Teddy said. 'Oh my darling. Look at yourself. . .' He took me tenderly by the arms and turned me to face the long (tarnished, spotted) mirror at the end of the boudoir. I stared into it. An empty room stared back.

'I'm not there,' I said in awe. 'I don't have a reflection. Darn, how am I going to check I look good now?'

'Don't worry,' Teddy assured me. 'I swear you have never been more beautiful.'

'Well, of course, silly!' I batted at his shoulder playfully. He flew backwards, through the window, and fell to the grass outside in a shower of broken glass. Whoops. It looked like my adorable clumsiness had crossed to the other side with me, only with the added complication of super-strength.

Oh well, the window was so filthy, it needed to be replaced anyway.

I bounded to the gaping hole, and leapt down to join Teddy. The sensation was incredible. I could feel everything. The wind rushed past me, and each hair on my head quivered in the breeze like an antenna. I felt dust particles hitting my skin, atomized against my hard marbley hardness. The smell of the evening air, the moon high in the sky... It was almost too much to take in. If I described everything with the appropriate level of detail, it would fill a book. Since we don't have time for that, I'll skip everything but the most transcendent parts; it'll help to keep the story ticking along.

Once he'd dragged me out of the resulting crater in the lawn and brushed off as much of the dirt as he could, Teddy embraced me with all his might. I saw abruptly how much he'd been holding back in the days when I'd been a puny human. Now, with no fear of snapping bones or bruising flesh, I knew we could be with each other, no holds barred, testing our stamina and our bodies to breaking point...

'Are you all right, Heffa? You've gone a little cross-eyed.'

I grabbed him by the shirt, pulled him with me, and we ran. Again, I could write you a really detailed and magnificent description of the forest, which would make you cry with the beauty of it. You would punch yourself in the face with joy, thinking, 'So this is what a forest is like, I never knew before, because of my puny mortal senses.' But I'm in a hurry to get to the good stuff. There were a bunch of trees, that's the essence of it. We were well matched in speed, and he chased me without pause through the forest, up the trees, down the trees, over waterfalls and through the occasional grizzly bear that got in our way. At length, though, he caught me (for the record, I let him).

A rather busy and exciting time later, we lay in the torn remains of our clothes, a canoe, and a party of adventurous holidaymakers who had unfortunately stumbled into the midst of our passionate lovemaking. I tenderly brushed an entrail or two off Teddy's dimpled thighs and said, 'I wish I still had my scorecard. Don't get me wrong, that was okay for a first go, but I'm pretty sure you can do better. I rate that at about 2.5

– I'd have given you the extra half-point if you'd lasted more than three minutes.'

'I'm sorry, Heffa. It's been thirty years; I got a bit carried away. But I'm glad to know that your personality has survived the transition unscathed.'

'Mmmm,' I agreed. 'If anything, I feel even more exacting and judgmental than I did before. It's as if all the most appealing aspects of my personality – my obsession with my appearance, my humble and overweening self-belief, my impossibly high standards and general all-round perfection – have only been enhanced by my immortality.'

'Indeed, for my eyes tell me that vampire adolescence has hit you hard – you've gained twenty pounds and your spots look like enormous pus-filled volcanoes, while your hair has the greasy sheen of an oil slick. Yet for some reason, I believe without question that you are the most attractive woman I have ever seen.'

I pondered this slightly bizarre disconnect between objective reality and the version Teddy and I believed. 'It's almost as if vampires get some kind of supernatural power when they turn, and mine is the ability to make everyone see me as the incredibly hot, mind-blowingly intelligent, fascinatingly wonderful, worth-dying-for woman I've always believed myself to be in the face of all evidence to the contrary.'

'We do not have superpowers – apart from strength, speed, poise, beauty and eternal life, of course – but I do find you entirely wonderful,' Teddy said, with an adorably loving leer. He leaned over to kiss me. One thing led to another, and then various things went into each other, and Teddy—

'That was amazing,' I said. I would have been either sleepy or breathless, if I'd been human. Mind you, if I'd been human, I'd probably also have been broken in two by the animalistic violence of Teddy's— 'Hang on a minute, where did all the description of our sexual activity go?' I demanded. 'I thought that was the most erotic, long, hard, pumping bit of narration ever. I was going to try to sell it to *Penthouse*!'

'Sorry, Heffa,' Teddy said. 'Stephfordy wants all our lovemaking to take place in discreet white line breaks so as not to give our teenage readership disturbing ideas.'

'You mean the disturbing idea that normal people can enjoy a mutually satisfactory bit of rumpy-pumpy without it necessarily resulting in bruises, broken bones, pregnancy and death?'

'Yes, exactly – if impressionable young folk thought that sex could be described and talked about openly and enjoyed in a straightforward fashion, what kind of world would we live in?'

'A non-repressed one?'

'Well, quite – and if there was no repression, who on earth would wade through page after page of unresolved sexual tension and buy the Teddy and/or Joe pin-up calendar to swoon over?'

'Good point. I'll stop trying to talk about it, and focus on the merchandising money instead.'

'That's my girl,' Teddy said proudly. 'Now, lovely as all this has been, the campers' blood is starting to get a bit sticky, and we probably ought to make sure our daughter is all right.'

'Oh, I'm sure she's fine,' I said. 'Bobbi and Jack and Joe are all there to look out for her, and Joseph can put her back together if need be. I don't see why the existence of the daughter we love almost as much as each other should interrupt us having fun.'

'You're right,' Teddy smiled. 'I feel another white space coming on, don't you?'

'Yes,' I agreed, 'oh, Teddy, yes, *yes*, YES, *YES!!*'

By the time we returned home, it had grown dark. Perhaps my eyes were becoming accustomed to the overwhelming grubbiness I could see all around me. My castle squatted reassuringly in the moonlight, looking slightly less shabby than it had earlier. Technically, it was still the Kelledys' castle, but I felt a strong sense of ownership, and my supernatural self-belief would break down Joseph's resistance a little more each day. I was sure he'd soon volunteer to sign the deeds over to me. Warm yellow light was pouring out of the sitting-room windows, and I knew that waiting inside would be our family, a safe full of cash, a wardrobe full of designer outfits, and a fridge full of sweet, delicious packs of O-Neg.

At last I knew for sure that I'd done the right thing in choosing Teddy over Joe, despite the occasional angst and melodrama the decision had cost me. Being a vampire was the best thing in the world, and I knew that from now on nothing bad would happen to us. And if it tried, well, we'd just snap its neck, whatever it was, drain its blood and stomp on its tattered corpse, because nothing was going to get in the way of Heffa Kelledy's happily ever and ever and ever after.

chapter 15

veni vidi vindicti

The weeks rolled by. Imagine a montage of blurred people whizzing back and forth, days falling off a calendar, and leaves turning from green to golden and finally falling, as autumn turned to winter on the Utensil Peninsula. Or maybe the leaves didn't fall from the trees. Are the trees round here evergreen or deciduous? Stephfordy hasn't ever bothered to think about it in that much detail. You choose, whatever, it's not that important. The point is that time was passing, and our happiness grew with every new day, until I sometimes felt like I would burst with self-satisfaction.

It was hard to believe that Teddy and Penissa and I could be together like this forever. But we could. Not like you; you've got a maximum of sixty years left in you, probably much less. And you'll be in constant pain for most of the last part. I know that's a depressing thought, but cheer up. Maybe hearing some more about how amazingly perfect my life is will make you feel better?

Penissa was a constant joy. Motherhood had turned out to be everything I had suddenly decided a few months ago that I had always dreamed it would be. We spent virtually every waking moment together, which was a lot of moments now I no longer needed to sleep.

I had achieved every dream I ever had in life, and I'd learned a lot along the way, so it was only right that I passed on my incredible bank of accumulated wisdom to my daughter. We sat and talked for hours. She would ask me charmingly naive questions like 'How do I get boys to like me?' and 'Is this my "fourth base", Mommy?' and I for my part would laugh my wonderful crystalline vampire laugh and answer as best I could. Which was totally brilliantly, of course.

Other days, we would sit together as a family, Teddy playing his mandolin, our daughter singing along in her charmingly shrill chipmunk-like voice, and me reading a fascinatingly intellectual and high-brow Victorian novel while they droned on. Penissa was so full of life – ironically – that even with our inexhaustible supply of vampire energy, we struggled to keep up with her. Well-balanced child that she was, she was just as happy to play with herself in the garden. Though it broke my heart when she ran back into the house clutching some body part or other that had come loose, Teddy and I both felt that she should learn to be independent. After all, we wouldn't be around forever. Even vampires get bored of their playthings eventually.

The joyous highlight of the week was the big family lunch that we had each Sunday. Penissa and I would go to the market in Spatula in the morning, and I would stroll along the aisles filling our cart with the finest gourmet foods while Penissa charmed the locals by reciting *The Little Book of Calm* for small change in the parking lot. When I had sated my lust for conspicuous consumption, I'd remind the manager how valuable my custom was to their humble enterprise, in terms of the free publicity they got from it rather than any actual money passing from me to them, of course! Then we'd return home with our booty and Teddy would laugh and remind me that we didn't actually need any food, being vampires and everything now. It was our little joke, bless our callous undead hearts.

This particular Sunday, though, he was wrong, as my pathetically still-human father was joining us to eat. I was eager to ensure that he was amply catered for. Penissa ran off to count the money she had earned in town, and I set about preparing lunch for her beloved grandfather.

I had only been a vampire for a few short months, but in that time I had drunk the blood of many different species of animal. From the 'cattle' that we supped on an average weekday evening to the exotic anteaters that Teddy had run down to South America to get for me as a treat one Saturday night, I'd tasted pretty much everything that walks, crawls, slithers or flies. They each had their own intoxicating flavor, which I could taste just by thinking about it. Being a bloodsucker was an incredible dining experience, it really was.

The only snag was that all these new flavors had shoved aside some of my knowledge about the human foods and ingredients I had known in my old life. This made cooking for company a bit of a struggle. Nevertheless, Dad was due, and I tried to remember the special Sunday Roast casserole recipe that I knew he loved. Dice some onion, chop the meat, make the stock. A handful of herbs, taste for seasoning, there we go. Still got the old magic.

I was so caught up in my cooking that I didn't notice the time passing until Teddy called to me from the living room: 'Your father is here, my little thorn bush!' I removed my apron and eagerly skipped into the other room to greet my father. He was standing there with the old expression of concern I knew so well. He hadn't seen me yet, so I waited patiently while Teddy untied him, and then I stepped in front of him, eager to consummate our reunion with a hug. He recoiled with surprise at my sudden appearance.

'My God, Heffa! I thought you were dead!'

'I am dead. It's the best thing that's ever happened to me, don't worry.'

He looked confused. 'But they found your clothes on the cliff top out at La Trine. And you left me that suicide note on the kitchen table. Why would you do such a thing?'

I hadn't seen Chump since my glorious ascendance to the ranks of the ever-living, but it was obvious that he hadn't spent the last few months getting any less dumb. 'I did it to protect you, Dad, obviously! When I agreed to become a vampire, it meant leaving everything about my old life behind – apart from still living in the same town – and I couldn't bear the thought of you disapproving of my choice. And so, to protect you from the pain of disagreeing with me, I just pretended to commit suicide. But then after a while I thought, what's the point of having all this incredible power and success if I can't share it with my dear old dad? Didn't I always tell you I was going to make it? And now I have. You see? I. Told. You. So.'

I prodded him in the ribs with each word to make sure he got the point; I'd sharpened my nails specially. 'There, makes perfect sense now, doesn't it?'

He shook his head. The poor simple man would never be able to fathom the subtle thought processes of us higher beings. 'I don't know, but I'm glad you're not dead.'

'I am dead, Dad. Will you listen when I'm talking to you, jeezus.' I grabbed his ears and gave them a friendly tweak to reinforce my point. When he had stopped howling in agony, I helped him to his feet. 'I'm a vampire now, with powers you can't begin to imagine. So think carefully before you give me any more backchat.'

'I'm sorry, honey,' he mumbled hesitantly. That was more like the Chump I wanted to see, placid and compliant. Even he was capable of personal growth when I was around. The effects of my vampire powers continued to astonish me.

I guided him to his place at the head of the table and pointed to his chair. 'Sit there, meat-sack, I'll call the others to the table.' I closed my eyes and concentrated on emanating the psychic waves necessary to attract the attention of my extended family. When no one had arrived after a couple of minutes, I decided to do it the old-fashioned way and hollered, 'Blooooooood!' at the top of my voice. It was time to serve up. 'Teddy, keep an eye on Dad while I bust my hump bringing in the dishes for your ungrateful family,' I requested sweetly.

The other Kelledys joined us at their own leisurely pace while I bustled back and forth carrying cutlery, bowls and finally the wonderful casserole that I had lovingly prepared for my father. They took their places at the table: Joseph at the opposite end to Chump, Jack and Bobbi on either side of him. Bobbi slouched in her chair scratching away on her cellphone, while Jack and Joseph exchanged desultory small talk.

There was no sign of our wonderful daughter; she was probably out in the garden toying with small animals. I called to her from the patio doors: 'Get your ass in here, young lady, or you'll be real sorry!' A moment later, she was scurrying gracefully across the lawn, waving a long stick with several frogs skewered on it. The games children play! I ruffled her hair, and after I'd sternly reminded her that she wasn't allowed to bring her toys to the dinner table, she wiped her feet and came inside.

As we walked to the table, she tugged my skirt and whispered, 'Momma, who ith that howwid wickle man, and why ith he thaking tho much?' while pointing at Chump. Oh my golly, I had nearly forgotten: they hadn't even met! I'd been pretending to be dead for the last few months, and before that I hadn't needed anything from Chump, so naturally I hadn't called or visited him. He didn't even know he was a grandfather!

I guided Penissa over to the seat in which Chump sat trembling with excitement and shoved his granddaughter towards him. 'Penissa, say hello to your grandpa.' She tried to bury her head in my skirts, but I encouraged her, 'Don't be shy, honey, ask him for some money.'

She nodded and held her hand out to Chump, palm up. 'Can I have a dowwar, gwanpa? Pwease?' she asked. Then she batted her eyelids and flashed her breathtaking smile, just like I'd taught her. Chump recoiled at the sight of so many wonderfully pointy teeth all in one mouth, and if it hadn't been for Teddy holding him down, I think he would have tried to flee the room with joy. He clutched spasmodically for the wallet that he kept in his shirt pocket and threw it to the ground at Penissa's feet.

'Here, take what you want, just stay away from me, whatever you are!'

She extracted the bills from the discarded wallet with the artful fingers of a piano-playing prodigy – they hadn't been cheap to get hold of, let me tell you! – and skipped off to sit down, riffling the wad of notes as she went. I bent over and kissed my father on the forehead.

'It's so sweet of you to contribute to the cost of lunch, Dad!' I told him, and took my place to Penissa's right. 'Okay, who'd like to say grace?' I looked around the table as the Kelledys shrugged in turn, but Dad came to decorum's rescue. I couldn't make out any of the words he mumbled to himself, but he made the sign of the cross with such enthusiasm, and so very often, that I figured it probably counted.

My vampire family passed me their bowls in turn and I asked, 'Red or white blood cells?' before serving them from the two large silver tureens that dominated the table – a wedding present from Joseph's cousin Eric Northman in Louisiana. Penissa, ever the fussy little madam, insisted on some of each. I served myself and then dished up some casserole for Dad. Then we feasted, my undead in-laws each according to their untamed vampire habit. Bobbi and Joseph always used straws, while Teddy and I preferred the silver soup spoons that went with the tureens. Jack, the wildest of us in many ways, fell forwards into his bowl and slurped away happily until it was empty.

Dad just sat there staring at his plate. I thought the sight of the first nice meal he'd seen since I'd – supposedly – taken my long walk off that short cliff probably stunned him. I was sure that his new scullery maid Lassie's simple rustic 'stews' could never match the Michelin-starred majesty of one of my casseroles. But soon we'd all finished and he hadn't even picked up his fork.

'Something wrong, Father?' I inquired. 'There'd better not be.' His reply was an inaudible mumble, so I asked him to repeat himself, at a volume that people other than dogs could hear this time, if he knew what was good for him.

'It's delicious, honest, darling. It's just a bit... raw.'

I threw my chair aside and pounced down to Chump's end of the table. How dare he criticize my cooking? I'd peel his skin from his bones like I'd peeled the onions for the casserole he was so rudely rejecting. I grabbed him by his hair, pulling his head back, and using the razor-sharp nails of my other hand I started to make the first incision down his chest. Then I realized that – incredibly – Chump was right. I had made a very minor mistake with the casserole recipe. I released my grip and he collapsed to the floor in a heap. Then I laughed, and the sound was like a flock of precious glass birds had flown suddenly into the room.

'Oh Daddy, how silly of me, I mixed all the ingredients together, but I totally forgot to cook it at all!' The rest of the table laughed too, and although the sound of their laughter was nowhere near as magical and musical as mine, they did their best.

'Heffa, you big silly!' Teddy chortled.

I turned to him with tears in my eyes. 'I know! Thank goodness we don't have to eat human food every night. We'd starve to death.' I gave my father a gentle kick in the ribs. 'Can you forgive me, Dad?'

He was quiet at first, but after a few more good solid kicks, he eventually groaned something that I chose to interpret as a yes. I knew from long experience that there was nothing Dad liked better after a big meal than a nice nap, so I thoughtfully let him slip into unconsciousness where he lay.

'Another wonderful family occasion, Heffa, well done,' Bobbi congratulated me before slinking upstairs. Penissa ran back out into the garden, flicking her frog-stick so that a frog flew off the end each time.

'Typical Bobbi, leaving the chores to others,' Teddy said. 'Will you do me the honor of keeping me company while I clean the crockery?'

I shrugged willingly and helped clear the table. It was nice to be alone together in the kitchen after another hectic family meal. As much as I cherished the warm and loving atmosphere that the Kelledy family generated wherever they went, nothing compared to the joy I felt when it was just Teddy and me. He washed the dishes happily, arms covered to the elbows in soapsuds, whistling along to the radio. I stood next to him drying the various items as he passed them to me. If they were too awkward to dry with a tea towel – things like bowls, knives, forks and spoons – I tossed them in the garbage. We didn't have all day to do chores.

Teddy was scrubbing away at one of the tureens with his typical vigor – dried blood stains silver like you wouldn't believe – when he suddenly stopped whistling and dropped the tureen back into the sink with a splash. He pointed at the radio, flicking a trail of suds across the counter.

'That's our song on the radio!' he exclaimed furiously. I gave him a puzzled look and listened. It wasn't a song I recognized. I was almost certain that this was a woman's voice. And come to think of it, I was absolutely positive that DJ Rockin' Ricky Rialto had introduced it as Lady CooCoo's new song 'Bad Skin'. I said as much to Teddy, who shook his head.

'No, you're not listening! It's our song "Bad Romanians", it's identical. Listen to the beat – I based that rhythm on the heartbeat of a grizzly bear as it slowly bleeds to death. And there, where she's put that... tuneful bit, that's where my tap dance interlude should happen!'

'So, what, Lady CooCoo has – what's that special word my teachers had for my homework? – she's plagueified you?'

'Yes, she bloody well has. She must have eavesdropped on our set at La Trine Fest. I am replete with outrage. What sort of a person would take someone else's hard work and transform it into a perverted parody, purely for their own selfish ends?' He paced the kitchen, lashing out impotently at thin air.

'Well, they're not called the Vindicti for nothing. They did say they'd be coming after us; maybe this is part of it?'

'Well, it's not on, and I'm not having it.' He called to Jack, who had remained sitting at the dinner table until such time as he had a narrative function once more. On hearing Teddy's cry, Jack ambled into the kitchen and gave his brother a blank look.

'Do you still retain the litigatory services of that lawyer in Port D'Angerous, Jack?'

Jack nodded. 'Sure, we go way back. Why, what's the problem? Hey, isn't that your song on the radio?'

'*That* is the problem, my brother. That malevolent flat-faced hussy Lady CooCoo has stolen one of our songs, and I shall make her pay. With money.'

Jack poured himself a four-finger scotch on the rocks from the previously unmentioned bar that stood in the corner of the kitchen, and leant against the counter. He lit a cigarette, and nodded sagely. 'Sure, sure, I get it. Happens all the time. I had the same trouble back in the day. Old Dino, we were pals, but this one time he rewrote my song "Ain't That a Bite in the Neck" and released it without my say-so. I was plenty sore about that, I tell you.'

181

'Yes, I remember, you have regaled us with the story in the wee small hours on many occasions. And your lawyer friend helped you seek recompense, did he not?'

'Of course, under normal circumstances, I just woulda bit the guy who gypped me, sort it out like men, but with Dino ... Sheesh, who knew what kinda freaky jazz was sloshing about in them arteries? But like I told you, I had this lawyer guy in my back pocket; I'd done a favor for some of his heavy friends back in my Jersey days. So I contact my guy...'

'Fascinating as these trips down the gin alley of showbiz nostalgia always are, I don't have the time at present. Kindly tell me how to contact your lawyer, in as concise a manner as you are able.'

Jack poured himself another drink. 'Well, okay, but it's complicated. He has two law firms: one for all his above-board business, and another for his more clandestine affairs.'

'Huh, most lawyers are happy to do their dirty deeds out in the open. What makes this guy so special?' I chipped in, feeling that it had been rather too long since I had made a contribution.

'You can't just go to his normal office,' Jack explained. 'What you gotta do is: you drive to his scumbag office, that's over there in the old crack factory district, across 112th Street. You hang around there for a bit, ask a bunch of nosey questions, and then eventually you'll be approached by a one-legged woman in a red dress. She'll give you the address of a bar where you go and meet a guy called Raoul; he'll give you a false passport. You take that down to the bus depot and show it at the lost and found. They'll give you a briefcase; the code to the lock is 411. Inside, you'll find a map of the city with a pentacle drawn on it. At each of the points of the pentacle, you'll find a woman walking a dog. You ask the women how old their dogs are, and when you've got all the numbers, that's the zip code where the lawyer's real office is. To find the street address, you—'

'Jack, this is all terribly exciting and mysterious, but a cynical person would say that it's rather a lot of aimless to-ing and fro-ing. It's quite clearly a smokescreen to delay the onset of the story's climax. We have precious little time available for your ambulatory shenanigans. It's Chapter 15 already.'

'Well, why didn't you say you were in a hurry?' Jack reached into his back pocket and pulled out a business card. 'Here, you can call him instead.'

Teddy snatched the card and examined it. 'There's no name on here; who should I ask for?'

'In the straight world, he goes by Richard Edgar Dickulous, but for a sensitive matter like this, you'd better use his secret name.'

'Which is?'

Jack lowered his voice to a whisper. 'It's R. E. Dickulous.'

'It certainly is,' Teddy said, heading for the telephone in the living room. He returned a few minutes later, his mood seemingly much improved by his conversation with the lawyer.

'He says we've got a promising case. I explicated to him about my song, and when it was composed and about Lady CooCoo being at La Trine Fest. He also said that because the Vindicti are the secret rulers of the supernatural world, they tend to remain out of sight, and often prefer to settle out of court.'

'That's great news, my darling.' I embraced him and his potential fortune eagerly.

'Either that or they'll avoid making recompense by having us all killed; he said it could go either way.'

'That's less great.' I de-embraced him with equal enthusiasm; then remembered my critical wifely role as an emotional crutch in times of need. 'But we're not scared of the Vindicti, are we? We've overcome every obstacle that's ever been put in our way, by brains or by brawn or by just standing there and complaining until someone moved it, and this won't be any different. You'll see.'

Teddy smiled and clutched me to his manly bosom. 'Oh Heffa, my darling, your insight and perky can-do attitude are a never-ending source of inspiration and comfort to me. With you by my side, I feel like I could take on and kill, strangle or mutilate the whole world.'

The doorbell rang. 'Who could that be at this hour?' Teddy said. I followed him into the grand entrance hall and watched as he effortlessly swung open the monumental oak doors of Kelledy Castle.

A small red-haired woman in a charcoal-grey business suit was standing on the drawbridge, holding a briefcase with both hands. She looked at Teddy through round wire-framed spectacles, cleared her throat and asked, in a voice as sweet as hickory-smoked ham, 'Tedward Kelledy?'

Teddy nodded warily. The woman opened her briefcase and handed him a bulging manila folder. 'Very good,' she confirmed to no one in particular. 'Mr. Kelledy, I represent certain parties who prefer to remain anonymous. If I told you that their dark ancient name is a curse in several languages, and that saying it out loud has been known to curdle vulnerable children and make milk spontaneously combust, I think that will tell you to whom I refer.'

'I bet she means the Vindicti!' I shouted helpfully. Teddy shook his head, but I don't know why. She totally did mean the Vindicti, as her next words proved.

'They wish you to know that it would be unwise to commence legal action against them. Unwise and unnecessary, as you are about to enter into a formal business relationship with them.'

'I am?' Teddy asked with genuine surprise.

'Not just you, Mr. Kelledy, but your wife and child too. You have always been of interest to them, as I'm sure you're aware, and the child Penissa is quite simply a remarkable creature. As for your wife −' she shuddered '− she is probably one of the most amazing vampires who ever lived.'

'Finally, someone said it! Thank you, sinister agent of the Vindicti!' I punched the air with gratitude.

'While she remained human, she was no threat. But now, with the combined force of the three of you, they feel your star potential. With the right help, you could be more famous than Marilyn Monroe and Michael Jackson put together.'

'Hah, my father tried that once.' Teddy smiled at the memory of an experiment gone hilariously wrong.

'What you hold in your hands is a contract, Mr. Kelledy. You will sign it, and become willing servants of Vindicti Talent Management Inc., or. . .' She paused for emphasis, removing her glasses so we could fully appreciate the malevolent glint in her eyes. '. . . You will be destroyed!'

I gasped and ran to Teddy's side. He looked at me, at the folder containing the contract, and back at the flame-haired agent of the Vindicti. I squeezed his arm reassuringly. The next words he spoke would seal our fate forever. We could either become rich and famous corporate puppets of the Vindicti, or we could keep our freedom and integrity, and have it murderously removed again shortly afterwards. I could see pros and cons with both, but as Teddy's loyal wife it was my job to support him whatever fate he chose for us. 'Pick the first one,' I whispered hopefully.

Teddy raised himself up to his full height, and threw the contract as hard as he could. It went sailing out into the night, disappearing over the treeline.

'There's our answer. Without creative freedom, an artist is nothing. You can steal my songs, you can threaten our lives, but you can never take our integrity!'

The Vindicti's attorney nodded. 'Destruction it is, then. You have until that bit of the month that's after the new moon, but before the full moon, when the moon is getting bigger each night.'

'Ah yes,' I said, suddenly remembering my days as a member of Spatula's Astronomy Society. 'I believe it's known as the Breaking Yawn.'

Teddy pretended to breathe a sigh of relief. 'Thank goodness we managed to get that in somewhere. Stephfordy was getting worried.'

'Yes, that's it,' the lawyer confirmed. 'You have until the Breaking Yawn, and then you will be destroyed!' She flashed her eyes malevolently once more, and then shuffled her feet sheepishly.

'Is that it, then?' I asked. She nodded. 'Aren't you going to disappear in a puff of smoke or something?'

'I'm an attorney at law, not a magician,' she snapped. 'I

thought you'd sign the contract, so I didn't plan a dramatic exit. Umm...'

Teddy smiled sympathetically. 'That's okay, I'll shut the door, and you can beetle off back to the Vindicti at your own pace.'

She nodded eagerly. 'Yes, please! Goodbye, Mr. Kelledy.'

'Righto, bye then.' Teddy waved as he hauled the doors closed. 'Nice lady,' he said, turning to me for affirmation. I grabbed the helmet from one of the suits of armor that lined the hallway and gave him an affirmative whack on the head with it.

'You've just signed our death warrant, Teddy Kelledy, you and your precious artistic sentiment.'

He looked shocked. 'My goodness, I have, haven't I? Sorry, love, I got a bit caught up in the moment. It was all so exciting!'

'Hmm, you don't get out much, do you?'

'Only when I need to follow you, my darling,' he simpered adoringly. He clutched my hands, and spoke in a resolute tone. 'Never fear: all will be well. We are not the only vampires who prefer to remain true to our indie roots. Summon the rest of the family; it's time for a council of war!'

chapter 16

gang bang

We talked late into the night. The whole Kelledy clan sat round the dining table while Teddy paced the room incessantly, stepping over Chump's unconscious body what must have been a thousand times as the hours ticked by and the debate raged back and forth. He explained the situation calmly: how the Vindicti had threatened to take away everything we held most dear, particularly our existence.

Bobbi pointed out that no one had threatened her or Jack or Joseph, so maybe they should all just trot off and leave us to our fate, but Teddy wouldn't hear of it. 'We are a family, Bobbi. We stand or fall together.' He was so noble in the face of adversity.

'I guess we fight, then. There goes my chance of a spin-off series,' Bobbi sighed, the perkiness leaving her petite vampire body all at once. 'It would have been great; *Sex and the City* with vampires, that was the idea. I called it *Vampire in Brooklyn*.'

Ignoring her self-centered whinging, Teddy's father piped up. 'But how can we fight them, son? The Vindicti are so powerful; that's why I've spent the last three hundred years trying to avoid pissing them off. Count me out; I'm going to hide out somewhere bleak and hard-to-get-to. Los Angeles is nice this time of year.'

Teddy was defiant. 'It's painfully simple, Father. They're coming here to destroy us, and when they do, we will fight them fang-to-fang, like proper vampires would. It's back to the old school, Nosferatu-style. As I believe the young folk say, "We shall totally own them!"'

'Good luck with that, my son. It's been nice knowing you,' Joseph said, slinking away.

'It won't be easy,' Jack said, shaking his head doubtfully as the sound of Joseph Kelledy's footsteps faded into the distance.

'We'll have to get help, then,' Teddy said, accepting his father's betrayal manfully and stepping into his rightful place as head of the family. Sweet, that meant the castle was definitely ours now!

'Heffa, I am sure that Joe Cahontas and his brothers – and that annoying girl – will help us in our hour of need. Will you call and ask?'

I waved a hand at him. 'No need; as soon as Joe hears that I'm in danger, they'll come a-running. Let's take their presence for granted, shall we?'

Teddy nodded. 'It's worked so far. Bobbi, are you still a member of that vampire social network, Undead Fiend Finder?'

'Where do you think I go for intelligent conversation – Jack?' she replied.

'Great, get on there and share the news. All freedom-loving vampires should make haste to Spatula, where they will shortly have the opportunity of fighting for their right to party.'

'But it's certain death. Why would anyone in their right mind come?'

'Good point. Tell them that Heffa Kelledy is in danger.' Teddy pointed to me and I tried to look threatened and pathetic. Bobbi regarded him skeptically, but said nothing. 'Oh, okay, then. Tell them... that it's a free bar between now and the Breaking Yawn. The citizens of Spatula will be a free-range blood buffet for anyone who stands alongside us.'

'Yeah, that might do it,' Bobbi said, hopping up the stairs two at a time. 'I'll put the word out.'

Penissa had sat silently throughout our discussions, but now she clutched my hand tightly and asked, 'Are we going to die, Mommy?'

'Don't worry, honey,' I reassured her. 'We're already dead.'

Then there was nothing to do but wait, and continue acclimatizing to my new vampire life. Being a vampire was, in a word, absolutely brilliant. I loved living forever, and having superpowers was really cool too. Best of all was being on a pedestal so far above humanity that they seemed like mere ants. Their concerns and petty morality were a joke to my kind. As perfect beings in our perfect vampire world, our every act, no matter how depraved, violent or unnecessary, was by its very nature a perfect act. It was sweet.

There was one thing that did bug me though, and that was the whole not sleeping anymore bit. By a rough calculation, I'd spent about ten of my eighteen human years asleep or otherwise unconscious, and so now, when there wasn't much going on plot-wise, the time did drag somewhat. The others started training, but as I was planning on letting them do all of the fighting, I didn't see the need to join in. I took my dad home – well, to the hospital – and then I came back and straightened up the castle for a couple of hours. It was always so dusty. Then I alphabetized Joseph's scalpels, and threw out some of his more disturbing creations.

Finally, I made my way to the balcony at the top of the castle's highest tower to gaze out at the forest and practice my windswept brooding. It still wasn't quite up to the required vampire standard, however kind about it Teddy felt obliged to be. I watched the sun rise and go down again several times from the solitude of this dismal eyrie. Each night the moon grew fuller in the sky. Or thinner. Whichever one of those marked the coming of the Breaking Yawn. I saw no one, and no one saw me. Teddy might have brought me something to nibble on; he was so selfish, forgetting about my needs like this. And on top of that, we had so little time left together before our almost certain destruction at the hands of the Vindicti. We should have been spending it together. It was hopeless, my husband didn't love me, I was about to die – for good this time – and the wind up here was playing havoc with my hairdo. Truly I was the most unfortunate vampire that had ever been. Oh woe, woe upon woe. I wished I had never been reborn.

It felt like I was starting to get the hang of the brooding, and I allowed myself a smile. Looking around me for the first time in several days, I noticed a cloaked figure emerging from the trees far below, heading straight for our home. Good gravy, was that some dread agent of the Vindicti announcing their

189

imminent arrival? Was our judgment at hand? Why hadn't I worn a watch to keep track of time?

I raced down the spiral stairs that led back to the living room, taking them four at a time. Initially, anyway, then I lost my footing and just sort of fell head over heels for the last few hundred feet. Gracefully, though. When I rolled out at the bottom, I dusted myself off and stood up with spectacular vampire poise. My head was spinning and my vision blurred, but there was no time to lose in warning the others, so I calmly screamed, 'They're here, run for your lives! Protect Heffa!' at the top of my voice.

'What are you talking about, my darling? It is another week until the Breaking Yawn.' Teddy was suddenly beside me. He threw a protective arm around my shoulders and guided me to a chair.

'But I saw someone coming!' I insisted as my vision slowly cleared.

'I expect it was Bjorn; he's our latest arrival.'

Teddy's words puzzled me, but as my vision cleared, I saw that we were not alone in the Kelledys' spacious living room, and things started to make sense. We were surrounded by vampires. Sitting on the couch, playing cards at the table, leaning on the fireplace glaring broodingly into the flames... There must have been at least a dozen.

'Isn't it wonderful? We called for help, and they answered,' Teddy beamed.

I looked from face to face. I was used to hanging out with freaks by now, but the Kelledys had nothing on this lot. Strange clothes, bizarre facial hair, all sizes, ages and sexes were present. Where were they all going to not sleep?

'But who are they, and where did they come from?'

'They're just ordinary freedom-loving vampires like us, my darling wife. They heard of the Vindicti's threats to our livelihood and continued existence on this plane, and from the four corners of the earth they rushed here to aid us in our struggle.'

'Well, who wouldn't want to sacrifice their lives for us?' I agreed.

'Come, let me introduce you to some of our new friends,' Teddy said, leading me over to the darkest corner of the room. A petite Japanese girl with orange pigtails sat curled up in Joseph's leather easy chair. Seeing us approach, she hopped to her feet and gave me an enthusiastic wave. She wore a skintight blue-and-white latex sailor suit and held a coil of red silk rope in her hand. 'Heffa, meet Reiko Shibari. She was the Far East's most popular undead idol singer. She was the hottest star in Japan for almost nine days – a new record.'

Reiko's red painted lips curled and with flashing fangs she said, '"Don't Stop Bereaving" was the number-one song across all of Asia. Until that gaijin bitch Lady CooCoo's single came out. Then I heard she was coming here, so I come to teach her a lesson, maybe poke *her* face, see how she likes it!'

She slapped the coil of rope against her leg. The depth of her commitment to protecting me was most impressive, and she deserved our thanks. I cast my mind back to my high-school Japanese classes for the appropriate words. 'Gojira mitsubishi, Shibari-san.' She looked slightly taken aback; she obviously hadn't heard that mastery of many tongues was yet another of my vampire talents. Then she smiled and stuck two fingers up at me. I was shocked, and was about to pounce on her and stick her fingers somewhere she wouldn't like, but Teddy pulled me away, insisting that it was a traditional gesture of vampire solidarity.

He led me round the room, introducing me to so many vampires that I would have struggled to keep track, if it hadn't been for the remarkable fact that they all had precisely one character trait, and were easily distinguished by their differing styles of clothes.

A man in a silver cowboy hat sat at the dining table with a huge stack of receipts and forms. 'That's O'Bone, the Irish vampire. He's been "on tour" for twenty years hiding from the taxman, but it looks like they found him,' Teddy whispered as we approached. He introduced us and O'Bone looked up from his paperwork. I could see his red eyes flashing behind his stupidly large sunglasses, and I was forced to remind myself that not all vampires were as nice as the Kelledys.

O'Bone fixed me with his gaze and said, 'Can you believe I'm not allowed to write this crate of landmines off as a charitable donation? The orphans were so grateful, no feet meant no more worries about their lack of shoes...' He scrunched the receipt up, and threw it onto the table.

'Come on, darling, before his fiery Irish temper flares up. Come and meet Larynx and Gisard; they're from France,' Teddy interjected, moving us on quickly.

'Oh, France, okay. They've probably got stripy jumpers and berets, haven't they, with big strings of onions round their necks?' I said, getting into the spirit of the occasion.

Teddy looked appalled. 'Credit Stephfordy with a little more originality, Heffa. It's 2011, what kind of cliché merchant do you think you're dealing with?' He pointed them out on the other side of the room, where they seemed oblivious to the vamp convention going on around them. One was fiddling with a complicated-looking set of turntables while the other tapped urgently at a keyboard. I realized that this was the source of the urgent pumping techno that filled the room. They wore matching black leather jumpsuits and featureless burnished metal helmets that made it impossible to tell if they were young or old. I waved a cheery hello. The one on the left nodded imperceptibly and the other played a short keyboard riff that Teddy assured me was a standard intergalactic welcome tune.

'Aren't there any vampires here who are normal like us?' I muttered, holding Teddy's hand tighter.

'Ooh, I know, come and meet John, you'll like him.' He pointed out a tall, long-haired man in a white suit who was standing barefoot in the ornamental fishpond at the far end of the room.

When Teddy introduced us, he returned my smile, his yellow eyes kind behind his round-framed glasses. 'How do, Heffa, very pleased to meet yer,' he said in a distinctive British accent. 'Great do, Teddy, but when you asked us to come together, you were talking about a revolution – don't let me down. Please, please me by letting me know we can start killing the Vindicti soon.'

'Patience, John, the time of the Breaking Yawn approaches,' Teddy replied.

The vampire known only as John nodded with satisfaction and indicated the polished wooden floor of the Kelledys' living room. 'That's dead nice, that is. Norwegian wood? Looks well flammable.'

'Okay, darling, I think you get the idea,' Teddy said, and tried to lead me away.

I liked John but he'd seemed so lonely when I saw him standing there. 'Why don't you mingle, John? It is a party. Have you met Reiko Shibari?'

He sneered sardonically. 'No, ta, I'm done with Japanese birds; you wouldn't believe what I had to do to get shot of the last one.'

Oh well, if he was the sort of social deviant who was happy on his own, that wasn't my concern. I flashed him the V-sign that Reiko had taught me and he laughed hard. 'Yeah, peace, love, good luck with that...'

Finally, Teddy took me over to a cloaked figure I recognized as the one whose silent approach had frightened me so much when I'd seen him from my tower. He was stacking his suitcases in a pile against the wall; he looked like he was planning on moving here, not simply helping us out and then clearing off again. I would have to watch this one. His task finished, he turned to us, pulling back the hood of his cloak to reveal a kindly round face with long hair and a scraggy beard. He seemed impossibly ancient, perhaps as old as forty. He shook my hand warmly. As warmly as an ice-cold vampire can, anyway.

'Hallo, I am Benny, and you must be Heffa. I've heard so much about you,' he said, in what I hoped would become the standard greeting for the newly crowned Queen of the Damned. (That's me, btw.)

He removed his cloak and tossed it on top of the suitcases. I could see why he'd been wearing it now. It was certainly a more subtle and practical option for traveling than the purple jumpsuit it had concealed. He looked at Teddy and then back at me as if a thought had just occurred to him. 'A good friend of mine married her stalker, too. Don't worry; it worked out just fine.' He patted his stomach. 'Teddy, I don't mean to be rude, but it has been a very long journey. You said something in your invitation about smörgåsbord, did you not?'

Teddy laughed and clapped him on the back. 'Fear not, my friend; Jack is going to get some take-out. Just tell him what you want, and remember, it's all you can eat.'

Benny laughed as though I had made a joke. At that moment, Jack came into the room with a pad and pen, twirling his car keys around his finger. 'Okay, you crazy cats, who wants what?'

Benny stuck his hand up and immediately shouted, 'I like two big plump blondes, and a small ginger guy on the side.'

Jack nodded and made a note. Reiko Shibari sidled up to him and whispered something in his ear, making a slashing gesture across her throat, a mangling gesture with her fists and what I thought I recognized as a groin-stomping gesture with one of her high-heel-clad feet. He shuddered and wrote it down, and she returned to her dark corner. I looked around at the other vampires as they made their orders. There was something slightly disturbing about this whole affair, and after a few seconds I realized what it was.

'Teddy, I thought that we Kelledys were decent honest vampires who never fed on humans because of our principles and stuff, but now you're sending Jack out to round up townsfolk for our guests. That's quite a sudden turnaround, isn't it?'

Teddy looked surprised. 'Huh, I hadn't thought of that, and clearly neither had Stephfordy.' He shrugged. 'Still, Jack's got it all written out now, and no one really cares about any of the characters here besides us, do they?' He stroked my face with his icy finger, and pulled me close to him. The simple honest passion of his deep lingering kiss freed my mind from all thoughts of inconsistent characterization and mass murder.

From the garden I heard a childish scream, and suddenly remembered my beautiful perfect daughter Penissa. Protecting her from the wrath of the Vindicti was the whole point of this plot line, and I had let her out of my sight. If anything happened to her, I would never forgive everyone else for failing to look after her. I tore myself away from Teddy and raced outside. He followed close behind.

Typically, it was a false alarm; nothing exciting had happened. Penissa was running across the lawn, chased by Bobbi and another vampire I didn't recognize. She screamed again as Bobbi pretended to pounce on her and rend her in twain, then they were both rolling on the grass laughing. Seeing me, Penissa wrestled herself loose from Bobbi's vice-like grip and ran over to me. 'Did oo thee, Mommy? We were pwaying pwedatorth and pwey, I wath the hooman and Auntie Bobbi wath helping me to be dead like she ith.'

'I saw, sweetie, you make a great corpse,' I said, ruffling her hair with relief. 'Who's that other lady you're playing with?' I asked, looking at the female vampire who was approaching with Bobbi. Of all the strange creatures I had met this evening, she was the weirdest. She was tall, taller than me, and statuesque, like a mythological figure from an episode of *Xena* or something. Long blonde hair tumbled down over her bronzed shoulders, and the fur bikini that was all she wore gave me ample evidence that she was the same rich caramel color all over. She carried a spear that was even taller than she was. Teddy hastened forwards to greet her, and I thought I could detect a very slight reddening of his pallid cheeks. Goodness, was he blushing?

He turned to me and with a voice that had suddenly gone up half an octave said, 'Darling, this is Sherakahira. She's got a Brazilian. I mean, she's a Brazilian. From Brazil.'

I regarded my new rival dubiously. There was no doubting the sincerity of her smile as she greeted me, but there was something about her that I didn't like. I decided to probe her a bit further, before Teddy had the same idea. 'Sherakahira, so glad you could make it. You're from Brazil?'

'Yes. It is sunnier than most vampires like, but it is my home.'

'And what's up with the fur bikini, exactly? Don't you have the Gap in Brazil?'

'My people live far from the city, in a remote jungle clearing. We are simple folk, happy to eat the coca beans from

195

the trees and the yams from the ground. For sport, we wrestle crocodiles and race elephants.'

'Elephants? In Brazil?'

'Oh yes. I have a pet chimpanzee also; his name is Sergio.'

I folded my arms skeptically. 'Sherakahira, I know you've traveled a long way to help us, and please don't take this the wrong way, but I'm not finding your Brazilian jungle home very credible.' The fur-clad vampire looked at her feet and twiddled her spear sheepishly. I went on, 'In fact, it sounds like a bunch of stuff that Stephfordy saw in Tarzan movies when she was a kid, and she figured probably no one knows the difference between Brazil and Africa; it's all just abroad after all!'

Before she could answer, I turned and stormed back towards the house. I was glad to have so many new friends arriving to protect us from the Vindicti, but I would have to keep a close eye on them. With so many vivid and well-rounded new characters being introduced, there was a real danger that I could get sidelined, and that could not be allowed to happen. It was a terrifying prospect, scarier even than the approach of the Breaking Yawn and the army of vengeful vampires that would come with it. On the other hand, the massive climactic battle was sure to end up with the death of quite a few of these new vampy-come-lately characters, so maybe it was all for the best.

I was pulled from my reverie by sweet little Penissa pulling at my sleeve. 'What is it, you little rugrat?' I asked tenderly.

'Can I thow oo my new twick, Mommy? Auntie Reiko showed it to me.'

'Of course you can, sweetheart.'

'Oh goody, wait here while I go get my ping pong ballth!' she yelled with delight.

Penissa scampered off upstairs with innocent childish glee, and I felt Teddy put his arms around me. This perfect happy family was what we were fighting for, and nothing was going to take it away from me. No matter how many had to sacrifice themselves to save us.

chapter 17

assuming the position

As dawn broke on the day of the Breaking Yawn, the Kelledy house was a hive of activity. There was so much to do before leaving for our fatal rendezvous with the Vindicti – preparations to be made, last-minute fight training... there were jobs that needed doing everywhere I turned, and vampires hard at work in every corner of the house. It was an overwhelming sight.

I found Teddy with Benny and John in the kitchen, a map spread out on the counter. He was briefing them on the ground where we would confront the Vindicti that evening. When he saw me, he smiled as encouragingly as he could manage, but the deep frown lines in his marbled brow told the real story. I took his hand and led him gently out of the kitchen into the hallway. He put his hands on my shoulders and sighed. 'There is so much to be done, my darling. Our chances are so slim, nothing that could give us an edge can be neglected, or we shall most certainly be doomed.'

I stroked his arm. 'It's such a burden on you, my love. You need to take a break, or you won't have the strength to protect me later. Why don't we go upstairs for a while?'

'I cannot desert my post, not at this gravest hour of our existence.'

'But Teddy, is this really how you want to spend our last day together? Come with me, I can show you that new underwear Bobbi bought for me.'

'Heffa, I cannot!' he said resolutely.

'Although "underwear" isn't quite the right word; "apparatus" is probably more like it...' I rubbed my hand down Teddy's chest. He looked back over his shoulder to where John and Benny stood, waiting patiently for instructions.

'Well, it does look like everything is under control down here. A quick break couldn't hurt. Lead on, my sweet rotten apple.'

I took his hand and led him to our marital bed. Not much time remains until the climax of my tale, so I will not detain you with further luridly overwritten descriptions of our passionate, unrestrained lovemaking. Especially since Stephfordy would only censor it right when we were getting to the best bit. But trust me when I say that you will never experience anything like it in your pathetic colorless human life, and if you did, your insides would explode with pleasure and as you lay bleeding to death on the floor, a prayer of gratitude would be the last thing to pass your lips. If you were as lucky as I am. Which you're not.

While Teddy and I were entwined in each other's arms, time seemed to stand still. Nothing mattered but the two of us and our sacred lust. I was so transported by desire that I was having trouble even remembering what was going on that had been so important. I looked for clues in Teddy's face, but saw only simple adoration in his bright orange eyes.

I rolled onto my back and saw the moon shining in through the picture window. It had been mid-morning when we'd come up here. Had it really taken us so long to satisfy each other? Teddy was lying with a contented expression on his divine face. I whispered in his perfect porcelain ear, 'We've been up here all day. It's dark out. Can you believe it?'

He sat bolt upright and gave a panicked wail when he saw the moon bathing us in its soft light.

'Yes, it is beautiful this evening,' I agreed. 'What's it called again, this phase of the moon that comes before the full moon?'

He was on his feet now, racing around the room looking for the jeans that he had eagerly thrown off a few hours before. His panicked expression suggested that he was concerned about more than his missing pants. He jabbed his finger at the moon. 'It's called the Breaking Yawn, Heffa! And if you remember, it presages the arrival of our mortal enemies the Vindicti, who have sworn to destroy us this very night!'

That was it! I knew there was something plot-related going on today. Why did we have to be tossed hither and yon by the vagaries of narrative events? Why couldn't Teddy and I remain here basking in the glory of each other's bodies for the next fifty pages? That wouldn't be boring to read about at all. I would certainly lap it up like I'd just lapped up Teddy's—

'Heffa, there's no time for whatever it is you're giggling about. Remove that item of "clothing" immediately and put something decent on. We need to leave. The moon has risen, and we've wasted the whole day when we should have been preparing our battle strategy.' He waved his jeans at me angrily before nimbly hopping into them.

'Wasted?' I pouted.

'Sorry, my love, sorry. Not wasted, of course, never wasted. Only perhaps we. . . allocated our remaining hours of existence rather less wisely than we might have done, given the perilous circumstances we are about to face.'

'That's better. I'll just have a shower, then; my hair needs washing.'

Teddy pulled his T-shirt on and his head emerged from the neckhole with a frustrated expression. He was about to say something ignorant and masculine about my bathroom routine, which I had pared to the very bone in an attempt to bring it in under an hour – if only he appreciated my sacrifices. But before he could, there came a series of long blood-curdling howls from the woods.

Teddy went pale. 'They're here already. Oh, crap.'

'No, darling, don't you recognize that gruff macho tone? It's Joe Cahontas and the other werewolves: Laddie, Fidaux and that pissy girl. They've come to help us in our hour of need.' I smiled at him and raced for the door, but with lightning-quick vampire speed he stood in front of it, blocking my path.

'That is good news, my darling, but please, put some clothes on. I don't think they should see you dressed like that.'

I quickly assembled an outfit suitable for a dramatic climax. A black T-shirt with a black see-through long-sleeved top over it. A black corset, for that essential touch of vampire chic. And my favorite pair of black sweatpants, for comfort.

When I came downstairs, the atmosphere was electric, with vampires and werewolves facing each other across the empty expanse of the Kelledys' minimalist living room. Joe sat on the large white couch as if he owned the place, while the others stood behind him, their powerful muscles stiff with tension. On the opposite side of the room, our vampire guests huddled together and conferred in angry hushed tones. Reiko Shibari stood apart from the rest, regarding the La Trine werewolves with intense, hungry eyes. Laddie smiled back boyishly, ever the friendly one. The petite Japanese vampire bared her fangs and snapped her coiled rope against her thigh like a whip. The young werewolf looked away, blushing.

Benny gestured for me to join the gaggle of vampires and with a subtle head movement in Joe's direction whispered, 'Your house is infested with werewolves, Heffa Kelledy.'

'But don't worry; we can kill them for you sure enough,' O'Bone reassured me with a hearty slap on the back.

'No, you idiots, these are our friends. They've come to help us in our hopeless struggle against the Vindicti.'

Shocked murmurs passed around the group, and I sensed that I was about to be subjected to a barrage of outraged insistence about the ancient blood feud between werewolves and vampires and all that claptrap that we really didn't have time for. I reached into the pocket of my sweatpants and pulled out the pamphlets that Bobbi had given me after she and Laddie started their merchandise store together. I thrust one into Benny's hands and said curtly, 'Come on, guys, it's 2011, not 1960. Your negative stereotypes are way out of line. You might be ancient, but you don't have to be dinosaurs.'

'*Vlad is Hard, George is Hairy: From Supernatural Fiends to Superspecial Friends*,' Benny read, then pointed to the crude illustration beneath. 'Hey look, they're having tea together!' He seemed puzzled, but also eager to understand.

I gave copies of the pamphlet to each of the other vampires and they retired to a corner of the room, intent on the leaflet's message. Bobbi added an extra audio-visual element by putting a DVD of *Being Human* on. Joe grinned at me from the sofa. 'You didn't have to do that, Heff, we could have taken 'em.'

'But you could have been hurt. Or they could, and then there would have been fewer of you to protect me and Penissa. I couldn't let that happen.'

At that moment, little Penissa skipped into the room, holding a bunch of brown and wilted roses. I frowned at her. 'How many times have I told you not to take things from the graveyard?'

She hid the pathetic bouquet behind her back and looked at her muddy shoes in remorse. 'It wath onwy the fwowerth this time, Mommy, I pwomith.'

She looked so sad and cute. I couldn't be angry with her, not at a time like this; I'd just have to be mad later on, if we survived. 'Say hello to your Uncle Joe, Penissa. But keep your distance; he's got that weird glint in his eyes.'

'Hewwo, Uncle Joe. Are you coming to get kiwwed wiv uth?' she asked.

Joe stood up and planted his feet wide apart. 'No one's dying tonight, baby, not if Joe Cahontas and his fearsome werewolf pack have anything to say about it!'

The other werewolves howled their agreement enthusiastically, except for Laika, who snorted and rolled her eyes in a gesture that I was sure the unoriginal bitch had copied from me. She mumbled something that made Joe turn and stare at her.

'What's that, Laika?'

She stuck her hairy chin out indignantly. 'I said, I wish the torch you're carrying would die. Then we wouldn't have to keep risking our lives for this ungrateful—'

'Dammit, we've been through this!' he snapped. 'We'd do the same for anyone we know. It's not Heffa's fault that she gets people declaring vendettas against her so very frequently.'

Laika snorted again, and went outside to glare at the moon. By now it had risen high above the treeline.

'I'm so glad you're here, Joe. I can't imagine a climax without my best friend being involved,' I purred platonically.

Joe blushed, then waved a hand dismissively. 'We just like a good scrap, don't we, guys?' The others howled once more, and exchanged handslaps with their leader. How lucky

Teddy and I were to have such loyal (and easily led) friends as these.

The huddle of vampires in the corner was breaking up, and Benny marched over, his expression much friendlier than it had been. The others followed him. He held his hand out to Fidaux and smiled. 'I'm sorry I called you a "mangy flea-bitten half-breed cur", my friend.'

Fidaux shook his hand with a shrug. 'Hey, sticks and stones, man.'

Benny continued, 'I understand now that my hatred of werewolves stemmed from my confused feelings about my own supernatural nature. Somewhere deep inside, I hate myself for what I am, but instead of dealing with those feelings, I externalized them and turned them on you. And that was wrong. Can you forgive me?'

Fidaux tried to wrest his hand free from Benny's grip and mumbled, 'Um, sure, I guess.'

Benny hugged him. 'Thank you, Fidaux, I love you!' He squeezed the werewolf hard. Fidaux looked disturbed, far more than he had been by the Swedish vampire's earlier aggression. After patting him on the back a few more times, Benny released his grip and turned to the assembled vampires to shout, 'I love myself!' They greeted this breakthrough with enthusiastic applause.

I hadn't seen Teddy join us, but now he was standing beside Benny with an arm around his shoulders. 'That's wonderful. I really think you've made a lot of progress today, Benny.' The smile left his face and his ivory brow developed a serious crease. 'But our conflict with the Vindicti will not be settled so easily. It is time, my brothers and sisters. Shall we go over the plan once more?'

We gathered round the dining table. I sat with Penissa on my lap, and the other vampires mingled with their new werewolf friends. Teddy stood at the end of the table, flanked by Bobbi and Jack. They wore matching black leather suits that made them look like members of a futuristic paramilitary organization. Gisard, one of the French vampires, stroked the sleeve of Bobbi's jacket and nodded with approval.

Jack wheeled over the blackboard, which showed a plan of our appointed meeting place with the Vindicti. Teddy looked at it for a second and then turned to us. 'This place will be known to some of you. It's that clearing in the woods where virtually everything significant seems to happen, from romantic liaisons and games of vampire tiddlywinks, to dramatic fights that could lead to our world being torn apart. I trust you have all familiarized yourselves with the arena of battle?' There were nods around the table. Teddy acknowledged them with a curt nod of his own, then indicated his sister.

Bobbi read from the clipboard she was holding. 'Okay, pay attention everyone. Joe Cahontas and the La Trine werewolves will run on ahead of us through the woods to Climax Clearing. Jack Kelledy will take O'Bone, Sherakahira and John in his car. I'll take Gisard, Larynx, Reiko and Benny in mine. Heffa and Penissa will ride with Teddy, as Heffa can't share cars, apparently.'

'Is that all understood?' Teddy asked. There was more nodding. 'Very well, then. To arms!'

There was a moment of silence, followed by some awkward shuffling of feet. Teddy had turned to march towards the door to the garage, but when he saw that no one was following him, he came back to the table. O'Bone the Irish vampire was sitting opposite me, his arm raised. Teddy pointed to him. 'A question. Of course, I should have asked if there were any questions. My apologies. O'Bone, what do you want to know?'

The vampire cleared his throat and adjusted his sunglasses nervously before speaking. 'It's a great plan, sure it is. Very reassuring for everyone to know which car they'll be going in, isn't it, lads?' There were murmurs of assent from around the table. 'But will we not want a plan for after we've arrived? You know, when the Vindicti turn up and try to kill us all? Have you not neglected that part, Teddy?'

Teddy took a step backwards as if he'd been struck. His face could not have been any paler than it already was, of course, but I could tell that O'Bone's question had rattled him. He looked at me with panic in his eyes and I shrugged as subtly as I could, mouthing, 'I hadn't thought of that,' to show that I had been caught out too. He looked around the room as if the answer might be pinned to one of the walls, but only the remains of last night's takeaway were there, hanging limply in their chains.

The silence was becoming awkward and some of the vampires had started to exchange nervous glances. Then the allegedly South American vampire Sherakahira stood up and shook her spear at O'Bone. 'One thing at a time. Teddy will brief us on the rest of the plan when we arrive at the rendezvous. Isn't that right, Teddy?' She winked at him. Teddy nodded with relief, and agreed that he would indeed share the rest of the plan when we had all rendezvoused in Climax Clearing.

I glared at Sherakahira with gratitude and shuddered as I realized that this attractive, exotic, helpful vampire was almost certainly going to be killed by the Vindicti in a few short hours. If I had anything to do with it.

Teddy glanced at his watch. 'No more time for questions; if we want to beat the traffic, we need to leave. Once again, my brothers: to arms!' Reassured by his firm leadership, our motley crew of vampires and werewolves got up from the table and busied themselves with their final preparations.

Bobbi approached Benny, carrying a bulky bundle of clothing. 'You're Scandinavian, aren't you?' she demanded.

Benny nodded, holding up the silver winged helmet that Bobbi had given him and watching it glint in the candlelight. 'Yah, I am from Stockholm.'

Bobbi tutted with disapproval. 'That's what I wanted to talk to you about. This —' she indicated his gold jumpsuit, which was unzipped to reveal swirls of chest hair '— well, it's just not saying "mighty Viking vampire" to me. Change into this armor; it'll be much clearer who you are and where you're from.'

She held out a glistening metal breastplate and red cloak for the puzzled vampire's approval. He looked uncertain, but I knew only too well that Bobbi was not easily dissuaded in matters sartorial. 'And this goes with it,' she continued, unabashed by Benny's reluctance. She handed him a huge metal hammer with a lozenge-shaped head, which looked like it was designed for more serious work than battering down coffin nails. 'You should use this in battle. Some say it has magical powers. It's called Mjol—'

Teddy snatched it away from her, and hurriedly retrieved the helmet, armor and cape from Benny. He scowled at Bobbi reproachfully. 'Sister, we are fighting the Vindicti for our lives and our precious copyright. I hardly think that infringing on a large corporation's intellectual property is going to help our cause. We may yet be able to persuade the Vindicti not to kill us all – but not everyone is so reasonable, so take that armor back to Asgard before you get us into any more trouble. Benny, you look wonderful as you are.'

The Swedish vampire stroked his beard thoughtfully. 'Maybe I could paint my face blue and yellow like Swedish flag; would that help?'

Teddy sighed. 'Yes, that's a super idea; you will be a total caricature of your nation then – perfect. Please attempt to make haste, though; we are going to be late.'

Bobbi led Benny away to find some face paint, and Teddy clapped his hands for attention. 'Very well, my friends, it is time to depart! Does everyone remember who their travel companion is?'

There was general assent, so Teddy and Jack started shooing our brave band of freedom fighters towards the garage. Penissa was still sitting at the table; there was too much going on for the poor little darling to take in. I took her hand and squeezed it reassuringly. It was so soft – squelchy almost – compared to my diamond-hard vampire skin, but she was my daughter, flesh of my flesh. Not literally, of course, her flesh was from all over the place, but nevertheless she was mine. She looked at me imploringly. 'Is it going to be okay, Momma?'

'Don't worry, darling, Daddy won't let anything bad happen to us. Even if he had to sacrifice himself, his family and every single one of his vampire kin to save us, he'd do it without a second thought.'

'Are you sure, Mommy?' She still looked worried. I picked her up and hugged her as tightly as I could without pulling something loose.

'I've never been surer of anything, Penissa. But I'll make sure Daddy gets a detailed reminder of his responsibilities while we're in the car, okay?'

She smiled, and Teddy joined us. He kissed Penissa and the three of us walked to the car together. His face was as still as a carved ivory mask, and I felt sure that mine was too. But behind it my mind was racing. There was so much I needed to tell him, and so little time left to us. I needed him to know how I felt, now more than ever. How I felt, and most especially how angry I would be if anything happened to me or Penissa because of his stupid selfish little argument with the Vindicti.

chapter 18

final release

We were the last of our group to arrive in the familiar forest clearing. Teddy's siblings had made better time because they did not share his insistence on driving at 20 miles an hour. Teddy had also had to pull over a couple of times to examine the diagrams I had helpfully drawn for him, showing precisely which circle of hell is reserved for those who fail to protect their families.

We pulled up by the other cars parked neatly next to one another at the clearing's edge, and then walked briskly towards the ragtag band gathered at the center. Joe and his gang had switched to their werewolf forms, and they stalked back and forth around the edges of the group, incessantly sniffing the cool night air, the moist grass, and Sherakahira's bikini bottom.

Larynx and Gisard had brought their full musical rig with them and were busily connecting their keyboards, turntables and mixing boards together with a bewildering array of cables. I looked at Teddy to see if he had any idea how this feverish activity was supposed to help us. He was whispering to his brother, 'I knew we should have invited Serge Gainsbleurgh instead of these two clowns. There's a vampire who knows how to sweet-talk his way out of a dispute.' Larynx suddenly yanked a bundle of cables from the sockets where his partner had plugged them, screamed something incomprehensible and hideously French-sounding and hit Gisard a ringing blow around the head with a large wrench. Jack nodded in regretful agreement.

I looked around at the other vampires who had come from around the world to help us in our hour of need. Sherakahira was chatting amiably to Benny over by one of the picnic tables. My sensitivity to other people's emotional states had always been acute, but since becoming a vampire it was even more amazing. I had already suspected that something was going on between the Brazilian beauty and the Swedish guy, and the fact that they were talking to each other confirmed it. I felt sure that they'd probably end up together after all this was over.

In accordance with their traditional national characters, John the English vampire and the feisty Irish O'Bone were engaged in a heated argument about which was better, a pint of Guinness or Queen Elizabeth. It was nice to have a spot of whimsical light relief on such a serious evening. I was glad that they were around to act so stereotypically.

On our arrival, everyone looked towards Teddy, eager to hear his brilliant plan to defeat the Vindicti and save us all from certain death. I pushed him towards the center of the circle that had formed around us encouragingly. 'Remember what I said, Teddy – if I die, termites will eat your spleen for all eternity. But I'm sure your plan is brilliant, so there's no danger.'

He resisted my loving shoves, turning instead and grabbing both my hands. 'But I do not possess a plan, do I? I was hoping to improvise one in the car, but your delightful wittering about how being slaughtered by the Vindicti would play havoc with your complexion, and what you wanted for Christmas, and a hundred other things prevented me from stringing two thoughts together!'

I was totally shocked by this unhelpful outburst. We had only been married a few short months and it seemed Teddy was already bored of listening to me. Sharing each other's cares and woes was supposed to be one of the cornerstones of a happy home. Wasn't I always ready to listen to him when he talked about all that stuff that he was interested in? And worse than that, he was trying to start an argument with me in public, in front of our daughter, and all our friends. *And* he hadn't thought of a plan and we were all going to die. This wasn't looking like a new entry on our list of top ten nights together.

Just then, there was a rustling sound from the far end of the clearing. We turned as one to see a few thin tendrils of mist reaching out into the clearing from the treeline. Then a young man holding a small boxy machine ran out of the woods in a half crouch. Smoke poured from a nozzle at one end of the machine, which he waved in wide arcs around him as he ran across the grass and disappeared back into the woods. Tense glances passed among us. Was this strange scuttling half-man a harbinger of the Vindicti?

Seconds ticked by before a voice from somewhere in the dark wood shouted, 'More smoke, darling!' and the man ran back across the clearing waving his smoke machine. Teddy whispered encouraging words to our small group as we waited for the inevitable onslaught. 'Little more smoke, please,' the voice came again, and the man ran before us one more time, now carrying a smoke machine in each hand. After he'd disappeared into the woods again, Teddy gestured for us all to fan out so as to be ready for an assault from any direction. Yet once more the voice called out: 'A little bit more, luvvie.'

'No, it looks fine, truthfully,' Teddy shouted back. 'Does it not, everyone?'

'Yah, very spooky,' agreed Benny.

'*Sugoi*!' added Reiko Shibari with a small excited clap.

'It looks proper gear, come ahead!' John shouted into the darkness.

The voice spoke again. 'Very well. Places, everyone. Ready in 3, 2, 1!'

The foggy darkness at the edge of the woods was bathed in blinding white light and I shielded my sensitive vampire eyes from the sudden brightness with my hand. As my eyes adjusted, I squinted towards the source of the light to see three silhouetted figures coming towards us through the mist. They were perfectly still and seemed to be gliding on air rather than walking. The Vindicti! Close behind them followed a larger group of figures, about which all I could make out was that they vastly outnumbered us. Crap.

'You can't beat dry ice for a dramatic entrance,' Benny whispered to O'Bone, who nodded nervously.

As the trio drifted closer, the smoke thinned out and I saw that they were standing on small, flat, wheeled platforms, each pushed smoothly towards us by a crouching man. This did spoil the effect somewhat, and a little of the tension in our group dissipated.

The middle figure pushed back his hood to reveal the familiar face of D'Arcy D'Acula, with his slicked-back hair and neatly trimmed moustache. The silent figures either side of the foppish vampire followed suit. Lady CooCoo's huge flat face was perfectly still and emotionless. The moonlight reflected from her too-shiny nose, and I thought to myself that the girl could really use another layer of foundation... but then I realized that her face was actually a mask: a perfect porcelain replica of her own features. Her crystal blue eyes were visible behind the mask, and they simmered with the brooding intensity of pure madness.

Cowl stood to D'Arcy D'Acula's right, his arms folded and his weight on one leg. I could hardly bear to look at his grim visage, as putridly repulsive as ever, and I shied away from meeting his gaze, knowing that the twin pools of pure evil that were his eyes would suck my mind down like a panda in a tar pit. His bored sneer suggested that he was thoroughly unimpressed with their attempt at a dramatic entrance.

D'Arcy D'Acula stepped down from the trolley he'd been wheeled in on and gave it a reproachful kick. 'You see, Kelledy, I told you we needed more bloody smoke.' He looked left and right as Cowl and Lady CooCoo stepped down from their trolleys and joined him. 'It's supposed to be the night of the Breaking Yawn, not amateur night at the Palladium.' His fellow Vindicti nodded sympathetically and Lady CooCoo put a comforting metal arm around his shoulders. D'Arcy D'Acula sighed deeply, regarded his shoes for a moment, and then looked back up at us, a smile fixed on his thin blue lips. 'Anyway, keep buggering on! Can't let it spoil the show, what?'

He snapped his wizened fingers and a minion ran forward holding a crimson briefcase with both hands as if it were a sacred offering. He handed it to D'Acula and scuttled off. D'Acula fiddled with the briefcase lock and the lid popped open. He pulled out a familiar-looking sheaf of documents, and held them out to Teddy.

'Why not take another look at the contract we're offering, Kelledy? I think you'll find the terms quite agreeable. I know we have a fearsome reputation, but you have to be tough to make it in business these days. Our people are more than mere minions, though: they're family, and we *so* want you to be part of that family. Don't we, chaps?'

He looked to the others for affirmation. Cowl shrugged and said, 'Yeah, your family is totally amazing, just what we're looking for,' but his bored tone didn't sell his words to me. Lady CooCoo remained motionless except for her left arm, held out in front of her. Her fist was clenched, but her thumb flicked up in what, from a less creepy person, would have been a positive gesture.

D'Acula continued his sales pitch. 'You see, we all feel the same! Your choice is very straightforward. Sign a contract with us and reap all the benefits of membership of a prestigious showbiz organization – such as fame, fortune, and the peace of mind that comes with surrendering your will entirely to those most qualified to make the right decisions.' He paused, holding his arms out wide as if struggling to encompass all the benefits of bowing down to the Vindicti. 'Or you can retain your precious integrity and independence, which we will gladly leave you to enjoy…'

Teddy and I looked at each other, in agreement about accepting the second option.

'Oh, that's very reasonable of you,' Teddy said. 'We'll do that, thanks.'

But D'Acula snapped, 'That was a dramatic ellipsis, you nincompoop! I hadn't finished. You've thrown me now. Where was I? Umm, integrity… independence, yes, right, which we will gladly leave you to enjoy… pause for effect… for the final few seconds of your pathetic existences!' He cackled at this punchline and exchanged satisfied diabolical glances with his fellow Vindicti.

'I knew it was too good to be true,' I whispered to Teddy. 'I don't trust these Vindicti, darling. Let's be careful.'

'Oh, do you think?' he replied, grateful as ever for my insightful wifely advice.

'You want to get yer grubby fingers in everything, don't yer?' John shouted from somewhere close behind us. 'Well, you can't. Some of us aren't interested in having our faces on magazine covers and all that rubbish you promise. Real artists like Teddy and the rest of us want to be left alone to create their art, without the Man bringing us down with his obsession with bread, man.'

There were encouraging shouts of 'you tell 'em, me boyo' and 'his lips don't lie' from the other vampires, but D'Arcy D'Acula seemed unimpressed by John's passionate speech.

'That's easy for you to say, John, but you had your time in the sun, didn't you? You made enough moolah to keep you going for the rest of your eternal life. But you're a bright lad. Look at Teddy and Heffa, and lovely gruesome little Penissa. So young and so very, very stupid... Don't they need all the help they can get to prevent them from making any more disastrous life choices?'

'They can get all the help they need right here,' said Sherakahira, slapping her chest with indignation. 'We will support them, and nurture them as they fulfill their artistic destinies.'

O'Bone stepped forward to stand next to her. 'Sure it's a journey they need to make for themselves. Their incredible powers could change the world forever – but if they let you drive the tour bus, they'll just end up changing your bank balance forever!'

The hot-tempered Irish vampire looked like he had more to say, but he was silenced by a frenzied keyboard solo from Larynx the French vampire. His passionate playing bespoke freedom and giving in to creativity's wild abandon more eloquently than words ever could. To make the unspoken message extra clear, his partner Gisard stood in front of the keyboard miming that he was trapped in an invisible glass box that clearly represented the Vindicti's imprisoning contractual grasp.

Cowl shook his head dismissively and turned to Teddy. 'What a load of old crap. It's very simple, Kelledy. Either you're in, and alive, or out, and dead. Which is it?'

Teddy raised himself up to his full height and gripped my hand tightly. He looked at each of the Vindicti in turn. 'We gave you our answer weeks ago. You dreadful parasites can never own us, because we already belong to each other. We're ready to fight for our freedom. By all means, step forward and do your worst.'

The Vindicti's army of minions moved closer to our small band of vampires and werewolves in response to a hand signal from D'Arcy D'Acula. Cowl was rubbing his hands eagerly at the prospect of imminent bloodshed, while Lady CooCoo threw off her cloak to reveal her robotic body beneath. The chrome glittered in the moonlight, lithe and deadly looking.

The silence of the surrounding forest was absolute as I looked around. The werewolves' breath was hot and steamy in the cool night air, and their claws scratched the dirt impatiently. Fangs flashed from behind parted lips as the vampires glared with belligerent resolve at the Vindicti and their minions across the dozen or so feet that separated us. Teddy had let go of my hand and now stood in the familiar half-crouch that meant someone was about to get pounced on, and subsequently bitten lots. The smell of tension in the air was intoxicating to me; I could almost taste the imminent violence on my sensitive vampire tongue. Every creature in the clearing was poised to fight for its life; we waited only for the final spark that would set Climax Clearing ablaze.

As if he was striking a match, D'Arcy D'Acula said, 'Very well, then. The time for talk is over. . .' and pulled a thin-bladed sword from the scabbard at his waist.

'Um, no, it isn't!' said a girl's voice that I recognized but couldn't quite place. I looked off into the darkness towards the source of the strangely familiar voice, as did Teddy and the Vindicti and everyone else, all equally startled by this sudden intrusion.

A petite teenager with lank brown hair and spectacles had emerged from the woods and was walking towards us. Around her ankles scuttled a mass of dark creatures. As she got closer, I realized they were an unknown number of mangy-looking cats. She stood before us, and I looked her over with my keen vampire senses, frantically trying to assess what hideous new threat we faced. She wore a black *Sandman* T-shirt and tight black jeans – so she might be a gatecrasher, but at least she was dressed appropriately. To human eyes, she would probably be considered pretty, once the acne had cleared up. She had butted in with an air of great authority, but there was something timid and birdlike about her movements. She carried a heavy-looking book which she shifted nervously from arm to arm, the silver skull pendants that hung from her friendship bracelets jingling as she moved. Squinting with my vampire-vision, I could just make out the title: *Buffy the Vampire Slayer: Complete Episode Guide.*

Unimpressed by her appearance, Cowl shouted, 'We're in the middle of something here, love. Do you mind?'

She looked down her nose at him dismissively, utterly unfazed by his indescribably ghastly appearance. Pushing her glasses back up, she said calmly, 'Stop! You're all making a big mistake.'

Where had I heard that voice before? It was thin and whiny but so very familiar, as much as the sound of the wind through the trees or the rain on my window. It was like I had heard it all my life, all around me, but it had just been there – part of the world, not coming out of the mouth of some skinny little fan-girl. I looked at the newcomer's purple Dr Marten boots and her pallid skin, and I felt a passionate hatred for her, unlike anything I had ever experienced before.

She spoke again. 'There's really no need to fight. Just think of how many beautiful, fascinating, three-dimensional characters will be in danger if you resort to settling your problems by violence.'

'Well, what's your big idea then?' I asked.

'You should keep talking about your issues some more. Maybe another twenty pages or so. I'm sure you'd find a way to resolve them, without the need for an exciting action scene. I'm a writer – trust me, audiences don't want simple-minded violence. They much prefer a well-crafted *anti*climax.'

Teddy looked slightly less confused by this interruption than the rest of us. He snapped his fingers and pointed at her.

214

'You're a writer! I know who you are now – you're Stephfordy Mayo!'

She gave Teddy an enthusiastic nod. 'I am, and as your creator I am here to tell you that you've got this dramatic denouement all wrong.'

D'Arcy D'Acula chipped in. 'Oh, I don't know, I thought it was going quite well. Frightfully tense. It's a bit rich to turn up and try to change it now, if you don't mind my saying so.'

'Well, now you know how it feels not to control your own destiny, don't you?' she snapped back. 'Come on, everyone, let's see if we can sort this out peacefully. . .'

My mind was in turmoil as I listened to this exchange. Was this petite geek-girl really Stephfordy Mayo? It would certainly explain why her voice had sounded so familiar. But even if it was her, it didn't change anything. The others might have been gazing in awe at the face of their creator, but all I saw was another person trying to take the attention away from me. And weren't there already quite enough of those? In truth, I was surrounded by them on all sides – friends and foes. In the final reckoning, they were all just getting in my way. Wasn't the whole point of this fight beneath the Breaking Yawn to thin out the ranks of the undead a bit, to make sure that none of them ever tried to swipe the narration from under my nose again? And Stephfordy thought she could just waltz in here and mess it up for me? Well, if she thought that, then she didn't know Heffa Lump.

I grabbed the sword from D'Arcy D'Acula's hand and, using all the power of my strong vampiric right arm, I struck her head from her shoulders.

'That's for not making me blonde!' I screamed with the full force of eighteen years of pent-up resentment.

Stephfordy's head landed at my feet, the light in her eyes extinguished forever. Now that she was no longer a threat, I realized what an incredible mind she must have had, to bring someone as wonderful as me into the world. As a last token of respect to my esteemed creator I gave her noggin a somber funereal kick, and it went bouncing off across the clearing into the dark, chased by several hungry-looking cats.

D'Arcy D'Acula grasped my wrist and retrieved his sword. 'Wonderful, darling, wonderful; Roland Barthes would be proud,' he commented; then he shoved me away. I was only prevented from falling by Teddy, who rushed to catch me in his strong hard arms. He whispered in my ear, 'I've been advised to clarify that all characters appearing in this work are fictitious and any resemblance to real persons living or decapitated is purely coincidental.'

I wasn't sure what he was on about, but there was no time to consider it: D'Acula waved his sword with a flourish, and the mood in the clearing instantly became as tense and as angry as it had been before what's-her-name showed up. 'Now, if there are no more interruptions, I believe we had a fight to the death scheduled!'

He raised the point of his sword and ran at us. Teddy pushed me hard to the ground, using the force of the shove to leap out of the path of the charging Vindicto. D'Acula sped between us, sword flailing, then stopped and turned for another pass. I could hear shouting and the sounds of violent conflict all around, but my eyes were fixed on Teddy's. He crouched on the damp grass, watching D'Acula prepare to attack again. I moved to join him, but he waved me away. 'Get Penissa, keep her safe; I'll deal with D'Acula,' he shouted. D'Acula charged again and Teddy neatly sidestepped the point of his sword, grabbing his arm as he passed. They fell to the ground and I lost sight of him as Benny the Swedish vampire ran past, chased by Lady CooCoo and a horde of machete-wielding minions.

I looked around frantically for our beloved daughter. She'd been standing right next to me before Stephfordy Mayo had arrived, but now there was no sign of her. Stupid kid, didn't I always tell her to stay close to me? Eager to give her the telling-off she deserved, I marched into the fray to find her.

A werewolf that I thought was Fidaux was encircled by half a dozen of the Vindicti's black-clad servants. They were armed with long silver-tipped spears, and Fidaux was desperately trying to keep away from their deadly lunges as the circle closed in around him. It didn't look too good for poor loyal

Fidaux; without immediate help, he was almost certainly doomed. I gave him a cheery wave of encouragement, and continued my search.

I pushed through the surging, struggling mass of bodies with increasing panic, lashing out blindly at whoever got in my way. Once I heard Bobbi Kelledy shout, 'Ow, thanks very much, Heffa!' so although I wasn't paying attention to what I was doing, I knew that I was making a positive contribution to our cause.

Suddenly the crowd parted, and I saw my beautiful daughter Penissa sitting alone on the grass a few feet away from me, seemingly oblivious to the mayhem. I rushed over and snatched her into my arms, then ran as fast as I could – which was pretty fast, thanks to my vampire super-speed – back to the car.

'Hewwo, Mommy,' Penissa said from under my arm as I ran. 'I made oo a daithy chain.' She held out the necklace of human ears that she'd been calmly collecting from the battlefield and threading onto a length of twine. Such a sweet child, and so creative – just like her parents. I stifled a tear and thanked her, promising I'd put it on just as soon as the ears had dried off a bit.

Then at last we were at the car, and I pretended to breathe a huge sigh of relief as I strapped Penissa into her child safety seat. 'You'll be safe here, my darling,' I reassured her as I climbed into the car next to her. I shut the door and locked it, then started to unwrap the small picnic lunch that Teddy had prepared for us.

Penissa looked at me with simple childish innocence. 'Aren't oo going to go and help Daddy?'

'No, my little maggot. I promised Daddy I would protect you; you wouldn't want me to break my, mmph, promise to him, would you? Besides, mmph, I can see him from here and he looks fine, over there on those rocks, mmph,' I said, shoving another handful of toffee popcorn into my mouth as I watched our titanic battle for survival play out in a series of vignettes across the clearing.

I could see from the bodies that littered the ground that there had been casualties on both sides, but it was impossible to tell who had the upper hand. Everywhere I turned I saw familiar faces locked in a desperate struggle for survival. Joe and the other werewolves were away to my right, tearing their way towards Lady CooCoo through a thick phalanx of Vindicti henchmen. My beloved husband Teddy was still struggling to survive the sword-wielding attentions of D'Arcy D'Acula. They were evenly matched now, Teddy having acquired a sword of his own from somewhere or other while I'd been looking for Penissa. Their fight had moved across the clearing to the large jagged outcrop of rocks, which jutted from the bare earth along one edge of the clearing. They leapt from rock to rock, lunging and parrying and stabbing. There was probably a fair bit of sword-fighting banter going on too, but I couldn't hear it from where I sat.

I rolled down the car window for better audio, but all I could hear was Cowl shouting. He was standing in the middle of his band of henchmen, who were holding their ground despite being assaulted on all sides by vampires of all nationalities. The vamps were rending hapless minions into unpleasantly clammy confetti with gleeful abandon, but it seemed that two more took the place of every one they killed, and they were getting no closer to Cowl. That repellent creature stood behind his henchmen offering helpful comments to the combatants around him. 'You call that fighting? You couldn't fight your way out of a baby's bladder.' 'Come on, that death rattle was pathetic – die like you mean it!' 'Oh, that was horrible, get out of my sight this instant.' I could certainly see how the Vindicti had held on to power for so long with such inspiring leadership. But no longer. Tonight they faced their Waterloo, as Benny had memorably put it.

Joe and two of his werewolves had made short work of the minions protecting Lady CooCoo, and now she faced them alone. She tried to back away, but Laddie had got behind her and she was trapped. Trapped, but not helpless, I saw, as the twin barrels of her machine-gun nipples fired a deadly barrage at Joe Cahontas. My heart leapt into my throat as Joe dodged nimbly back, the bullets kicking up a red mist of blood from the corpses of her followers. She fired again, and only Joe's preternaturally sharp werewolf reactions kept him alive. He growled with frustration and continued circling his prey, now leaping forward to try to get Lady CooCoo within the reach of his powerful claws, now leaping away to avoid being hit by her deadly breast bullets. This stalemate continued for some time, before the third werewolf made a sudden hasty dash right in front of the murderous robot Vindicta. Lady CooCoo's breasts spat death once more.

I hadn't been sure which of the clan it was, but as the bullets tore into the rash werewolf's soft flesh and sent geysers of thick warm delicious blood spurting from its sides, I recognized the tiresome whine of pain as one that could only have come from Laika. Her pathetic inability to dodge the deadly bullets was typical of her incompetent and second-rate efforts at werewolfing which had led the rest of the clan to turn against her, but Joe didn't let her latest failure get in his way. He had worked his way round to the side of Lady CooCoo while she had been distracted by Laika, and now he leapt forwards with all the strength he had in his mighty werewolf haunches, knocking his foe to the ground. She struggled to get up, but Joe held her head in his powerful jaws, and Laddie rushed to add his weight to Joe's. Lady CooCoo could only fire a volley of bullets helplessly into the air. Joe cocked his leg and a steaming jet of werewolf pee splashed down onto her chrome breastplate.

I had assumed this was the latest in a long line of inappropriate 'Inflicting' incidents, but then I saw blue lightning start to crackle over the surface of CooCoo's stricken body. Joe and Laddie leapt back as she thrashed around wildly, her limbs shaking like that epileptic kid at school we'd all found so amusing. Then smoke billowed out from behind her cracked porcelain mask, and she was still.

Looking back over to the rocks where Teddy and D'Arcy D'Acula were dueling, I saw that their confrontation was reaching a similarly dramatic conclusion. It was a good job both fights hadn't happened at the same time; otherwise I wouldn't have known which to narrate. Teddy, a fine swordsman as I knew to my delight, had forced D'Arcy D'Acula back step by step until they both teetered on the narrow summit of the highest rock. D'Acula's fine silk shirt was drenched with sweat, and criss-crossed with a dozen or more bloody marks where Teddy had injured him. Teddy attacked again and D'Acula fell back once more. Now only a few inches stood between him and a long fall onto the impressively spiky rocks below.

The exhausted vampire dropped his sword and, pointing first to the crotch of his own trousers, then at Teddy's, shouted something at my husband that was swallowed up by the distance and the sounds of battle closer by. Teddy scowled, span on one foot and planted a supremely powerful roundhouse kick square in D'Arcy D'Acula's chest. The ancient vampire was thrown backwards off the vertiginous cliff top. He landed among the almost unbelievably spiky rocks at its base, and was skewered right through the heart by the longest and spikiest of them. He thrashed about for the briefest second, before exploding in a shower of silver confetti: a showman to the very end. Teddy looked down at the drifting cloud of confetti, and made an inaudible but surely hilarious quip.

His gaze searched for Penissa and me. He saw us sitting snugly in the warmth of the car and I waved at him, but he shook his head, pointing towards the center of the clearing, where the battle with Cowl was conveniently about to reach its climax. I understood that he wanted me to meet him there, probably so we could make sure that our stupid vampire cousins didn't make a hash of dealing with Cowl. I'd finished the last of the popcorn, so I thought it couldn't hurt to keep a closer eye on things.

Teddy needn't have been concerned – Bobbi and Jack had things well under control. The last of the henchmen had fled, dragging their severed limbs behind them, and Cowl was surrounded by Benny, O'Bone and the rest. He turned and tried to make a run for it, but Reiko Shibari finally did something useful with the coil of rope she carried, and threw a lasso around Cowl to prevent him from escaping. She yanked him off his feet and pounced on top of him, securing his hands behind his back.

He thrashed around in the dirt like the repellent slug that he was, his earlier calm mood absent as he looked from face to face, pleading for his life. 'Benny, me old mate. Help me out here. I can get you that TV series you wanted, no problem. O'Bone, I've got friends in government; I can make your tax problems disappear. Just untie me, eh, there's a good lad?'

None of the other vampires met his gaze, and eventually he fell silent. Having me stand on your windpipe will do that. Teddy joined us in the circle and hugged me hard, before announcing, 'You see, I told you my plan would succeed. Good work, everybody!' There was a ripple of applause and some spontaneous good-natured backslapping.

'What are we going to do with Cowl, Teddy?' I asked, indicating the muddy trussed-up choking figure at my feet.

Teddy looked off into the distance for a minute, deep in thought, and then said, 'Well, my love, I don't think we need to worry about Cowl anymore. You see, the Vindicti were bullies who used their power to make other people feel small, and bad about themselves. But now look at Cowl, groveling there in the dirt, his face turning blue. He doesn't seem like such a big man anymore, does he?'

'No, I guess he doesn't. So, what, we're going to let him go?'

Teddy turned to his sister. 'What do you say, Bobbi?'

She thought for a moment. 'Well, it's been great to have him here tonight, and the show wouldn't be the same without him. What would they do; draft in David Hasselhoff? It doesn't bear thinking about.' She shuddered. 'I think we should let him go.'

'You're crazy!' I asserted reasonably. 'He was horrid on television, mean to everyone for no reason, all the time! Then he turned on us, and I went right off him. He's too dangerous to live; we must destroy him – it's the only way I'll be safe!'

Teddy nodded as he heard our judgments, then addressed Cowl. 'One says you live; the other says you die. It appears the casting vote falls to me. I will now decide your fate, one excruciating syllable at a time!'

There was a long pause before Teddy spoke again. The rest of the vampires were pretending to hold their breath with anticipation, and I swear I could hear tense music building to an emotive climax in the background. Cowl looked unsure whether to be relieved or terrified. I stared at him, and back at Teddy, and then back at Cowl, drinking in every sweet drop of tension as the moment stretched out interminably.

'Cowl, I've made my decision,' Teddy said finally. 'You... are ... going...' He paused again. Cowl grinned with sudden elation.

'... to the eternal damnation of Hell which you so richly deserve!' Teddy finished, pouncing on Cowl's throat and tearing at his exposed jugular vein with his sharp fangs. With his chin covered in Cowl's dark blood, he spoke to the assembled vampires once more. 'This isn't the sort of vampire that explodes in a shower of confetti, folks. We need to deal with him the old-fashioned way. Who's hungry?'

After our impromptu early breakfast, I let myself rest, sitting on the rocks with Joe and Teddy, taking in the scene of carnage that lay all across the clearing.

'All worked out pretty well for us in the end, huh?' said Joe.

'I was sorry to hear about Laika. She died bravely,' Teddy said solemnly, a hand on Joe's knee.

'Enough about her. She wouldn't want us to dwell on her embarrassing death forever,' I added, nobly trying to help Joe get over his loss.

'It was only thirty minutes ago, Heffa,' Joe pointed out.

'But look, Joe –' I indicated the horizon '– it's a new day now. Time to forget our troubles, and get on with our lives.'

'Looks like it's going to be sunny today too,' Teddy said, as the light started to break through the early morning mist.

Bobbi called to us from below. 'Get down here and help tidy up, you three. There's enough spare meat here to keep Dad's shop in business for a year!'

I exchanged amused looks with my husband and my best friend, and then the three of us walked hand in hand down the cliff side, ready to leave all the horrors of the Breaking Yawn behind us.

After turning the leftovers into delicious sausages.

heffaly ever after

After the battle with the Vindicti, peace descended on our little pocket of paradise – at least, it did once we'd managed to evict our staunch allies and helpers. A bigger lot of freeloaders and layabouts it would be hard to imagine! They almost bled Spatula dry before we could persuade them (with holy water and flaming arrows) to get lost.

Joseph Kelledy wired to say that he was terribly pleased we were all still living, but that Los Angeles rather suited him now that D'Arcy D'Acula's death had left a hole in the undead movie magnate world. Disturbing rumours had reached us that he was busy creating an unholy army of child stars; but if it were so, we would deal with that when it became a problem, or unnecessary competition for Penissa.

My father was slowly coming to terms with my changed way of life. The doctors had cut his meds significantly, and were hopeful that, in time, they could let him out of the straitjacket.

And, best of all, now that my mimsy creator Stephfordy was no more, I was free – free to do whatever I wanted, whenever I wanted, however I wanted. Brilliant, huh? I'm sure you're all insane with jealousy right about now, but don't worry. As a last gift to you, Reader, here are my top tips for finding your own perfect life:

1. Move to a town where you are literally the most exciting, hot person who's ever lived there.
2. Find vampire.
3. Persuade vampire that you are the most exciting, hot person he's ever met (not hard; vamps don't get out that much).

4. Avoid being killed by various horrible creatures that don't understand your eternal union (this may include your friends, family, local priest...)
5. Convince vampire to turn you into an unholy bloodsucking fiend.
6. Hope that he follows through, and doesn't simply drain you drier than the Sahara on a hot day.

Some of you lesser mortals may have trouble with steps 1–3, but what can I do about that? It's not my fault you're just not as amazing as I am. What am I, a lifestyle coach? You're on your own.

I was chuckling about the millions of readers who would read my teachings and dream hopelessly of improving their own pitiful existences when Teddy came upon me.

'Heffa, darling, what are you doing out here?'

I put my notebook to one side. 'Oh, just struggling to provide resolution without Stephfordy around to do the heavy lifting. Honestly, one teensy moment of sudden death and her attention to detail went right out of the window.'

'Enough of that!' Teddy exclaimed with the rash impulsiveness that was such an attractive and occasionally dangerous part of his nature. 'We are free to write our own destinies now: you, Penissa and me. What shall we do? Fly to the moon? Descend to the deepest reaches of the oceans? Travel the known world imparting wisdom and tasting all the local cuisine and the locals?'

I considered it. He was right. The world was our oyster, to open and slurp as we liked.

'Oooh, I know! Can we go into Spatula and get ice cream sundaes with special blood sauce direct from our server?'

Teddy sighed with resignation. 'Whatever you want, my love, whatever you want.'

And with those perfect words – the words any woman wants to hear – he took my hand, and together we went off into our eternal, blissful, amazing, forever perfect future.